SENSIBLY WED

Also by Kasey Stockton

SENSIBLY WED

KASEY STOCKTON

GOLDEN OWL PRESS

First edition: June 2022
Golden Owl Press

Library of Congress Control Number: 2022911468
ISBN 978-1-952429-22-4

This one has to go to Jon—for choosing me every day. This is, what, your third dedication? That's because I keep choosing you, too.

CHAPTER 1

London, 1817

There was nothing in the world less enjoyable than a ball. Well, perhaps almost as awful was an intimate tea with Mama's friends, their shrill voices relaying more gossip than the whole of the *ton* could be depended upon to accurately produce. I surveyed the lively gathering in the Hutton's London townhouse and followed my mother toward a pair of empty chairs beside one of her friends. Apparently I was being punished for my dislike of dancing, for I now had to endure two of my least favorite things: listening to gossip *at* a ball.

Mama lowered herself beside Mrs. Ormiston, and I remained standing, searching for a way out of this stuffy, overheated ballroom. My skin prickled with unease, and my heart ticked up in speed. So many people gathered in such a small space—so many strangers and haughty, discerning eyes—was enough to send me into one of my quiet fits. I swallowed my discomfort and shook

1

the feeling, straightening the fingers of my gloves to give me something to focus on.

I needed to calm my racing heart, for I would not be escaping this room quite yet. The Season was nearing its end, and I had yet to make a match. Mama was unlikely to agree to leave the ball before I had danced twice, which put us at an impasse. For I did not intend on standing up with any of these gentlemen tonight. I would simply have to wait out the evening until it drew to a blessed close.

Mr. Peel caught my gaze over the top of Mama's quivering feather, and I quickly dropped into the seat beside her. I retracted both of my previous statements; unwanted suitors, *that* was most deplorable of all. For suitors always led to dancing.

"And you say he is here this evening?" Mama leaned against me so she might look out over the gathering for the man she was surely gossiping about with Mrs. Ormiston.

Mrs. Ormiston nodded vigorously. "It is said he has six thousand a *year*."

"Goodness." Mama was breathless.

I craned my neck to peer in the direction Mr. Peel had been standing, hoping to find him inquiring with someone else for a dance, but I could not locate the man from my current position. Drat. If he was making his way toward me, I only had a minute to make myself scarce.

It was not that I deplored Mr. Peel himself. He was a kind enough man. But he smelled extremely strong, and he was not my Mr. Bradwell.

Not that Mr. Bradwell was mine to claim, exactly. But he was the handsome creature who had wiggled his way into my heart last summer. My family had suffered a carriage accident and took refuge in his hunting box, and I had yet to determine how I might find him in polite society to resume our acquaintance-ship. Thus far, I had tolerated an entire Season hoping to see him again, but to no avail. The man was not fond of social functions.

Our chance encounter last summer had produced a *tendre* that I had not yet been able to fully snuff out—and might never have the opportunity to grow.

I lifted my reticule and allowed it to rest on my lap, giving my wrist a respite from the heaviness.

"I wish you would not bring that to every ball, Felicity," Mama whispered, her eyes darting to my small, beaded bag.

And be caught without a book? Absurd.

"He is also said to be on the hunt for a wife," Mrs. Ormiston continued.

Mama waved her fan in front of her face and resumed her search of the room. "A man *looking* for a bride, now that is refreshing."

"Indeed." Mrs. Ormiston leaned forward and eyed me behind her looking glass, squinting one wrinkled eye while the other was enlarged. "Shall I find the man and provide an introduction?"

I shrank back, my stomach fluttering unpleasantly. "No. I thank you, Mrs. Ormiston, but I have no interest in six thousand a year."

"Of course not," Mama tittered, shaking her head ruefully. "Unless it was six thousand *books?*"

"Well, yes, that does sound rather enticing."

Mrs. Ormiston looked at me shrewdly. "His six thousand could purchase you as many books and more, I wager."

That was an attractive prospect, indeed. I gave the women a patient smile. I needed to move soon, or Mr. Peel would request a dance. And I could not dance. "Mama, this heat is unbearable, and I am feeling rather faint. Can I interest you in a walk on the terrace?"

Mama hesitated. She shared a look with Mrs. Ormiston

before letting out a soft sigh. "Very well. Perhaps we will find a willing partner on our way across the room."

Given the heat, that was a risk I was willing to take. Besides, the only man who consistently sought me out for dances was last seen on the opposite side of the room.

We rose, and Mama took my arm, pulling me close as we navigated through the crowd. "I only want you to find a husband, Lissy. I am not asking you to marry the first man who smiles at you."

"That is fortuitous. I would certainly be Mrs. Peel already if that was the parameter from which we chose my husband."

Mama was not amused. She was not fond of Mr. Peel, either, for the man always emitted a ghastly cloud of garlic wherever he went. Truly, did he bathe in it?

"But if you are unwilling to meet *any* men, you will never find someone to love you. I only want you to be as happily cared for and adored as I am, Lissy."

My heart lurched with longing. I wanted to love and be loved in much the same way, but as of yet, only one man had entered my heart, and he was not in this ballroom tonight. Nay, he was likely up in Northumberland in solitude, reading beside a warm fire. He was so similar to me in tastes and preferences, I could not imagine another in his place. It was not as though I could merely choose a man who would love and understand me, as mother believed. She was also under the impression that I could simply *choose* not to fall into a fit of nerves when placed in the center of attention or forced to dance before crowds of strangers.

If only it were so easy.

We passed the table of refreshments, and I pressed closer to my mother to avoid bumping my shoulder into a man retrieving a drink. He presented the dainty debutante beside him with a glass of lemonade and a startlingly handsome grin, and she giggled.

I refrained from scoffing. That young woman made all of us look ridiculous when she laughed over the sake of a grin. It was preposterous. *What* was so funny about lemonade and a dashing smile? Perhaps I was too practical for romance.

"A refreshing drink for a refreshing young woman," the man said, his deep voice inciting another round of giggles. He was tall, his shoulders broad and his bearing relaxed but dignified. His brown hair framed a pair of greenish brown eyes that were fastened on the debutante before him, and I suppressed an irritated huff from the sheer insipidity before me.

Mama was unfinished in her campaign. "I want you to find a man who loves you as much as your father loves me."

I nodded toward the romantic scene we were passing. "I can guarantee that *none* of these men would love me as Papa loves you."

The man looked up and caught my eye, and I swiftly turned away, tugging Mama's arm to move us more quickly through the room. Had he heard what I said? I'd been speaking softly, the same as Mama, but the way he'd looked up and held my gaze had dropped a stone into the pit of my stomach. His eyebrows knit and eyes narrowed as though he'd heard my censorious thoughts.

Oh, dear. I needed to remain on the terrace for the remainder of the evening.

Mama released a long-suffering sigh that reached into my chest and filled me with remorse. She wished for a daughter who would enjoy social functions as much as she did, and I wished for nothing more than solitude and the comfort of dear friends. If I could change my innate desires to better fit the daughter she wanted me to be, I would. But as it stood, I could not. My heart raced and my fingers shook anxiously, and I needed to be removed from this overcrowded room immediately.

Mrs. Plumpley stepped into our path, her bright eyes fixed

on my mother in a way that spoke volumes to the prime piece of gossip she wanted to share. One look at Mama proved how dearly she would prefer to remain indoors and hear it.

"Cynthia, have you heard?" Mrs. Plumpley asked.

I cleared my throat. "Why don't you remain here, Mama. I just saw Miss Hutton step outside, and I can join her for a quick reprieve."

Mama looked at me doubtfully and leaned in so Mrs. Plumpley would not overhear. "I do not want you to sneak away and read for the remainder of the evening, Lissy. You recall what happened last time you did so?"

The book I had brought for that very purpose weighed heavily in my reticule, digging the corded handle into my gloved wrist. That was exactly my goal, but I planned to be more discreet this time so I would not be discovered by a pair of ardent, newly engaged lovers.

It had been a blessing neither of them had wanted to be caught out or I could very well have landed myself in hot water.

Mama's worried brow needed smoothing, however, so I delivered my most conciliatory smile. "I only intend to ask Miss Hutton to walk in the garden."

"In view of the servants?"

"In view of everyone," I said, indicating the open terrace full of people.

Mama held my gaze. "It is my duty to guard your reputation, Lissy. I am not trying to ruin your evening."

"I must hurry, or I will be unable to find Miss Hutton in that crowd."

Mama looked unsure, but Mrs. Plumpley stepped in to unknowingly aid me. "Truly, Cynthia, you will never believe what I heard this evening."

Mama nodded. "Very well. But return quickly."

"If I have not returned by the end of the set, it is because Mr. Peel has finally cornered me and begged a dance."

She shook her head, but a small smile formed on her lips. "I suppose that would be better than not dancing at all."

That was where we disagreed. I slipped away toward the open terrace doors, though I could feel Mama's gaze hot on the back of my neck. I would need to find Miss Hutton swiftly and pray that she allow me to join her conversation.

The cool, evening air rushed over my warm cheeks, and immediately my lungs took it in. How many more Seasons would I yet be forced to endure before I found the match Mama dreamed for me? It had nearly been a year since I'd met Mr. Bradwell, and the likelihood of seeing him again was growing as slim as my chance of marrying a man possessed of six thousand a year.

My cousin Jane had suggested that I write a letter to Mr. Bradwell and post it to him with the book I had borrowed. It was a reasonable course of action, but the forwardness of penning a letter to an unmarried man had consistently stopped my quill before I could put ink to paper. When we'd parted ways, I had promised Mr. Bradwell I would return the book he'd lent me, and he had replied with a sparkling smile that he looked forward to it. That alone was the encouragement I'd received, the sole endorsement for believing a match possible—and it was thin.

What if Mr. Bradwell had not felt the same connection I had from our conversations? What if he was uninterested in pursuing a relationship with me, or, worse, had met and married a different woman in the nine months since I'd met him?

All were possible scenarios that blocked me from having the courage to write to him. And as a result, I was still in possession of the book he'd lent me.

Surely, he must believe me a thief by now.

I spotted Miss Hutton on the far end of the terrace and turned in her direction when a motion inside the ballroom caught my eye. Drat! Mr. Peel had found me again. I pretended not to see him and spun the opposite way, edging closer to the house. A potted tree was situated near the wall and behind it was surely my shadowed respite.

I slipped past the tree and could not believe my good fortune. I would not be forced to hide in the foliage, for there were French doors closed to a dark room just beyond it. I glanced through the branches toward the ballroom and found Mr. Peel paused in the center of the terrace doors, looking about for me.

If he found me, I would have to dance, and I would give anything to avoid dancing.

Quietly, I turned the handle on the door, glad to find it unlocked and not at all squeaky. I slipped silently inside and shut the door behind me. The stillness in the dim, empty room was a balm on my anxious nerves. I stepped softly, fearful of anyone following me in here, and moved further into the room.

A low-burning fire smoldered in the hearth, emitting enough light to faintly see the shelves lining the walls, brimming with books. I removed my gloves, giving my damp palms a respite, and tucked them into my reticule. I took a candle from the mantel, lighting it with the hearth's fire. Surely I was not disobeying Mama by looking *at* books. I did not intend to read them or even remove any from the shelves.

And there were so many wonderful books to look at. The Huttons' ball was officially my favorite of the Season, now that I found myself alone in the library. I truly could not think of a better way to pass the remaining hours of the ball.

I would simply have to beg forgiveness at the end of the night. Mama might be angry with me for a spell, but if it saved me from dancing, I would suffer her—admittedly reasonable—indignation for the next few days.

Minutes passed in quiet bliss as I walked slowly along the shelves, absorbing the different titles and making a note of which ones I would later like to acquire from the lending library.

Contrary to what Mr. Bradwell could potentially think of me, I was not a book thief. I did intend to return his novel one day, after all.

I crouched low and brought the candle with me to look at the titles along the lower shelves. Quite a lot of Byron and no Shakespeare thus far. Hmm. I supposed not everyone could be counted upon to have taste.

The door at the far end of the room creaked open, and I blew my candle out, slinking down to hide behind the thick, wooden chair. My heart raced. I peeked through the carved back of the chair to see a man enter the room and close the door behind himself, and I cursed silently.

This was much worse than a pair of ardent lovers—this one would not be as easily distracted.

He crossed the room toward the fire and lowered himself on a plush seat near the hearth. Scrubbing a hand over his face, he let out a long, drawn out sigh. "Lady? She was an absolute *child*," he mumbled.

He looked familiar, and I leaned closer to the back of the chair to better see him. His dark hair gleamed in the soft orange light, and his eyes were closed, but I recognized him at once as the man at the refreshment table earlier—the flirt.

Or perhaps his greater flaw wasn't that he was a flirt as much as he was unoriginal. *A refreshing drink for a refreshing young woman*. Revolting. How *unrefreshing* of him.

My feet were beginning to fall asleep in my crouched position, and I shifted to find a more comfortable way to sit. Judging by this man's sudden need for a nap, it was safe to assume that I would be hiding here for a while.

I certainly could not try to escape until he had gone from the room first. I would not be found alone again. It could have almost been ruinous last time.

As I shifted, my foot snagged on the underskirt of my gown, and I yanked softly to remove the hindrance. Hot, searing wax dripped over my hand. I yelped, dropping the candle with a clatter on the wooden floor.

The man beside the fire sat up swiftly. "Who goes there?"

I shut my eyes and breathed in, my heart racing from the impending confrontation.

He rose to his feet and repeated himself. "I say, who goes there?"

Sucking in a quiet breath, I reached for the discarded candle and holder and stood. "Forgive the intrusion, sir. I only dropped my candle."

He watched me with a discerning glare, his face impassive. "I suppose I did not mishear you earlier in the ballroom, after all, when you said you would make me love you. Forgive my blunt criticism, but this is a sorry way to entrap a man."

CHAPTER 2

Entrap a man? I scoffed at his ridiculous statement. Surely, he could not be in earnest. "I said nothing of the sort!"

"I heard you state that you could make one of these men love you as your papa loved your mama. Do not think I missed the pointed look you sent my direction." He spoke in measured tones as though he hoped to stave off a feral cat.

Me. A feral cat. It was absurd. "I believe you mistook the word *none* for *one.*"

His skeptical look drove frustration through my chest. Was he silent because he was running over the possibility that I was telling the truth? I could not help but press my case further.

"You forget I was in the room first, sir," I said, my defenses rising.

He shook his obnoxiously handsome head. "No, you must have followed me in here. I only saw you in the ballroom minutes ago."

I could not restrain the laugh that bubbled from my chest. Of all the ridiculous notions. "I must have been quite stealthy to manage such a feat. You had hardly entered the room before I dropped my candle—a candle which had been burning long enough to pool wax at the base."

He looked down at my hand. "That is what happened to cause your outburst? Did you injure yourself?" His voice, laced with a hint of compassion, fooled me briefly.

I set the brass candle holder on a nearby table with a thunk and held my hands behind my back. "It was only a bit of wax. My hand is perfectly fine."

"How can you be certain of that fact when you are in the dark?"

"You wish for me to come into the light, sir? How can I be certain you are not the one who is attempting to entrap me?"

He scoffed, his dark eyebrows rising a fraction. Heavy silence pushed against us briefly. "I suppose we can safely come to the conclusion that neither of us entered this room with nefarious intentions, hmm?"

"On the contrary. None of my intentions for sneaking into the library were very innocent." I clamped my mouth closed and gripped my hands tightly behind my back, causing the burn on my hand to pinch. What possessed me to be so contrary? It was entirely unlike me.

A small smile ticked up the side of his lips and drew my attention to their perfect symmetry. This man was objectively handsome, his jawline firm and eyebrows thick and expressive. There was something about him that tugged at a chord within me, something about his face that rang familiar, but I could not place it. I had never before met him in my life, but I must have seen him about London or other balls hosted by the *ton*, for I was positive he looked like someone I'd met before.

"Might I ask what corrupt plan caused you to seek refuge in the library?"

"You may ask," I said, "but I do not think it wise to tell you."

His head tilted to the side, intrigued. "Now I feel you must, or I will be forced to believe you hid here lying in wait for whatever unfortunate soul should happen upon you."

"Unfortunate?" I asked, raising my eyebrows.

"Indeed. I pity the poor sap who is trapped into marriage, and I pity the desperate woman who fell to such lengths to do the trapping."

"Your charm is simply astounding, sir." My voice dripped with sarcasm, and I squared my shoulders. "It tempts me to keep my reasons safely hidden from your censorious ears."

"Have I been too blunt?"

"Well, yes. But it is quite . . . what is the word? Ah. Refreshing."

If this man noted my reference to his flirtation earlier at the refreshment table, he did not indicate so. "If I promise to refrain from criticizing your reasons, will you share them?"

I could not help but be intrigued by him. I wanted to know why he had escaped a ballroom that seemed curated to praise and adore him. "Only if you will share yours in turn."

He gave a curt nod and extended his hand. "We can shake on it."

I stared at his hand. A gentleman's shake would require me to cross the room into the light and expose my injury. Perhaps if I was quick about it, he would not notice anything amiss. I did not take false sympathy well. Though, I had not been able to see if the wax left a mark as angry as it felt. It *could* look perfectly normal.

"You can trust me," he said.

"I cannot trust a man I do not know."

He held my gaze, and I considered the situation. I did not need to put my trust in him entirely, but the fact remained that if he proved to be anything other than the gentleman he appeared, a quick scream would alert anyone standing on the other side of the French doors walking the terrace.

Besides, I *felt* safe, and as a woman prone to fits of nerves, I had grown accustomed to listening to the feelings deep within my body. My curiosity won out, and I crossed the room into the light of the small fire. Drat my passion for mystery novels—I could not leave this room without having my curiosity satiated.

His strong hand was still extended, and I placed mine into it, curling my bare fingers around his gloved hand. He looked into my eyes, and I blinked away my surprise at the subtle way he stole my breath.

If being alone with a man caused such heady sensations for everyone, it was no wonder young ladies were admonished to never find themselves in this situation.

I moved to tug my hand free, but he held fast. "Was this the hand you injured?"

I scoffed. I had been right not to trust him. "You cad. Release me at once."

He looked at me with sincerity. "*After* I verify that you are unharmed. It is safe to say I am the cause of your injury, yes? I assume you were attempting to hide from me when you spilled the wax on your skin. By the by, where are your gloves?"

"In my reticule, not that it is any of your business," I said through a blatantly fake smile. "I had not anticipated being interrupted during my perusal."

He regarded me a moment longer before pulling my hand gently toward the fire. He turned my palm until he found the red mark over the back of my hand and sucked in a breath. His dark eyelashes fanned down, his attention lowered, and he ran a thumb gently around my injury, driving a shiver up my arm. "You must put some ointment on this straight away."

"It looks worse than it feels." I pulled my hand free, shaking away the feelings he infused in it. "My skin is pale, so the mark is bound to be more conspicuous." I would not admit that it stung something fierce.

He cleared his throat and held his hands behind his back—a

gracious gesture no doubt designed to put me at ease. "Your reason for escaping the ballroom?"

"I do not dance."

His eyebrows shot up. "You do not *enjoy* dancing?"

"No, sir. It is as I said. I do not dance."

He appeared to have trouble understanding me, his handsome countenance wrinkling in confusion. "Has no one taught you to dance?"

"I have taken lessons and know all the steps. I simply do not dance."

"Hmm." He looked to the fire and the small flames twirled in his eyes. His brow puckered, then cleared, and he looked at me. "You are not . . . *talented* at dancing?"

Was that his polite way of asking if I was awful at it? I did not wish to share my true reasons, so this would have to do. "I suppose not, no. I escaped onto the terrace, and in order to"—I cleared my throat and glanced away—"*avoid* a suitor, I slipped in here. When I saw the books, I could not help but tarry a little before returning to my mother."

"You like to read."

"Yes."

He smiled broadly, and I closed my mouth. It was no wonder that insipid young miss had giggled at this man's smile. It was irritatingly handsome.

He leaned forward a little as though he meant to impart a secret. "I do believe you feel for dancing the way I feel for books."

He fell in my esteem at once. I lifted my eyebrows. "Then why, pray, have you escaped to a library?"

"Because this is my godmother's house, and I knew the library would be empty."

"You needed an empty room during a ball so you might take a nap? Was the dancing too wearing for you, sir?"

He chuckled a little, and a thrill shot through my chest. It was *not* an achievement to make this man chuckle, despite how my body had reacted. He was only a man.

"It was not the dancing from which I required a break. It was the ardent young misses."

I recalled what he had said when he believed himself to be alone in the room. *Lady? She was an absolute child.* Had the poor man been set upon by an eager young woman fresh from the schoolroom? Surely, the woman I'd seen him giving the lemonade to had been seventeen or eighteen at least—old enough to wed.

"Were the misses too ardent or too young?"

He looked up sharply. "Both."

I couldn't fault him for that belief, for he appeared to be closer to thirty than twenty. I could only claim two and twenty years myself, but I felt much older most of the time—especially when surrounded by young girls masquerading as women.

Women who were now likely wondering where the handsome, dark-haired gentleman had escaped to. "We ought to return to the ballroom before we are found alone and the worst conclusions are drawn."

He nodded in agreement. "Will you find something to ease your burn? I can request an ointment from my godmother. I am certain she will have something in her kitchen to use."

"That is unnecessary. I do not live far from here." I pulled open the drawstring closure on my reticule and retrieved my gloves.

"I would ask you for a dance, but we have yet to be introduced."

I paused in the motion of pulling my glove up to my elbow.

"And of course there is the barrier that you do not dance," he added.

That pulled a small smile onto my lips.

He watched me straighten my glove. "Would you not make

an exception to your rule for a new friend? I have it on good authority that you do know the steps."

"If you'll recall, it has nothing to do with my *knowledge* of the dances."

"But perhaps you do not enjoy dancing because you've yet to acquire the correct partner."

Impertinent. I focused my attention on the glove in my hand. Was this stranger implying that he could be the correct partner for me?

"Or perhaps," I said, "I will never dance, regardless of who partners me."

"Care to place a wager on it?"

I slid my fingers into my second glove and glanced up to find him watching my hands still. "What sort of wager?"

"If I prove that dancing can be enjoyable, you will allow us to be properly introduced and dance the next set with me."

"How are you so certain we will find a mutual acquaintance?"

"I remind you that this is my godmother's ball. I'm assuming you are familiar with the Huttons or you would not be here."

He had me there. Miss Marianne Hutton and I possessed something of a friendship. It was her company I pretended to seek out in order to escape to the terrace, after all.

"And if I dislike it as much as I expect to?"

He rubbed a hand over his strong jaw. "Then I suppose I must pay a forfeit."

"There is nothing I want from you, sir."

"Nothing?" The way he looked down at me, his head cocked to the side, was endearing. The only thing I wanted was to be home, safe in my room, and away from the Hutton residence completely.

Ah, that was it. He could be my ticket out of the ball early this evening. Surely, I could force myself to move through the motions of one dance without issue? We were alone, lacking an audience. I had always done perfectly fine with my dancing master when we were alone. I would simply imagine this tall, handsome gentleman as a wrinkled man of sixty with awful breath.

"If I win, which I shall, then you must fetch my mother so I can convince her to leave the ball without having to reenter the ballroom. Mrs. Hutton will surely provide you with the introduction to make that possible."

"Deal."

This was far too easy.

He bowed to me, then held out a hand. "May I have this dance, Miss . . ."

"Certainly." I ignored the question in his tone, for I would not supply my name to the stranger. But I had to swallow my moral high ground, since evidently my strong proprietary convictions did not extend to *dancing* with a stranger. I glanced over my shoulder at the French doors and felt his hand slide around mine.

"No one can see us in here. It is too dark."

He was correct. The fire had slowly faded to a faint burn. I could hardly see him, and my eyes had gradually adjusted. "Which dance are we meant to be doing?"

"The waltz."

"By ourselves?"

"It can be done without a room full of people."

"And the music?"

"I needn't any. Just follow the moves that you evidently know well." He took my hand and led me in a promenade about the small rug before the fire, then moved into the following motions, pretending that other couples danced the set with us. "What do you have in this?" he asked, nodding to the reticule that dangled heavily from my wrist.

"A weapon in case a strange man asks to dance with me alone in the library."

"It is a book, is it not?"

How did he know that? His smile was evidence that my surprise had given me away.

We continued to move through the motions of the dance until we found ourselves before the fire, our hands raised above our heads, our other hands around the others' waist. It was with great dismay that my heart beat quickly and my cheeks grew flushed—though I didn't at all feel faint. I was *enjoying* this ridiculous demonstration.

But if we were in public, among the other couples the dance normally included and the crowd of spectators, I would not be enjoying it at all. My hands would grow increasingly clammy, my heart slamming against my breastbone, my breath shallow and head faint. It was the same every time, without fail. I did not dance because I would faint. Nearly *every* time. I could not help the biological reaction so much avid attention caused any more than I could help growing hungry on an empty stomach or sleepy after a late night.

He looked down at me, holding the position, and my heart raced. "Do you dare say that you are not enjoying this dance?"

I could not speak the truth of things now—it would require that I obtain an introduction and dance with him in public. If his earlier flirtation at the refreshment table was any clue, the man was something of a flirt. I did not wish to fall into his trap, and I certainly did not wish to faint this evening in the center of a crowded ballroom, particularly during such a crush.

And there was a niggling at the back of my mind that reminded me that this was not my Mr. Bradwell. Any of the sweet flirtations this man tossed at me were cheap in comparison to the depth of connection I shared with Mr. Bradwell last summer.

There was nothing else for it. I had to lie.

I swallowed, nervous that he would discern the tremor in my voice. "Actually, I—"

The door swung open, and a volley of feminine laughter filtered into the room. His hands tightened on impact, and then we sprang apart, but not before the women who entered the library stopped in the doorway and stared, the light from the corridor bleeding in and washing over us. Mrs. Hutton paused, her hand moving to rest on her chest, and the two women behind her gasped.

Oh, dear. This could not be good.

"Godmother," the man said. He stepped back again to put more space between us and cleared his throat.

"What is the meaning of this, James?" Mrs. Hutton demanded.

James. It was such a fitting name for the man, strong and sturdy. He looked at me, then back at the women. "It is not what it appears."

"Indeed," I said, my voice small and nervous. "He was only teaching me to dance." To *enjoy* dancing, specifically, but I needn't be that explicit.

One of the women in the back scoffed quietly, and I cursed her silently. She was not being unreasonable. Had I walked in a darkened room and found two people seemingly in an embrace, I would have jumped to conclusions as well. But I hated her reaction all the same. The other two women slipped away, leaving us alone with Mrs. Hutton.

"Come, Miss Thurston," she said to me. "We must retrieve your parents."

"It is only my mother," I corrected. "Father could not make it this evening."

Mrs. Hutton narrowed her eyes at James, then nodded at me. "Come."

I left the room obediently, casting a look at James over my shoulder when I reached the doorway. Surely there would be no dire consequences. The three women could keep this to themselves. If they cared at all for either of us—and it was clear Mrs.

Hutton cared for James—then they would desire to keep this secret.

James's eyebrows were drawn, his expression uneasy. If he had the same fears I did, he certainly did not hold the same hope. He looked like a man awaiting conviction.

But he was innocent. And I would prove it.

CHAPTER 3

"Mrs. Hutton," I implored, reaching for her arm when she closed the library door behind me. "I speak only the truth. I have never met James before tonight. I sought respite away from the ballroom, and—"

"That was your first mistake." She shook her head and began down the corridor. "Your mother is going to be devastated."

"But we did nothing untoward—"

Mrs. Hutton paused and turned back to me, her eyes wide, her head shaking. "It does not matter. I cannot stop the tidal wave of gossip that is now spreading about my ballroom. Did you not see who was just behind me when I opened the door and discovered you together?"

"I'm afraid I am unacquainted with both of those women."

She closed her eyes and pressed her gloved fingertips to her temples. "I trust James. If he says it was naught but a dance, I believe him. But it hardly matters what *I* believe. You and he will be the talk of London by midnight. Your mother needs to be made aware, and you need to leave as quickly as possible."

My heart raced, and I moved to follow her toward the ballroom. When we reached the end of the corridor, she put out a hand to stop me. "Wait here. I will fetch your mama, and you must think of what you intend to say to her."

I nodded and stepped back, resting my back against the wall. My eyes drifted closed, and I tempered my breathing. How ridiculous of me to agree to the dance. How stupid and naive to believe that we would not be found, that my behavior was at all without reproach. I'd been wrapped in the warm feeling of having a handsome man's full attention, and I allowed the heady sensation to cocoon us, falsely believing that we were untouchable in our own little sphere.

"My deepest apologies," a low voice said, and I opened my eyes to find James standing apart from me, contrition written in his downcast gaze.

"James," I whispered.

His eyes flicked to me, his lips parting.

I swallowed. "I'm not sure the best course of action—"

"This is not it," Mrs. Hutton said, appearing again, my mother just behind her.

Mama looked from James to me, confusion and hurt splashed across her raven eyebrows. "Come, Felicity. We are leaving."

I pushed away from the wall and passed James without another glance, directing my attention at our hostess. "Forgive me, Mrs. Hutton."

She sighed, shaking her head, and the weight of my mistakes laid like boulders over my shoulders. She stepped past me. "Come, James. Mr. Hutton keeps brandy in the library, and you appear as though you could use a glass."

I followed Mama outside to our awaiting carriage and climbed inside. My foolish actions had brought shame upon my family name, and there was nothing I could do to stem the tide that would only flourish and grow on the *ton's* gossiping tongues.

"The gossip will be everywhere by morning."

"Indeed," I agreed. No thanks to Mama's friends and their affinity for spreading information—false or otherwise. Twice that evening I had witnessed a hushed conversation between Mama and a friend, had witnessed my mother greedily lapping up the *on-dits* supplied to her. It had repulsed me then, and it disgusted me now.

"What will your father think?"

"I am certain he will tell us when he returns from the club." Suddenly, the burn on my hand reminded me of its presence, and I welcomed the distraction from my terrible predicament. I looked to my hands and traced the places James had held them. I was certain never to see him again, which I was grateful for, but my skin buzzed where he'd touched it. The way his thumb had gingerly wiped around the perimeter of my burn as though by some magic he hoped to sap it of pain.

I shut my eyes and shoved the feeling away. Was I now destined to become an old maid? What gentleman of good standing would accept me as a bride with this stain now splashed over my name? Surely Mr. Bradwell would not. I ought to post his book back to him tomorrow without a note at all. My chances of marrying were dashed tonight—and it was my own fault.

"There is no way to come back from this, is there?"

"We have a few options," Mama said. "But your father will have the final say."

Hope bloomed within me. "Options?"

Mama sighed, and the carriage rolled to a stop in front of our townhouse. "If you married the man—"

"James?" I asked, appalled. "I cannot marry him. I do not know him."

Mama's mouth pressed into a firm line. "Yet you call him by his Christian name."

"Only because I do not know any other name to call him by,"

I defended. "I do not even know his surname. Mrs. Hutton called him James, and that was all."

Mama's eyes closed, and she looked to be searching for patience. "We cannot track him down if we do not know who he is."

"If Mrs. Hutton is to be believed, our names will be irrevocably connected by morning. I am certain you will not struggle to learn it then."

Her eyes snapped to me. "True."

"But I will not marry him, and we cannot expect him to agree to marry me. It was only a dance, Mama. We were each escaping the ballroom. That one foolish choice should not force us to spend the remainder of our lives together, surely."

She opened the door and took the awaiting footman's hand before stepping out onto the street. I followed her up the steps and waited when she paused at the door to our townhouse. She turned to me. "You have placed us in a very uncomfortable position, Felicity. Whatever your father says, you must agree to it. Do you understand?"

"Yes," I said, doing my best to keep the shame and regret from my voice. We were in a mess of my own doing, and I would find a way to crawl out of it and restore our good name. Short of marrying a stranger. "I will do whatever it takes."

My father was a soft-spoken man. He enjoyed quiet outdoor pursuits like hunting and riding, and he never raised his voice. Typically, I appreciated his calm nature. But the quiet, thoughtful way he watched me this morning, his eyes cast away and sorrow seeping over his brow, nearly destroyed me. I had disappointed him, and that hurt far worse than any anger he could throw at me. I wished he would rant and rave and yell.

He stood by the fireplace, fingering his pocket watch. "We

cannot rely on this man's good character, Cynthia. He has so far proven that it is anything *but* good."

Mama's lips pinched, and her shadowed eyes looked to the morning light filtering through the drawing room window. She paced behind the sofa. "Perhaps an extended holiday would be best."

Papa nodded, moving to sit on the sofa opposite me. I was present, but neither of my parents were really speaking to me. "Surely your sister would be glad to receive Felicity at Arden Castle," Papa said. "She must be lonely now that Jane has married."

Mama looked less convinced, continuing her pacing. "Or perhaps a visit to Jane and her new husband would be the thing. It would only need to be a year or so."

"Visit Jane and Ewan in Scotland?" I questioned, gathering the attention of both my parents. I adored my cousin, but I was unsure if I could bear to live apart from my family for an entire year—and so far away. "You wish to send me away to Scotland for a *year*?"

Mama crossed to where my father sat on the sofa opposite me and lowered herself beside him. He took her hand and held it in his lap. They had always appeared a united front, their relationship strong and healthy and exactly what I had wanted to emulate in my own marriage one day. But now I felt the sting of separation wrought by my thoughtlessness and presented by the space between us. A chasm had opened, and my parents were completely out of reach.

"It will only be until the gossip has settled," Papa said. "Then you can return, and we will rejoin Society and prove—"

"No. That will not work." Mama frowned. It lifted a burden from me to hear her objection. Might I be allowed to stay with them? "If we send Felicity away for a year and then have her return, it will only confirm the rumors. The entire *ton* will believe she left to deliver a baby. If she remains in Town, at least her waistline can prove her innocence."

My relief was short-lived. If I remained in Town, I would be subjected to the *ton's* censure. I took a little relief in the simple fact that my parents believed me to be innocent, but there was no course of action available to me that was not entirely distasteful.

"If Felicity was to marry," Mama said quietly, "at least she could go away and not bear the slights or the cuts from her friends in Town."

Slights? Cuts? My own friends—few as they were—would stoop so low over a rumor?

"Do you not believe we are perhaps worrying for nothing?" I asked lightly. I could not imagine Marianne Hutton or Eliza Gould giving me the cut direct.

"No," Mama said without hesitation.

"But the Pickering ball is this evening. What if we were to attend, and—"

A knock at the drawing room door cut my words to the hilt, and I clamped my mouth shut. My parents looked at the door as though it held their reckoning.

"Enter," Papa called.

A footman let himself into the room and crossed to Papa, bearing a silver tray with a card. Papa lifted the card, and Mama read the name over his shoulder. She looked to me. "You mentioned last night that his name was James?"

I nodded.

"Then he has come to pay a visit."

My lungs squeezed, unable to draw a full breath.

Papa stood at once. "I shall meet with him in the study." My parents shared a glance, and Papa nodded in an unspoken code. Whatever they had agreed on, I did not believe I would find it very pleasant.

My father's click-clack of shoes across the wood-planked

floor set the beat to my racing pulse. I could not believe James was now in my home, that he awaited a meeting with Papa in the entryway two floors below us. The silence was thick in the room, and I could not bear to sit still a moment longer.

Mama lifted her head when I stood. "Where are you going?"

"To join in the meeting. They are discussing me, are they not?"

"It is better to leave this to your father, Felicity."

Felicity. My mother rarely called me by my whole name, and yet *Lissy* had not been spoken from her lips since before I disappointed her. I drew in a breath. "I cannot leave my future in the hands of other people. Surely they would not begrudge me an audience, at the very least."

I had always been quiet and reserved, often opting to read over any social option presented to me. I never made a fuss, and I did not give my parents much grief. I had always been a proper daughter, and my actions before now had given my parents cause to believe me immediately when I told them I did nothing untoward with the gentleman in the library. Should that not extend to now?

"Your father would not like it."

"Then he may turn me away," I said and left the room. I was grateful Mama did not stop me.

CHAPTER 4

F ather's study was on the ground floor of our townhouse, and my heart raced by the time I reached it. The thick, oak door was closed, and I stood in the corridor before it, staring at the embossed, brass knob and begging my pulse to slow. I tended to avoid confrontation at all costs, but more than that, I feared what I would step into.

Although a flirt, James had seemed a kind man last evening. What would the harsh morning light reveal?

Drawing myself up, I considered Esther from the Bible and the way she approached her king unbidden. I was not breaking a law in approaching my father, but I surely was unwanted.

I could be brave like Esther.

My hand curled into a fist, and I rapped on the door twice before turning the knob and letting myself inside. Father sat at his desk, James across from him, and both men turned to face me at the door. James's eyes were murky, his dark eyebrows drawn and serious. He wore a brown coat over a bronze waist-coat, and his clothing was very well made, if simplistic in design. He did not appear pleased to see me, and I could only imagine how deeply he regretted our dance.

"It is not a good time, dear," Papa said.

I cleared my throat and considered Esther again. This was my life and my mistake. I would see that a resolution was found that suited all of us. "I feel it is important that I am included in this conversation, Papa. It is my fault we have found ourselves here, after all."

James stood as if in afterthought and ran a hand through his hair. "I am equally to blame."

The softness in his deep tone surprised me, though I did not know why—he had given me no reason to believe he would be angry with me. His apology in the corridor the evening before only proved that further.

I tried to swat away the butterfly that was currently dashing around my midsection. I did not like the feeling, but I knew it was a product of James's compassion.

"I suppose it is no matter now," Papa said. "We have come to a decision that pleases both parties."

I looked between them. "How can it please both parties if I was not included in the making of the decision?"

Papa's eyebrows drew together, and I realized immediately that he meant himself as one of the parties in question. It pleased both James and *my father*.

"We will need your permission of course in order to move forward," James said.

It was a kindness neither of my parents had so far offered me, and I shot him a look of gratitude.

"I will leave you to it, then," my father said, rising from his seat.

No. Oh, no no *no*. The only reason Papa would leave us alone was if James needed to formally ask me to marry him.

"Are we not moving too swiftly?" I asked, though my words did not slow Papa's escape.

"We have come to an accord, Felicity."

"Yes," I said, taking my father's sleeve before he could fully desert me. "But have we not escalated at an alarming speed? We have not yet tested the strength of the rumors—"

"On the contrary," James said. "I did so last night, and they are just as rapid-moving and volatile as my godmother predicted."

Cold dread settled in my stomach, and I clutched my father's sleeve tighter, hoping to keep him with me. I could not be alone with James again so soon. My heart raced, and my limbs felt weak.

"But perhaps we ought to try one more time before making a decision that will impact the rest of our lives. Surely if we attend the Pickerings' ball this evening, our willingness to attend a social function will prove that we have nothing to hide."

"It hardly matters that we have nothing to hide," James said. "This is about our good names."

Our good names. I'd forgotten, in my stressful state, that my family was not the only one who would suffer from these rumors. James could have sisters hoping to wed that would be harmed by a scandal. I did not have sisters and thus felt I could withstand becoming a social pariah—I did not care for attending social functions anyway.

But . . . my mama did. She adored Society. Anything I agreed to was purely for her sake and that of my father's. They thrived in London, and I could not take that away from them.

I pleaded. "Can we not at least test the volatility tonight before we take these drastic measures? Surely one more ball cannot harm us so greatly?"

Papa looked to James, but when I followed his gaze, I found James looking at me. His gaze was steady, the gloom now missing that was present earlier. "I can agree to postponing for one more day, if that is what Miss Thurston requires."

My father did not appear to like it. "I would prefer the matter settled."

James took a step toward us, holding his hat in his hands.

"Suppose we settle the matter now, but we wait to make any announcements until we have . . . tested . . . Society this evening at the ball. If we are in agreeance to move forward, it would be the ideal place to make our announcement."

I tightened my hold on Papa's sleeve, and he looked down at my hand, then at me. "Very well." He vacated the room and closed the door behind himself, leaving us in the thick silence.

"This is all so ridiculous," I said, lifting my gaze to find James regarding me thoughtfully.

"And to think most people will believe that you have artfully managed to trap me into marriage, Miss Thurston."

My cheeks bloomed with heat, and he must have realized the thoughtlessness of his words. He stepped forward. "Forgive me. That was void of tact."

"Indeed, it was."

"I only meant that our situation *appears*—"

"Yes, I do take your meaning. It is unfair, truly, that I will be blamed when it was I who tried to leave the library early, and *you* convinced me into a compromising position."

"Perhaps we ought to refrain from pointing fingers. We do not wish to start a life together under such an accusatory tone."

Start a life together. Black spotted the edges of my vision, and my stomach turned over itself. I could not marry a man I just met. What if he was truly forty years old and only *appeared* young or had a strong affinity for stargazy pie? I could not stomach sitting at a table with fish heads popping from a golden pie crust for the rest of my life.

"You look pale."

"Thank you," I said with some sarcasm, but allowed him to take my hand and lead me to a chair.

He knelt before me so we were nearly eye level and set his hat on Papa's desk. His brow bent in concern. "Are you ill?"

I shook my head. "Merely coming to accept this awful situation."

James smiled. "If nothing else, I can see that you are determined to keep me a humble man."

"I did not realize you already possessed that admirable trait. I rather thought I was teaching it to you."

He chuckled and took my hand in his. Our proximity robbed me of breath, and I struggled with where to place my gaze. I settled on looking into his eyes and noticed that they were a lovely mixture of green and brown, the flecks mingling into gold at the center.

It was ridiculous how easy they were to find myself lost in.

"I appreciate your thoughtfulness," he said, "and I can see that you do not take action without thorough evaluation. I take equal blame—"

I lifted my eyebrows, and he smiled.

"Very well, I take a *majority* of the blame for the situation we have found ourselves in, and I would like to rectify it in the only way I can think to."

"Have you put enough thought into this?" I asked. "Perhaps there is an answer we have yet to stumble upon."

James's mouth ticked into a half-smile. "I sacrificed sleep last night working over our situation in my mind. I consulted trusted confidantes, and I think this is the best way forward."

I thought of the woman I saw flirting with him at the refreshment table the evening before and realized how little I knew of his life.

He still held my hand, and I covered his with my other one, my bare fingers curling around his. He seemed to draw still, but I did not remove my hold. "I am not naive enough to expect love, but I cannot move forward if I know that you hold another woman in esteem."

Mr. Bradwell was well and truly out of the question for me now, so I could safely admit that I entered into any agreements uninhibited.

James cleared his throat, his gaze darting between my eyes. "I do not have anyone in my heart, Miss Thurston."

"But yesterday, when I passed you in the ballroom, you seemed . . ."

"There is no woman who has any claim on me, I vow it."

I relaxed and removed my hands from his. He retook them and looked down, lifting my burn to better see it. "Have you put any ointment on your injury?"

"No, but as you can see, it already looks better."

"It looks quite as red at present as it did last night."

"Well, it hurts far less."

He looked up. "So you admit that it hurt last night? Why did you insist otherwise?"

"Because I could not have you storming into the ballroom in search of ointment."

"I can see that we will not have a boring marriage, Miss Thurston."

"I did not realize we had agreed to have any marriage at all," I whispered.

James held both of my hands, still on his knees. It was the most romantic gesture of my two and twenty years, and I forced myself to recall that he had no choice in the matter. This was not about me, not really.

"Why are you agreeing to this?" I asked. "Surely you could leave Town for a few months and return next Season, your reputation intact."

"Potentially, but I once made a promise to my mother, and it requires that I not walk away from you. I could not live with myself otherwise." He gave a little smile. "I did come to London with the intent of finding a wife, so it is not as odious an arrangement for me as you might believe."

I nodded. Curiosity nipped at me to ask him the nature of the promise he made to his mother, but it seemed an intimate question, and I could not bring myself to speak it aloud.

There was something oddly relieving in the knowledge that James felt himself ready to be married, that I had not forced him into a situation that he was not yet prepared to be in.

He squeezed my fingers. "Miss Thurston, will you agree to become my wife?"

My stomach swooped like a flying dove, and I sucked in a breath. I was ill prepared for how this would feel. Despite my protestations, I enjoyed the way James lifted my spirits with seemingly little effort.

"Yes, James. I will."

He smiled softly, and I continued. "But only if our situation appears irreversible on its own."

He tempered his smile and nodded. "Very well. I will see you tonight at the Pickerings' ball."

He stood and crossed to the door, and I stood as well. "James?"

"Yes?" He turned and waited.

"What is your surname?"

He smiled. "I am certain in all of your childhood fantasies of what your wedding would be, you did not imagine that you would need to ask your groom to supply his surname *after* becoming engaged."

I chuckled softly. "No, I did not."

"It is Bradwell, Miss Thurston. My name is James Bradwell."

Robbed of speech, I could do no more than nod while James dipped a soft bow to me and let himself from the room.

It turned out I was meant to become Felicity Bradwell, after all. The trouble was I was marrying the wrong Mr. Bradwell.

CHAPTER 5

Mama sat across from me in the carriage, her gaze uneasy. "Are you certain you wish to do this, Felicity? We can simply walk inside and announce the engagement straight away. Perhaps we can curb some tongues before they wag excessively."

"I am certain." I fiddled with the embroidery trim on my gown's sheer overlay. The blue flowers were meant to brighten my strawberry blonde hair, but I wasn't sure they did much of anything at all except add great expense to an already costly gown. I hadn't needed the embroidery, but Mama had wished for my gowns to be the best so we might escape censure from the overactive snobbery present at most Society events.

Papa watched me expectantly, and I turned my attention to him. "Does Mr. Bradwell have sufficient funds already or were you forced to supply a handsome dowry?"

"I supplied a generous amount that will remain in your name, regardless of what happens to your husband."

"It is merely a precaution," Mama explained. "Should your husband die suddenly, you will not be left destitute when his holdings are passed on to the next heir."

I nodded, aware of the purpose. "James did not require any more for himself?"

Papa shook his head. "He did not want it."

Our carriage rolled to a stop, and I followed my parents from the conveyance and into the townhouse. I had spent the duration of the day considering my situation, but still could not make sense of it. Was James related in some way to the Mr. Bradwell I met last year in Northumberland, or was it a mere coincidence that they shared a name? I had spent the previous nine months developing a *tendre* for my Mr. Bradwell, and recent events had forced me to put aside those feelings for the new future that loomed ahead of me. I could not reconcile the fact that I would possibly become *related* to the man in some way.

We stepped into the house and joined the receiving line to greet our host and hostess. The ballroom doors sat open ahead of us, orange light bleeding from the room into the corridor, and I leaned closer to my parents as we neared it.

"Do you not think it odd that Mr. Bradwell shares a surname with the gentleman who aided us when our carriage broke last year?"

Papa looked at me strangely. "Odd? That was one of the reasons I felt comfortable enough to agree to the match. We had already met a member of Mr. Bradwell's family and the man had proved himself to be of excellent character during our ordeal last year."

"They are related?"

"Gracious, dear, you did not know?" Mama whispered, the feather bobbing on her headdress. "The men are brothers."

My heart dropped to my stomach, and I looked up as we entered the ballroom to find James standing squarely across from me, watching me enter the room. My shoulders immediately straightened, and I held his gaze. Brothers? They were equally handsome but looked nothing alike, apart from their dark hair. But more than half of the men in this ballroom were possessed of dark hair, so I could not be blamed for failing to see that distinguishing feature.

"Ah, Miss Thurston," Mrs. Pickering said, curtsying to me. Her tall, white feathers quivered as she lifted her head again, and I returned the gesture. "I did not know if we would have the pleasure of your company this evening."

"I am exceedingly glad to be here, Mrs. Pickering, and your ballroom looks simply stunning."

The woman preened much like the bird whose feather adorned her hair, and I slipped away, followed by my parents. I wanted to test my social acceptance and prove to my parents that marriage was an unnecessary action, but I searched the room and could not find anyone who I would call a friend.

Mama came to my side, her smile nervous, as Papa slipped away to locate the card room. "I am uncertain where to go. I see a multitude of my friends, but I cannot bear to be rebuffed."

"You will not be," I said with more confidence than I felt. Another sweep over the ballroom, and I noted James walking toward us.

He bowed once he reached our side. "Good evening."

I extended my hand, and he took it, laying a kiss over the back of my glove. The pressure of his lips was directly over the burn I'd received from the candle, and it stalled my breath. Had he done that intentionally? When he lifted his head, the sparkle in his eye proved that he had, indeed, known exactly what he was doing.

My spirits could not help but be buoyed from the blatant reference to the meeting which had catapulted us into this mess to begin with.

"Have you found Society to be to your liking?" he asked quietly.

"I have not had sufficient time to gauge it," I replied. "And my mother is too afraid to do so."

"May I have your supper dance, Miss Thurston?"

"I do not wish to cause you disappointment, Mr. Bradwell, but I feel I've already made myself clear in regard to my opinions about dancing."

"And yet you find yourself at a ball."

"Oh, Felicity," Mama scolded softly. "You cannot refuse the man."

"Yes," James added with a grin. "You cannot refuse me. Besides, I believe you owe me a dance."

A quiet scoff ripped from my throat. "You did not win the wager last night."

"I believe I did, but we were interrupted before you could admit as much."

It was not good to begin our marriage on a lie, so I could not argue his point. But I could not do it. I could not stand up with him until anxious energy filled me to the point of fainting. My nerves were frayed already—fainting would only frighten him and make me look a fool.

"I must find Marianne or Eliza. I need to prove that nothing has altered for me."

James's smile grew tight. "Ah, yes. Do not let me stand in the way of your chance to remove yourself from any obligation to me."

It was impossible to tell for certain, but it nearly sounded as though James was hurt by the very idea. I could not reconcile it. Perhaps he was unused to rejection or the concept that a woman would not want to change her entire life to marry him, stranger or not. He was exceedingly handsome, well-regarded and from a respectable family, and he was flush enough in the pockets to not require an enormous dowry. So his confidence was seemingly warranted.

It was plain that he was settling for me—or for the prospect of no longer needing to seek a wife—and yet, he did not act as though that was the case.

Marianne Hutton entered the room on her mother's arm. "I

must go to my friend. I will . . . find you later, James, if that is what you wish."

"It is," he said quietly.

I slipped away before I could think deeply on the meaning behind his behavior this evening and crossed the ever-filling ballroom toward the Huttons. Mrs. Hutton had stopped to speak to another woman, but Marianne stood a few feet away, and I approached her, dropping into a curtsy.

"Good evening, Marianne."

She looked startled, her gaze snapping from me to her mother. "G-good evening, Felicity."

"I did not have the opportunity to speak to you last night, but your ball was beautiful."

She swallowed hard, her gaze darting again toward her mother. Leaning in, she lowered her voice. "I cannot be seen speaking to you, Felicity. Not until the scandal has passed. Please do not make me walk away. I value your friendship too greatly to treat you so abominably."

My stomach dropped clear to my feet, and I gave her a strained smile, dipping my head before turning away again. At least she had done me the courtesy of explaining herself instead of delivering a cut. I found Eliza Gould not far off among a group of young ladies and stepped in their direction, but each of them turned away before I could move any closer.

I had never felt comfortable in a ballroom, but neither had I ever felt so isolated as I did in that moment. My hands trembled, and my lungs failed to secure a full breath. I searched for my mother and found her standing equally isolated on the other side of the room.

Mr. Peel's copper hair stood out among the crowd, and I decided—in a fit of pure lunacy, obviously—to pass before him on my way back to my mother's side. If he ignored me as well, then I was well and truly sunk.

If not, then I would pay for the relief of having something of a reputation remaining to my name by being forced to accept his plea to dance, as he undoubtedly would offer. It was worth the prospect of fainting in order to prove to my parents and to James that things were not so dire as they seemed.

The entirety of my walk across the ballroom provided me with enough proof that I was the center of tonight's gossip. My name was whispered in conjunction with Mr. Bradwell's everywhere I stepped, and people moved out of my path as though I was Moses and they the Red Sea. By the time I reached the area where Mr. Peel stood, I found myself pleading silently that he would step into my path and halt me, but I continued to walk by, and he turned his head away after catching my gaze.

I could not even pretend to myself that he had not seen me, for I'd caught his panicked expression.

My vision sparkled darkly at the edges, my breath coming rapidly from the stares directed at me throughout the room. I reached for Mama's arm like a beacon and clutched her, willing my heart to calm and the black to recede.

Mama took my hand and squeezed my fingers. Tears welled in my eyes, and I did my best to blink them away, then closed my eyes and focused on controlling my breathing. "I was a fool to suggest this."

"No, you were full of hope," Mama corrected gently. "A fool has lost all hope."

"Mr. Peel would not even look at me."

"That is entirely his loss," James said, appearing at my side at once. Instruments tuned in preparation to begin the dancing, and he lifted his hand toward me. "May I have my dance now, Miss Thurston?"

I looked from his outstretched hand to his earnest face. "I was not being modest, sir. I truly cannot dance."

Mama scoffed quietly. "Yes, you can. Of all the times to submit to your nerves, *now* is not the moment to give up." She turned to James. "Only, be prepared to catch her, should the need arise."

"Catch her?"

My cheeks warmed, and I did not want to explain. "We better not."

Mama was not even apologetic when she whispered, "I am afraid after the way you were just thoroughly rebuffed, you no longer have a choice."

James looked as though he agreed with my mother, and I let out a shaky breath. Perhaps this time would be different. Dancing with James last night had not induced any fainting. It had been enjoyable. Perhaps that was all I needed tonight.

I slid my hand into his, and he held it tightly, placing it over his bent arm to lead me to the dance floor.

We took our places for the quadrille and waited for the music to begin. My skin burned from the many eyes set upon me, and already I could feel my heart rate increase from the attention.

"I am not certain I can do this," I whispered.

James looked down at me, faintly alarmed. "What did your mother mean when she asked me to catch you? Are you prone to tripping?"

"No. I am prone to fainting."

His eyes widened. "Gads, woman. Why?"

I shook my head. Two of the other couples had begun their steps, but I could hardly hear the music for the heavy pulse that thrummed in my ears. My hands shook, and I managed to move through the motions well enough when it was our turn.

We returned to our original places, and James leaned close. "Shall we sit out? We can leave now."

I could not speak. My mouth had gone dry, and within a few moments I would need to step forward and perform a few steps with the stranger on my other side. James watched me move away from him, his gaze on me as we moved through the motions the quadrille required. I turned to find him on the opposite side of the set, using him as a beacon to keep myself focused on the task at hand.

If I kept my attention on James, maybe I could ignore the crowds of spectators.

But as the dance continued, my nerves heightened. I danced back to James's side, and his hand squeezed mine. "Are you well?"

"Yes," I said, my voice breathless. I could not inhale fully, but so long as I could breathe, I could dance.

"Are you certain?"

The stares of the inhabitants around the room ran down my spine like tiny insects, and my stomach squirmed. "Yes, I'm well," I said. Though, I was anything but.

We moved to the center of the set and stepped away again, and I felt James's attention as deeply as I did the gossips about the room.

He was right. He and my father had been correct, as loath as I was to admit it. There was no pulling ourselves out of the depths of this scandal without some casualties. It was better to sacrifice myself than that of my parents' happiness.

"We need to make the announcement," I said.

He turned to me sharply, misstepping. He was light on his feet, though, and it was hardly a noticeable blunder. "Are you certain?"

"We have no other choice. Not unless you should like to remain the center of attention in such a horrid way." To be so utterly watched yet ignored by my friends was the worst kind of torture.

"I haven't noticed," he said.

I laughed lightly, but the black spots were already threatening the edges of my vision, and I did my best to focus on James. Somehow, he seemed to keep the darkness at bay.

We found ourselves moving steadily to the music, in and

around the other three couples, and so long as I focused on James, I could block out the rest of the room. When the end of the dance arrived, I was forced to move around the man beside me, opposite what James was doing, and did my best to keep him in my line of sight.

Instead, I caught the glare from the young woman who had tittered last night when James had given her a glass of lemonade. Her scowl was deep, marring her pretty brow, and at once I noticed each gaze of the surrounding spectators watching me. My heart sped, my vision blurred, and I turned the wrong way, running into another dancer.

The man righted me, but my breath was coming too quickly. I searched for James among the dancers, but he was missing.

The blackness quickly took over, my legs turned helpless, and I fell.

CHAPTER 6

"Where might I lie her down?"

The voice reached my ears as awareness slipped back into my mind, and I shifted against the firm, but padded, sofa.

"Is she stirring?" a woman asked.

"Yes. Do you have a retiring room, madam?"

The rumbling of James's words were close, vibrating through my arm, and I struggled to open my eyes.

As soon as I did, I closed them again. James's face was only just above mine, and his arms were wrapped around me. I felt the rumble of his words because the man was carrying me from the ballroom. It was not a sofa I leaned against, but James's shoulder. If I could sink into the floor and escape this horror forever, I would.

The gentle sway of his steps lulled me, but I did not allow myself to succumb to the sleepiness that generally overcame me after a spell. I inhaled sharply and instantly regretted it when my nose was assaulted with James's spicy cologne. It was incredibly delicious, and now I could never forget how great he smelled.

We followed a woman into another room, and James bent to lay me on the chaise longue. Cool air rushed in when he released me, and I immediately missed the feeling of being cradled in his arms. He crouched beside me and lifted a hand to move hair from my face. "I see now why you avoid dancing at all costs," he whispered.

I could not help but smile. "I am glad you can be taught to see reason." I swallowed, a real fear moving in to take over my drowsy state. He had now seen me at my worst. "If you no longer wish to move forward with the engagement—"

"On the contrary," he said, before I could utter another word. "I think it wise to announce our good news as soon as it is reasonably possible for you to do so. Can I retrieve for you a glass of ratafia or perhaps a cool cloth for your forehead?" He glanced up to the woman who stood in the room with us, and I noticed it was Mrs. Pickering.

"Oh, of course," she said at once, her feather bobbing with her jerky motions. "I will send for both of those at once."

When she left us alone in the room, James smiled ruefully. "I am glad you've agreed to the engagement, for now that Mrs. Pickering has overheard our mention of it, she has surely begun to spread the news about her ballroom."

"Devious," I whispered.

He laughed lightly and took my hand, bringing it to his lips. "I am only glad you appeared to recover so swiftly. You cannot know how dreadful it was to watch you fall."

"Did I not hit my head this time? Sometimes the accompanying headache can last for days."

"No, you did not hit your head," he confirmed softly.

The door opened again, and Mama stepped inside. "Oh, drat. I had hoped you would be able to complete at least one dance tonight."

"Forgive me, Mama."

She waved away my apology and turned to James, who rose

in her presence. "Thank you for catching her, Mr. Bradwell. Sometimes she hits her head, and the resulting headache will linger for days."

I looked at him sharply. "You caught me?"

He nodded. "It was nothing. I appreciate the warning, or I might not have known to keep an eye on you."

He caught me? I had been looking for him and unable to see him in my final moments of lucidness. He must have been paying close attention to me. I could not determine why the thought of that caused a shiver to run through me, chased by a warmth in my chest.

"Can you stand yet?"

I swung my legs over the side of the chaise and waited. I was no longer dizzy, but I was weak. "Nearly," I said.

"We would like to announce our good news," James said.

Mama looked sharply to me. "Is that so? I shall fetch your father from the card room. He will want to be present."

We watched her leave, and I expelled an airy breath. It was amazing how quickly mothers were willing to leave us alone once they learned of our official engagement. It was as though the one thing we were admonished not to do time and again was immediately acceptable. Though I felt no different, and our circumstances hardly felt changed.

I craned my neck to see his face. "Thank you, James."

He bent to look at me. "Truly, it was nothing."

I held his green-golden gaze. "It was something to me."

A maid entered the room with a small bowl of water and a rag, and another followed her with a glass of ratafia. I took the drink and sipped a few swallows before setting the glass on a nearby table.

"Are you ready to face the hordes?" James murmured.

"I don't think I have a choice."

We met my parents in the corridor, and James offered me his arm. I leaned on it more heavily than I intended, but the fainting weakened my legs, and it was nice to have someone beside me.

Papa held the doors open for us, and James and I stepped into the ballroom together. Conversation amongst the occupants nearest the doors came to a swift halt, and James leaned down to whisper in my ear. "Smile, darling, or they'll think you are not happy about this arrangement."

I smiled naturally and glanced up at him. "You would hardly credit it, I am sure, but I have not felt this well in some time."

He held my gaze, a look passing over his face that was entirely unreadable.

I swallowed hard. Had I said the wrong thing?

Mrs. Hutton approached us, a tentative smile on her lips. "Have I heard correctly that congratulations are in order?"

"You have, indeed," James said, loudly enough for all nearby to hear. "I am a fortunate man this evening, for Miss Thurston has agreed to be my wife."

Wife. The word was solid and thick with meaning. It held so much more weight to it than the measly four letters warranted . . . so much expectation and requirements that spanned the remaining decades of our lives. I was sobered immediately by the duties and responsibilities awaiting me, and yet free at the same time.

"When do you plan to marry?" Mrs. Hutton asked.

"As soon as we are able," he said. "I am eager to take Felicity home with me."

"Oh," Mrs. Hutton said, clearly pleased by this pronouncement. It was a credit to her that she appeared genuinely glad and relieved for James. "I do think she will adore Chelton."

"Undoubtedly," he agreed.

We moved further into the room, and I leaned close. "Chelton?"

"My estate. It is in Cumberland."

Cumberland? "Good heavens, that is a fair distance away. I might as well have gone to Scotland."

He looked at me strangely, and I bit my tongue. "Do you usually remain in Cumberland, James, or do you spend a good deal of time in London?"

"I prefer Chelton. I think you might as well once you've seen it."

That would certainly explain why I'd yet to see the man before now. But the reality that I was to be so great a distance from my parents was concerning.

"Is there room to entertain?"

He glanced down at me. "Yes. Who would you like to invite?"

"Only my parents."

James looked over my shoulder at the group surrounding Mama, and I followed his gaze. The women who had refused to speak to her upon our arrival this evening were now making themselves up to her, undoubtedly hoping for scraps of information, and it sickened my stomach. They were fickle in their attentions, and it angered me that the tide of their feelings could be so easily altered.

"Your parents will of course be welcome as often and as long as you wish."

"That is very generous of you."

He slid his fingers around mine, and my heart stuttered. "It will be your home too."

The music continued to fill the room and dancers moved about the center of the floor as friends and acquaintances approached to congratulate us.

My feet were tired, but I remained standing beside James, impressed by his ability to diplomatically navigate the many different conversations. Most of the people who approached us were hardly better than acquaintances to me, but James seemed to know them all. Charisma emanated from him in waves, and I was able to remain quietly beside him as he bore the burden of carrying the conversations.

The blonde woman—who I'd seen with James the evening before at the refreshment table—approached and dipped in a curtsy, her wide eyes trained on my betrothed. "Good evening, Mr. Bradwell."

James bowed. "Good evening, Miss Norland. Are you familiar with Miss Thurston?"

"I am afraid not," Miss Norland said. She gave an uncomfortable titter. "In fact, I had never before heard her name prior to last night. Tell me, sir, where have you been hiding her?"

James stepped just a little closer to me, and I was grateful that he did not move the opposite direction. "She is a rather well-kept secret, is she not? Now forgive me, Miss Norland, but I promised Mrs. Thurston I would return Felicity to her by the end of the evening. If you will excuse us." He dipped a nod of acknowledgement and led me away from the young woman.

"That wasn't polite to so quickly extricate us from her side," I said softly. "But I believe I must thank you all the same."

He shot me a small smile.

I cleared my throat, allowing him to lead me through the crush. "Was she a good friend of yours?"

"No. In fact, all Miss Norland did was help me realize how little I know of you, Miss Thurston. For example, how long you have lived in London, or if it is not your primary residence."

"*Felicity* will do just fine," I said. We were to be married, after all. "And we have time to discover those things."

Though, I knew what he meant by the discovery. I had wondered the same things about him.

James nodded, but his mind was elsewhere. He deposited me on a chair near my parents.

"We have much to discuss, Mr. Thurston. I will call on you in the next few days."

Papa nodded. "Thank you. We look forward to your visit."

"I will write to my family and ask them to prepare the house for our arrival."

"Your family?" I asked, hoping to know who all that entailed.

James flashed me a brief smile. "Everyone will be delighted to meet you. And you will love my brothers, I promise."

I looked down, unable to hold his steady gaze. I had no doubt that I would love at least *one* of his brothers. The problem was that I already did.

CHAPTER 7

I stood in the courtyard of St. James Church beneath the shade of overarching branches, the leaves now beginning to turn green after a winter stripped the tree clean. The new life above my head was bright and fresh, and I hoped it was indicative of the marriage I was about to seal myself into—clean and full of potential.

Mama spoke to Mrs. Hutton not far away, and Papa waited patiently at her side. It had been four weeks since the Pickering ball when our engagement was announced, and nearly four weeks since I had seen James.

He had sent around a note the following morning that he felt it best to return to Chelton straight away to prepare the house for my arrival. It was written between his finely penned lines that he also had some business up north which required his personal attention, and I could not help but wonder if that business was another woman. Was there a young lady in his parish who needed to be let down carefully in a way that only he could accomplish? Was his family not going to openly accept me into their home the way I wished?

Something had occurred after the Pickering ball to give

James reason to believe he needed to make a week-long trip across the country prior to marrying me.

And the more frightening prospect—had he brought his brothers with him to London for the wedding?

Each new arrival in the small churchyard caused my nerves to heighten, though so far none of them were James. We'd chosen this particular church because it was where my parents were married more than two decades before, and they liked the sentimentality of carrying on the tradition, but each new arrival was dressed more finely than I, and I wondered at the purpose of such a fashionable venue for my wedding when I was not quite fashionable myself.

Each guest was either a friend of my parents or my groom, and I would do well to remember that. This wedding was for the benefit of my parents and the good of our reputation. It was not for *me*.

"Perhaps we ought to wait indoors," Papa said.

I ran my hands down the pale blue silk of my gown and straightened the lace overlay. "You've spoken to the vicar already?"

"Yes." He looked out over the stone-covered churchyard. "You're certain this is the date?"

I nodded, though Papa was beginning to worry me. "James chose it himself."

Mrs. Hutton left to walk inside, Mama close behind her, and I drew in a concerned breath. If James jilted me, would I feel relieved or only disheartened? I did not know which I dreaded more: to see James's brother on the morning of my wedding, or to not have a wedding at all.

Loud footsteps clipped down the walkway, and James appeared around the corner. He was dashing in his crisp, black coat and clean cravat, and once he located me beneath the tree, he crossed to me directly. My heart jumped when he smiled, and

I did my best to temper my sudden, overwhelming relief. I was not to be jilted this morning.

I glanced over his shoulder, but no one accompanied him. James delivered a handsome bow. "Good morning, Felicity. Mr. Thurston."

"Your family has not chosen to join you?"

James glanced away. "I told them that they needn't bother. It is a long journey from Chelton, and since we are leaving for Cumberland directly after the wedding breakfast, I did not think it necessary."

My shoulders relaxed, and I was grateful not to have to face anything but my impending marriage this morning.

James swept an arm toward the red brick church. "Shall we?"

I set my white gloved hand over his bent elbow. "Please."

We followed Papa inside, and I grew more anxious with each passing pew full of Mama's fashionable friends. I had not employed a ladies' maid, having no need of one, and my hair was simply done up, my toilette far from extravagant. I'd allowed Mama to select my gown, but she had selected a simple blue gown with an abundance of lace. It was stunning, but not extravagant.

Did James realize his mistake now? I was not the sort like Miss Norland who took great care to appear lovely. I would never be that sort of person. I did not mind being plain. It suited my need to remain out of the general spotlight. But for the first time, I wondered if my husband would be at all bothered by it.

James smiled to those he knew as we took our places, but his expression was far more contemplative than disappointed. He caught my eyes when the vicar stood before us, and I found a refuge within his gaze. My lungs filled smoothly, and my worries fled.

"Dearly beloved," the vicar began. "We are gathered here together in the sight of God, and in the face of this company, to join together this man and this woman in holy matrimony."

My heart sped as he continued, and despite my fears, I could not allow myself to believe I was making a mistake.

The vicar's attention turned to James as he asked if he would take me as his wife to love, comfort, and honor me.

"I will," James said, his eyes fastened on me.

The vicar asked if I would take James, and obey, serve, love, and honor him. I looked to James. "I will."

His mouth tipped into a half-smile. This man, this near-stranger, had just pledged himself to me, and I, in turn, to him. We were bonded now in a way that I could never be with anyone else.

Papa stepped forward to give me away, and the vicar directed James and me to take one another by the right hand. We vowed to one another, and when it came time for the ring, my heart stalled.

James pulled a small, gold ring from his pocket with a blue gem in the center. It was remarkable, and far too costly to adorn my plain finger. My breath caught when the minister took the ring to place on my finger, and James spoke. "With this ring I thee wed, and with all my worldly goods I thee endow: in the name of the Father, and of the Son, and of the Holy Ghost. Amen."

The finality of his words rang through me. It was through, and we were married. The vicar proceeded to pray, but my attention was riveted by the ring upon my finger. It was heavy with the expectations and the vows I had only just made, and I wanted to live up to its worth.

But I could not help but glance at my mother and wonder if I would let James down in the same way I had done so for my parents over the last few years. I was not the daughter they wanted, for I did not desire the same things they did.

Panic laced my body, and I glanced up to the white ceiling, tracing my gaze along the gilt edges and pleading with my panic to subside. As much as I enjoyed James carrying me from the ballroom a month ago, I did not wish to repeat the situation during my wedding.

The vicar took my hand, drawing my attention back to the ceremony, and I looked at James. His brow was drawn, and I attempted a smile while the vicar completed the ceremony. James and I turned toward the gathering, and he slid his hand into mine. I anchored myself in that feeling and allowed him to lead me from the church.

When we reached the churchyard again, we paused under the tree, the red-brick church emptying its occupants around us. James leaned down until his lips rested near my ear. "Are you well?"

I could only nod, fearful that any words would escape my lips scratchy and uncouth.

He hesitated before turning and pressing a kiss to my cheek. "I am glad."

Warmth bloomed from that spot and filled the entirety of my body. I shuddered from the sudden reaction and swallowed hard despite my scratchy throat.

James's smile was sweet, and he directed it to the well-wishers who approached us in turn. He carried the bulk of the conversations, and all the while, he never let go of my hand.

Mama wanted to rush home to prepare for the wedding breakfast, and by the time James and I reached my townhouse, there were twice as many people within its walls than the number of attendees at the actual ceremony.

"I am famished," James said absently, holding the door for me.

"Cook has spent the last few weeks on the rum cake. You must try it." I paused, realizing that I was unaware if James enjoyed cake or not. "But I know Mama has gone to great expense to see that there is a wide variety available, if that does not suit you."

"Rum cake suits me just fine," he said. "You will soon learn that I am not difficult to please in regard to meals."

We moved further into the house and up the stairs toward the rooms designated for the breakfast, and I assisted James in finding a plate and loading it with an abundance of food. My appetite had not yet returned.

"Do you not wish to eat?" he asked.

"I cannot," I said softly, aware that we were surrounded by well-wishers. "I will do so once the people have left us on our own again."

He looked mildly alarmed. "Surely you will eat something before we travel?"

My stomach squeezed, and I nodded. We had designated one hour to the breakfast, and then James's carriage would arrive to carry us to Chelton. My trunks were packed and waiting in the study downstairs, and my goodbyes would need to be brief so I did not leave my parents with a tear-stained memory.

James seemed to sense my unease. "Would you prefer to leave tomorrow?"

What would one day matter when I would have to leave my home today anyway? James only rented rooms when he was in Town, and I did not wish to sleep in bachelor's quarters. It was better this way.

"No." I tried to soften my words with a smile. "I will be more comfortable when this breakfast is over, I swear it."

He seemed to take me at my word.

"I would like to find Marianne, if that is agreeable to you."

He took a large bite of sausage and indicated that I could go.

I had not even left the room when two other men had slid in to my place to speak to him, and James's voice could be heard down the corridor, his laughter contagious.

Marianne was seated on a tufted sofa in the sitting room,

and I lowered myself beside her, aware of the many other men and women surrounding us. "I do believe my mama has invited every person she knows in London."

Marianne sipped her chocolate. "You are her only child. Can you blame her for going to such an expense?"

"I suppose not."

"Have you had any chocolate yet? It is divine." She sipped her drink again, and my stomach flipped.

"I'm afraid I cannot eat anything until this is over." I pressed a hand to my stomach, and she looked at me with compassion.

"A little bread might help you to stave off the nausea," she said. "I cannot know firsthand, but my sister did nothing but nibble on rolls for the duration of her pregnancy."

I looked at her sharply. Did she think I was with child? "I am only nauseous because large gatherings make me nervous."

Marianne's face paled, the color draining from her rosy cheeks. She lowered her cup to her lap and regarded me with wide eyes. "I've blundered."

"Is that what everyone thinks? Who has told you this?"

She glanced around, and I did the same, wondering which of the women in this room believed the same of me as my friend had.

Marianne leaned closer. "I cannot recall who told me, but I did not realize it wasn't true."

"You did not think to ask me?"

She tilted her head to the side. "As though I could do such a thing."

But it was undeniable that Marianne had spoken to me as though my being with child was common knowledge—as though my marriage was a rushed affair to hide our greater sins. What little warmth I had yet remaining had since seeped from my cheeks, and I was woozy from the implications of this revelation. I wanted to be out of this house at once—James and I only married to *save* our reputations, not to solidify them.

Rising from the sofa, I moved to leave when Marianne reached for my wrist and stopped me. "Please, forgive me. Truly, I did not know."

I nodded to her and turned away, slipping from the sitting room and down the stairs. I heard someone call my name, but I could not be relied upon to socialize with my parents' friends now that I knew what they thought of me. I slid quietly into my father's study and shut the door, then leaned against it. Dropping my head in my hands, I did my best to temper my heavy breathing. A knock, though soft on the door, startled me.

If I pretended not to hear, would they go away?

A moment later another knock came.

"Felicity?"

It was difficult to tell through the thick oak door, but that sounded like James.

"Please, allow me in."

I hurriedly wiped the moisture from my eyes and inhaled through my nose before turning to open the study door. I could not force James to remain in the corridor, but I wasn't sure I wanted to see him just yet, either.

He stood in the entryway, lines between his eyebrows that spoke of his concern. "Are you—"

"Nothing has happened. I am merely overwhelmed by the splendor and magnitude of the day."

"You realize that you cannot fool me, yes?" He stepped inside and closed the door behind him. "I did not ask if anything had happened, but you gave that away yourself."

Drat. I moved over to the window and pushed the drapes aside to allow more light in. Shrubbery outside the window protected us from view, and I turned to lean against the frame. "It has come to my attention that we are to have a baby."

My goal had not been to shock the man, but I had succeeded all the same. His eyes widened and he tucked his chin. He rested his other fist on his hip. "I do realize that is a natural part of marriage."

"Yes, well, I only meant . . ." I cleared my throat. "It is believed that I am *already* with child."

"Ah." He nodded as understanding fell over his features. "Who told you this?"

"Marianne Hutton. She did not realize that it was untrue. Evidently in our attempt to save our good names, we have only confirmed the worst in everyone's minds. Do you not realize how contradictory that is? I am now accepted in Society— applauded, even, for making such a splendid match—and yet I have only proven that the actions which previously made me a pariah did, in fact, come to pass."

"It is unfair."

"Exceedingly," I said with feeling. I shook my head and looked to my father's bookcase, noting the adventure novels I'd consumed time and again, and wishing I could be lost in one of them right now.

If I'd considered any of this, would I have begged my mama to allow me to travel to Jane's estate in Scotland instead of saving our reputation with a rushed marriage to a near-stranger? Perhaps then I could at least have had a chance to secure a love match. As it stood now, the *ton* still believed me to be a woman of lesser morals—only now I had a ring on my finger and their blessing.

"I cannot change the prejudices against us," James said, and guilt swept over me.

"It is not your responsibility to do so."

"No, but I could have considered other options."

My lips formed a tired smile. What did other options matter now? "We are married, James. It is done."

"What if it isn't done? Not yet, I mean."

I straightened. Was he proposing an annulment? I could never do that to my parents, to *him.*

He took my hand gently in his and turned it over. Sparing me a brief glance, he lowered his attention to my glove and pulled at the fingertips one at a time to loosen the garment before sliding it free of my hand and setting it on a nearby shelf. His skin on mine was a heady, warm feeling. He brushed his thumb over the place where I'd spilled the wax on our first meeting, the skin now pale and healed.

Directing his attention at my hand, he said, "We can still prove your innocence, Felicity. If you do not have a babe or show signs of carrying one in the first six months of our marriage, then all will know that you are as faultless as you claim to be."

He glanced up and held my gaze.

My breath caught. "Are you implying—"

"Yes. We will not"—he cleared his throat—"be together as man and wife until the six months has passed. We can return to London for the Season next year and your good name will be restored in every way that matters to you."

It was a sacrifice for him, and I could not believe he was willing to agree to it. Nay, not agree, to *suggest* it.

"Is that not strange?"

He chuckled softly. "Nothing about us so far has been typical, why would we start now?"

A weight lifted from my chest. "Six months."

James lifted an eyebrow. "This could be good for us, you know. Perhaps we can spend that time courting."

Time felt suspended. "You would like to court your wife?"

"I did not have the chance before, so why not now?"

Butterflies flapped about my empty stomach, and my breathing grew shallow—but in an entirely enjoyable way. We were now bound to spend the remainder of our lives together, and this seemed a good way to begin.

"I suppose that would be good. You can, for instance, tell me how many of your family members live at your house, or whether or not you enjoy stargazy pie."

He laughed, his thumb rubbing lazy circles over my hand. "And you might inform me about whether or not you enjoy riding or playing battledore and shuttlecock."

I would not disappoint him further this morning by explaining how deeply I disliked both of those activities.

"Six months of courting," he said again, as though he was warming to the idea, "and six months to prove our innocence."

"Indeed. Shall we seal our agreement?" I pulled my hand from his grasp and straightened it.

James's gaze fell to my lips. He swayed forward slightly before seeming to shake himself. "Yes, I think that would be best." His voice was raspy, and my heart jumped. Had he nearly meant to kiss me?

Surely we would not need to wait the six months for *that*.

James took my hand and shook it.

"Shall we rejoin our breakfast?" he asked.

With him holding my hand, I believed myself capable of it. I nodded, and he released me in order to retrieve my glove from the shelf. When I tried to take it from him, he shook his head and proceeded to slide it back over my fingers. "I vowed only an hour ago to honor and care for you, Felicity. Allow me to do so."

I nodded, my throat too thick with emotion to argue that I was capable of putting on my own glove.

Once he finished, he took my hand to lead me back upstairs. I pushed aside my staunched concerns and did my best not to think about the very perfect man beside me, and his brother I would be seeing again in a week's time. Perhaps James's brother already knew to expect me as James's bride and did not care—or perhaps I would soon find myself in an uncomfortable situation.

Regardless, I couldn't help the hope that grew like vines around my heart. My husband wished to court me.

CHAPTER 8

The journey to Cumberland was not entirely foreign to me. I had spent my summers traveling to my aunt's estate in Northumberland for her yearly house party, and the slow, tedious road to Cumberland was nearly the same. The distance certainly was comparable.

James leaned against the carriage wall opposite me, his eyes closed. His soft snoring had ceased, so I was unsure if he was still asleep or simply resting. His legs were stretched out, and his knee bumped mine with every rut and turn on the road, but after a week together in the carriage, I'd grown accustomed to sharing such a small space with him.

We were nearing the end of our journey now with no one else for company, both of us doing our best to remain polite and stay out of the other's way. This was in no way how my parents acted around one another, and I hoped that one day the discomfort and politeness between James and me could meld into a real friendship, at the very least.

I was not foolish enough to hold out for love, but I would content myself with calling James a dear friend and companion.

Our beginning felt promising and proved we had the makings for compatibility, at least.

Except, of course, for the fact that James did not enjoy reading.

Dratted odd, that.

He drew in a deep breath and shifted on the squabs across from me, and immediately I was aware of myself. The way I sat, how loudly I breathed. My affinity for fainting and dislike of social activities were unfamiliar to James, and I did not wish for him to take displeasure in anything else I did so early in our marriage—especially since he had so far proven himself to be a paragon of perfection.

His eyes blinked open and sleepily rested on me. "Good morning, Wife."

A thrill ran up my neck. I did not think I would ever grow accustomed to the title. "I believe you mean good *afternoon*."

"Indeed." He looked to the window. "We have almost arrived."

Excitement drained from me. I had learned that James had two brothers who both lived at Chelton more often than not—Henry, the middle child, whom I met in Northumberland last summer, and Benedict, the youngest. The only other resident was their mother, Lady Edith, who was titled because her father was the late Earl of Claverley. James's father had died at Waterloo, and since he and Lady Edith had no daughters, there were no other family members at Chelton.

Though they did have a cousin and his wife—the current Lord and Lady Claverley—who lived relatively close.

"Do you have a very formal household, James?"

His head tilted to the side. "Whatever do you mean by formal? We are not prone to dining by rank or anything of that nature. Though my mother has long insisted that I preside at the head of the table. It is tedious, but I oblige her."

"I suppose I was only wondering how many members of your family would be present to greet us when we arrive."

"All of them, I imagine."

I did my best to appear pleased by this revelation. It was perhaps a blessed thing that the first time I would see Henry as a married woman would be in the presence of the rest of the family. Surely, I worried for nothing. Henry likely did not even recall who I was.

My childish infatuation was just that—young, naive, and very much in the past.

"Tell me of your brothers," I said.

James straightened in his seat. "You will be able to make your own opinion about them soon enough." He pointed through the glass window on the door. "We have arrived."

I leaned forward and peered through the thick glass. The carriage rolled over a wide, stone bridge, and sheep scattered to either side of us. Chelton sat in the distance up a shallow hill, its golden stone exterior a neat square with three rows of windows above a split, curved staircase. I lost the ability to breathe from the grandeur before me.

James crossed to sit beside me on the bench, but my attention was rapt on the house we approached. "Do you like it, Felicity?"

"Good heavens," I breathed. "I cannot *like* it. I am amazed by it."

"Then you approve?"

A short laugh burst from my chest, and I turned to James, grinning. He watched me earnestly, immediately sobering my delight. This was his home, and for some unknown reason, he cared what I thought of it. As though I could find *anything* to criticize about such a glorious house.

His hand rested on his leg, and I reached for it, curling my fingers around his. "It is truly magnificent."

James squeezed my hand, and I allowed the action to infuse me with strength while the carriage pulled to a stop on the brown gravel drive.

A footman opened the door and let down the step, and James exited the vehicle first. He offered me his hand, and I stepped from the safety of the carriage. Four people stood in a line at the top of the stairs, the men's arms resting on the balustrade before them, its pale stone matching the house and lined with thick, even columns. Two women bookended the men, one regal and the other simply dressed—the latter of the two was likely the housekeeper.

"Come, meet my family," James whispered, offering me his bent arm.

The procession up the grand, stone staircase was tediously slow. When we reached the top, I avoided looking at the man who was obviously Henry Bradwell, his eyes watching me earnestly. James paused before a woman with gray hair pulled back into a knot, a few curls left dangling near her temples. Her burgundy muslin gown was immaculate, and her movements graceful. She reminded me of my mama in her bearing, but in little else.

"Mother, allow me to introduce Felicity Bradwell."

I looked to James sharply, but he was correct. It was my name now, though it still sounded odd to my ears.

"Felicity, this is my mother, Lady Edith."

We each curtsied in turn and moved forward down the line as James introduced each person by name.

"My brother, Benedict." The man bowed. He was taller than either of his older brothers and equally as handsome, with a thick head of curly brown hair and a decided twinkle in his blue eyes.

"And my brother, Henry."

Henry dipped his head, but when he raised it again, he sent

James a soft smile. "We have met before, actually, just last summer. How do you do, Miss Thur—Mrs. Bradwell?"

My stomach flipped under the scrutiny of his blue eyes. His curly hair was slightly mussed, and he looked just as handsome as he had last summer. "I am well, I thank you. The ride was long, however, and I am grateful to have arrived."

James looked from his brother to me. "You've met?"

"Yes, last summer in Northumberland," I said.

He appeared confused by Henry's revelation but gave a nod and continued down the line. He gestured to the final woman. She was tall and thin, her black dress hanging from a bony figure, and her gaze, while severe, was not unkind. "Meet our housekeeper, Mrs. Prescott."

I dipped in another curtsy. "It is a pleasure."

"Do not let us keep you outside any longer, my dear," Lady Edith said, moving to my side. "If you would like to come with me, I will show you to your room and send for some dinner. I imagine you would like to take it in your chamber this evening? Prescott can manage your things."

Was it so obvious that I desired a reprieve already? "That would be lovely, Lady Edith."

James remained behind with his brothers as his mother led me into the house, and Mrs. Prescott started down the stairs toward where footmen were unloading the carriage.

We stepped indoors, and I did my best to cover my awe. The ceiling was tall enough to reach the attic, with a black and white checkered floor that spread across a gargantuan hall and opened up to an enormous staircase. Gilded, baroque-style carvings adorned the ceilings and alcoves on either side of the stairs, and I immediately felt small.

Tall windows punctuated the wall and doors opened into what appeared to be an enclosed courtyard. It looked peaceful and serene, a square space with only a shallow fountain in the center.

"It does take some getting used to," Lady Edith said softly. "But I promise it will come to feel like home."

How this massive building could ever earn the descriptor of *home* was beyond my comprehension. It ranked among the museums and palaces in London in my mind, for I had never seen such opulence or grandeur in any other setting.

And I was to be its mistress? I felt more suited to donning a gray gown and white cap and scrubbing the checkerboard floor.

But perhaps I would not be called upon to take up that role, for Chelton already had a mistress. Lady Edith began up the carpeted steps, and I followed her. She turned her head to speak over her shoulder as she ascended. "I did not realize you and Henry shared an acquaintance. Tell me, how did that come about? He does not go to Town often."

"My aunt has an estate in Northumberland. On our way to visit her last summer, our carriage broke an axle. The rain was awful, and the roads were unpassable, but Mr. Bradwell allowed my family to take refuge in his hunting box for a few nights."

"Hmm," she said. "He's never mentioned it."

My back straightened, and I swallowed the initial umbrage that followed her remark. Perhaps Henry had not mentioned it because it meant nothing to him. If that was the case, then I was exceedingly glad I had never posted him the letter that my cousin pressed me to write. It would have been forward, indeed, and worse still when the recipient was uninterested in pursuing an acquaintance.

I wanted to shift the conversation away from myself, and away from my connection with Henry. "I've been told you have a nephew nearby."

"Yes, he lives with his family on the other side of Bakewell. It is not very far, so we must include them when we go about delivering your cards. You have brought them with you, I assume?"

We moved across the landing and through another door. "I

haven't had any cards made yet." In truth, I had been hoping to avoid bride visits. I realized I would need to find a way to introduce myself to local society, of course, but I had not realized I was marrying into such opulence. I needed time to readjust my perspective before presenting myself as a member of such a family.

James had never before made his wealth clear to me, and it was plain, after looking at his house, why he had not pressed Papa for a larger dowry. If he had not needed money from me, then his estate must be flourishing. It was a level of wealth I had never before contemplated for myself—I had never even imagined it.

"Well, it is no matter. I can see it done tomorrow."

We paused before a tall door with a small knob in its center, and I searched for the words to adequately portray how I felt without giving offense. "Is it necessary to begin bride visits quite so soon? I am afraid my mind has not yet caught up with the changes to my life of late."

Lady Edith watched me with a discerning eye. "I am not sure what James has told you, but our standing and reputation as the Bradwell family is immaculate, and I do not wish to stain it at all by offending our neighbors. We will not be able to deliver cards until they are made, of course, and I would not wish to put you out by expecting you to begin your visits as soon as tomorrow. But we have a reputation to uphold, Miss—Mrs. Bradwell, and I do hope that will not be too much of an inconvenience for you."

"Please call me Felicity." I could not bear to steal her name. I had already stolen her son.

She gave me a tight smile and opened the door. "This is your bedroom, Felicity. I do hope it meets your satisfaction. I have chosen the colors myself, but if there is anything you do not like, you need only say the word, and we will have it made over."

I stepped past Lady Edith and into a room covered in varying shades of blue and cream. At a glance, it greatly resembled the gown I wore to my wedding, with its pale blue wall hangings and cream drapes. The tall bed was surrounded by blue and cream brocade, tied back away from the four posts, and the plush carpet spread out in varying shades of pink.

Each table possessed a vase of pink and white roses, and the scent was faint but pleasant.

"This is beautiful."

"Thank you. Prescott will be up shortly with your trunks, and a tray should arrive soon after. I will leave you now, unless there is anything you would like to know?"

Was there? I could not wrap my mind around the room that was meant to be mine alone. We could easily fit an entire floor of my parents' London townhouse in this room. "I cannot think of anything."

She pointed to a white door set in the wall near the fireplace. "That will lead into James's room. Breakfast is served in the parlor, but you are welcome to ring for a tray if you prefer."

I stared at the door connecting my room to my husband's. It would not be in use for the next six months, but no one else need know that.

Lady Edith paused as though considering something, a line forming between her eyebrows. "Have you brought a maid? I do not recall seeing anyone else in the carriage, and I know James left his valet here."

"No, Lady Edith. I do not have a maid."

She gave a nod. "Then I will see to hiring someone from Bakewell tomorrow when I go in to town for your cards."

"You needn't go to the trouble. I have been managing well enough without one for so long."

She seemed to measure her words, and I wondered in what way I had erred. "I will see to it that you have a maid, Felicity. We should, perhaps, pay a visit to the modiste, as well. You are a Bradwell now."

And with that edict, she left the room.

I spun in a slow circle and took in the majesty of the room, my shoulders heavy with expectation. I closed my eyes and heard the words repeated over again.

You are a Bradwell now. But would I give my new family cause to be proud, or would I spoil everything?

CHAPTER 9

D arkness had long since descended, and the fire in the large hearth blazed in my new bedchamber. Mrs. Prescott had emptied the measly contents of my trunks into the wardrobe and refused my help, despite my persistent attempts. She hadn't seemed comfortable with the offer, and I realized I had much to learn about the expectations of living in such a house.

I should have inquired better with James about the state of his home and income prior to accepting his proposal, but at the time, it had not mattered to me.

A knock rapped on the door, and I drew my dressing gown tighter, tying the sash in the front to keep it closed. Perhaps Lady Edith had already procured a maid and sent her up for comportment lessons.

I swallowed a snort at the very thought and went to the door. "Yes?"

"It is only me," James said, but his muffled voice sounded as though it came from behind me.

I pulled the door open to find an empty corridor and closed it again, turning to face the door that led into James's bedchamber just a few feet away. Nerves danced over my skin, and I crossed toward James's room. It was unlocked, and I turned the knob easily and opened it to reveal James framed by the open doorway in his shirtsleeves and waistcoat, his cravat discarded elsewhere.

The sight was possibly the most manly thing I had ever before seen, and it took great restraint not to stare at the triangle of skin visible at his open shirt collar or the way his skin dipped at the hollow above his collarbone.

"Good evening, sir."

He smiled softly. "I only wanted to say goodnight. I missed you at dinner, but I do not fault you for retiring early." He glanced over my shoulder at the rumpled bedclothes. "I worried I would be waking you."

"No, not at all. I haven't been able yet to fall asleep."

"Is that typical for you?"

"Yes." I had always struggled with falling asleep quickly. "Though I did wonder if I would be so tired from the journey that tonight would prove different."

"It can be difficult to adjust to a new bed."

We both grew silent, and I searched behind James for something to say. His chamber caught my interest, and I noted it was done similarly in blue, but on a darker scale. The walls were wood-paneled instead of painted white, and the silk hangings were navy instead of pale blue. It complemented my chamber well, though it maintained a masculine feel.

"Would you like to see the room?" he asked, noticing where my attention had drawn.

I shook my head and took a small step backward. Entering his chamber would feel intimate in a way that I was not quite ready for. Truly, I did not even know this man's favorite color or least favorite meal. How could I explore his personal things before I had explored his mind?

"Perhaps another time, then. I do not wish to keep you."

"I am not sleepy, James. It is only that I do not feel . . . well, we are strangers."

A look flashed in his eyes that I could not decipher. Had it been sorrow or perhaps understanding? He relaxed a little and rested a shoulder against the doorframe, crossing his arms over his broad chest, and I smelled a whiff of his spicy cologne. It was different this time, however—less pure, as though it had mixed with James's essence to give off an entirely unique scent.

"I would like for us not to feel as though we are strangers. How best do you think we might accomplish this?"

"Courting," I said.

He nodded. "Of course, it will be a trial to find time alone with you. Mother's list of things she would like to teach you spans the entirety of the desk in the library."

The very notion caused me to step back. He seemed to sense my hesitancy and straightened. "You only need to do that which you are comfortable with, Felicity. No one will press you beyond those bounds."

His eyes were earnest, and I knew I could trust him. "I want to do my best in this role, but I admit to being overwhelmed. It will take me time to learn what is required of me."

"Mother has been mistress of Chelton for a long time, and she has much wisdom to pass on. I recommend learning from her, and I will do whatever is in my power to support you." He smiled. "I even promise to steal you away from your lessons as often as you need me to."

My lips formed a smile on their own accord. "So we might mend our way toward not being strangers."

"Indeed. In fact . . ." He rubbed a hand over his stubbled jaw, the full day's growth appearing in a faint, dark shadow. "Perhaps we shall agree to share one fact each day."

"One fact about ourselves?"

"Yes. Just think, by the end of our first year of marriage we shall know more than three hundred things about one another. We could hardly call our spouse a stranger at that point."

"It is a reasonable idea."

"Shall we begin tonight?"

"Yes. But you must go first. I have no idea what to say."

He tilted his head to the side. "We can keep it very simple. Tonight, I will share with you that my favorite color is blue."

"I am not surprised after looking at your room."

He glanced over his shoulder. "Ah, yes. I had it done over a few years ago. You like it?"

"I do. Mine is lovely as well, though your mother told me that she chose these colors."

He nodded.

"Tell me, James. Did I remove your mother from her chamber?"

His mouth gave a tight smile. "No. She left it once I returned from Cambridge with a desire to call Chelton my main residence again, shortly after my father died. She had the room done over in preparation for my bride, but it has sat empty for more than a year. I am sure it does her heart glad to see it being used before the colors could go out of fashion."

I couldn't help but laugh at the notion, though my stomach tightened. "Did you have a bride in mind when you returned from Cambridge?"

His brow puckered, then cleared. "Oh, no. I did not. Mother only wanted me to marry and prepared the room accordingly, but I was not yet ready. That is to say, I did court some women to appease her. A few still remain in Bakewell, and I'm certain you will soon come to count them as friends."

"They are married now?"

He glanced away and cleared his throat. "One of them is, yes. The other has remained unwed. She is a lovely woman, but we did not suit."

And the poor woman had undoubtedly dreamed of becoming

the mistress of Chelton. Surely James was mistaken, and we would not easily become friends.

I looked to the waning fire. It took me back in my mind to the night I met James at the ball and all that had transpired since. This entire situation began because I wanted to look about a man's library. Perhaps that is what I would share tonight.

"My favorite pastime is reading."

"I did surmise as much," James said, his voice soft. "Given the way we met. Perhaps you can share something different?"

"Different. Very well." I searched my mind for something to say, but the only noteworthy things about me were my love of reading and my innate discomfort of finding myself the center of attention in social situations—both of which he was familiar with. "My cousin, Jane, is my dearest friend. She was married last summer and now lives in Scotland, which had previously felt like a whole world away."

"Though now, you probably live closer to her than you do to London."

"I would have to consult a map, but I do think you might be correct."

"How did Jane meet her Scottish husband?"

"They have known one another their entire lives. Their mothers are good friends, and they attended the house parties every summer at Arden Castle, just like we did."

"Ah, yes. The house party you were traveling to when your carriage broke." He chuckled, but the sound was strained, uneasy. "When your father spoke to me of the connection between him and Henry I did not realize you had met my brother as well."

I opened my mouth to speak, but James continued.

"Not to say there is anything the matter with it, for I should have made that assumption. It was odd, however, that I did not connect the points before we arrived. But Henry never mentioned anything about it."

"I can only assume our meeting did not make a strong enough mark on your brother for him to consider sharing it with you."

"Yes, well . . . I did arrive at the hunting lodge with Benedict only a few days later. It would seem the sort of thing a man shares simply because it is of interest." He shook his head. "There is no understanding Henry sometimes. He and I have never seen eye-to-eye on most matters."

My stomach swooped uncomfortably. I had formed what I'd believed to be an immediate bond with Henry last summer merely because we had understood one another so fully in our short conversations. If what James said was true of him and his brother, what could it say for James and me?

"You look as though something is troubling you. Is it something I said?"

I shook my head. "No, of course not. I suppose I am weary."

He paused briefly. "So long as you are always honest with me, and I with you, I believe we can make something of our marriage."

His words rang with truth within me, but I did not want to share my concerns and put the idea into his mind that perhaps I was better suited to his brother than I was to him. It was late, and I was much better off going to sleep. Or attempting to, anyway.

James remained in the doorway, but he lifted his hand, reaching toward me, and I stepped forward to place mine in it. He raised my bent knuckles to his lips and pressed a kiss on my skin, directly where I had spilled the wax on our first meeting. Lightning shot up my arm, and I squeezed his fingers softly on impact.

"Goodnight, Felicity."

I retook my hand and rested it on the door. "Goodnight, James."

Once he stepped back and the door closed with a click, I released a breath that had been lodged in my chest. How could one small kiss—on my *hand*, no less—have the power to rob me of breath? More than likely it wasn't the kiss, but the way James tended to make me feel, that held the power.

I returned to my bed to attempt sleep, but staring at the fireplace and the wall that divided my bedroom from James's, I did not imagine I would be able to accomplish that feat anytime soon.

CHAPTER 10

The following morning was sunny and cloudless, and I took extra time in my room to attempt a more intricate hairstyle than the simple knot I typically wore. I twisted pieces of hair and gathered sections together, but nothing appeared in the mirror as I'd imagined in my mind.

It was hopeless. *I* was hopeless and bound to appear a dowdy simpleton beside Lady Edith and her effortless elegance. Surely, she would not want to take me into Bakewell appearing like a governess.

I puffed a hair away from my forehead and groaned. There was nothing for it. I would need to put my hair up in the way I knew how and await the maid Lady Edith intended to select for me. I could only hope I would not be an embarrassment to my new family in the meantime.

It would be a blessed relief when my parents arrived in a fortnight and brought a sense of normalcy with them. I was already working on my arguments to convince them to stay longer than the few weeks they intended to stay.

Once my hair was secured in a knot, a few tendrils left loose beside my temples that would not fit into the bun, I donned my green muslin dress and pulled on my slippers. The gown was one of my nicer day dresses, and it was the best I could do without sporting evening wear in the morning.

Windows along the corridor outside of my room were opened to the morning light. I tried to retrace the steps I had taken with Lady Edith the day before, but quickly found myself lost. The house was a veritable maze, and within a quarter of an hour I found myself exactly where I'd started, but with no clear idea of how I had gotten there. I had even used a set of *stairs* at one point.

A moment's temptation begged me to knock on James's door and ask him to direct me to the parlor for breakfast, but I did not wish to wake him if he was still asleep. I would try to find my own way one more time.

I walked down the corridor and turned, exactly as I thought I had with Lady Edith, and ran directly into a man.

"Oh, forgive me!" I stepped back, pressing my hands to my midsection.

Henry stood apart from me, his curly, brown hair in disarray and his blue eyes on me. "There is nothing to forgive. I should have watched where I was walking."

I glanced down to find a book in his hand, his thumb pressed between the pages. "I can well and truly understand the desire to continue reading after reaching a pivotal moment in the story, Mr. Bradwell. It was I who should not have turned the corner so swiftly."

He looked past my shoulder and then at my hands, seemingly unable to rest his gaze on my face. "Were you heading toward the breakfast parlor?"

"That was my goal."

"Then allow me to direct you." He gestured behind me. "You were going the wrong way."

"Ah, of course." My cheeks burned, and I stepped aside to allow him to walk beside me. We retraced my previous steps and passed my chamber, turning down the opposite corridor and finding the entrance to the wide stairs there.

I had been turned completely around. "I feel I shall never learn my way about."

"You shall. We can post footmen in every corridor if you feel the need, though."

I glanced up sharply, but the twinkle in his eye exposed his jest. "I will let you know if that becomes necessary."

We traveled to the breakfast room in silence, and Henry paused at the entrance. The room was empty, though a sideboard sat against the wall teeming with covered dishes. Henry indicated that I should precede him into the room, and I stepped forward.

We gathered our plates and filled them in silence before carrying them to the round table in the center of the room.

Henry pulled a chair out for me and sat in the seat beside mine, laying his book down beside his plate. "Are your parents well?"

I took great care in slicing my stewed tomato to give myself something to focus on. Could he not have sat across from me in order to give me space to breathe? Or perhaps that would have felt more odd and pointed than this close proximity.

What had he asked? Oh, my parents. "Yes, they are both in good health. Though my father has mentioned returning to your hunting lodge a handful of times since last summer."

"Had I been there to receive him, he would have been most welcome."

"You better not say as much when he arrives in a fortnight, or you will find him finagling an invitation out of you."

Henry laughed. "Perhaps I will suggest it, and we can escape for a week or so. Benedict is always looking for a reason to go to Sedwick Lodge, so I am certain he would be happy to join us."

"You wish to escape?" I asked, popping a bite of tomato in my mouth.

Henry's gaze fell to my mouth and quickly looked away.

"I wonder if it will perhaps become necessary," he said quietly. He fidgeted with the kippers on his plate and cleared his throat. "The heat can sometimes become unbearable in June, and there are so many trees at Sedwick, so it is much cooler. Though I admit I would prefer a warm summer to the deluge of rain we endured last year."

"I do not mind the rain." I cut my tomato into even smaller pieces. "It makes for a good excuse to remain indoors and read."

Henry chuckled. "There is no arguing with such sound reasoning."

"Perhaps we can pray for a little more rain so I won't be required to attend my bride visits."

Henry's responding chuckle did not sound as cheerful as before, and he pushed his kippers about a little more on his plate. "I do not know why I selected these," he said softly. "I cannot abide fish of any type."

I glanced up sharply and laughed. "Indeed? Perhaps you are as nervous as I."

He scrubbed a hand over his chin, and the gesture reminded me of James last night in my doorway, his shirtfront open and his handsome eyes on me. The brothers did not look at all similar—their noses and the shapes of their eyes were nothing alike, one had curly hair and the other relatively straight—but they shared some of the same mannerisms.

"Undoubtedly more so," he said.

"Mr. Bradwell—"

"Call me Henry, please," he said, softening the request with a smile. "We are brother and sister now, after all."

I swallowed. "Very well, Henry. I wouldn't wish to make you uncomfortable in your own home. If my presence here is causing you distress or making you feel the need to escape—"

Benedict came into the room with James on his tail, both men in riding clothes and windswept hair, and I clamped my mouth closed. The interruption was ill-timed. I could not despair about their riding attire, however. What a blessed relief. If James rode with his brother, then I would never be forced to tell him how very much I disliked the activity.

Henry rose. "I am going to fill a new plate."

James glanced from me to Henry's plate. "Kippers? You hate fish."

"I wasn't thinking," Henry said.

"What is new?" Benedict grinned from the sideboard. "You likely had a book in your hand while you filled your plate. Am I wrong?"

Benedict raised his eyebrows to me, and I couldn't help but smile. "You are not wrong, sir."

"Please, call me Benedict. We are brother and sister now, you know."

"Funny." I gave him a smile. "Henry said the same thing. You will call me Felicity, I hope?"

James took the open seat beside me. He reached over me for Henry's untouched plate and slid the kippers onto his own. Benedict winked from the sideboard, and I turned my attention to James. "How good of you to avoid waste."

He sent me a soft smile. "Henry would never eat them. He must have been extremely distracted in order to dish kippers for himself."

I had nothing to say. There was no true reason for anything to be uncomfortable between Henry and me, anyway. We had never come to any sort of understanding. In fact, if I had not married James, I might never have seen Henry again.

James speared a kipper. "I have an activity in mind for us this morning, if you are available."

"I'm not sure I am. Your mother would like to order cards so I might deliver them to your neighbors for bride visits, and she mentioned finding a maid for me."

"Perhaps I can convince Mother to forego that for today. We can go for a ride this afternoon, instead."

I choked on a bite of my toast and coughed, taking the glass of water James offered to clear my throat. That was his intended activity? "Ride? On a horse?"

"Well, I would not mind riding a stag, but that might prove tricky."

I couldn't help but laugh and covered my mouth with my napkin. After taking another sip of water, I leaned back in my seat. Henry and Benedict were seated now, Henry's plate now devoid of fish.

"Did you not just return from riding?" I asked.

"Not exactly," James said.

Benedict lifted an eyebrow. "That was not a *bruising* ride, Felicity, but merely an exploration mission to determine the depth of the repair we'll need to order for the rut."

"I noticed a large rut in the road near the bridge when we returned home yesterday," James said by way of explanation. "It ought to be fixed."

"And who better to fix it than me?" Benedict asked, his voice dripping in sarcasm.

James grinned. "You must earn your keep somehow."

He lifted his glass. "That is far easier than finding an occupation, I will grant you that."

The smooth banter between the brothers flowed naturally and was easy to follow. When I assumed one of them had said something hurtful or gone too far, the other simply laughed louder. I would never understand them, but I did not need to.

James leaned in and lowered his voice a little. "What do you think about that ride later? There is something I wish to show you."

I swallowed. "If you can accept that I am not very good on a horse, then I suppose it will be fine."

He smiled, endeared. "Splendid. I am certain you are better than you lead me to believe."

"I am not prone to false modesty."

"Indeed. It is one of the things I admire about you."

Lady Edith swept into the room and each of the men stood at once. Their gentlemanly behavior was a credit to their mother. She motioned for her sons to sit again. "I have already eaten. I was only looking for Felicity so we might go into Bakewell together."

I set my napkin on the table. "I am finished."

"We are not in a hurry, dear."

"I truly am finished," I said. "I only need to fetch my gloves and bonnet."

Lady Edith fiddled with her gloves. "I will meet you in front of the house in a quarter hour, then?"

"Very good."

She left, and I pushed back my chair and went to leave the room when it occurred to me that I did not know how I had reached the parlor because I'd been following Henry. I paused in the threshold.

"Did you forget something?" James asked.

I smiled sheepishly. "I am not quite sure how to locate my bedchamber."

Benedict laughed loudly, pulling a chuckle from my chest, and James rose. "I will take you."

"No, you mustn't. You need to finish your breakfast. Direct me where to go, and I will find it."

He looked over at Henry. "You are finished eating, Hen. Do you mind?"

"Of course not."

I could certainly not use Henry as a guide all day. At some point I needed to learn my way around this house. And I was tired of feeling uncomfortable around him. "No, truly. If you tell me which way to go—"

"I do not mind," Henry said. He followed me to the door and pointed down the corridor. "That way, first."

I trailed behind him in silence, doing my best to memorize each corridor and staircase and room we passed through, focusing on the path and not the man. "I rather think I shall be forced to draw myself a map. I will never remember this all."

"You will," Henry said. "Someday."

We stopped before my door, and I reached for the knob. "Thank you for guiding me."

"Felicity?"

I turned, struck by his earnest gaze.

"Our conversation at breakfast was cut short." He turned the book he still carried over in his hands. "This is your home now, and I do not wish for it to be an uncomfortable place for you to be, either. While at one point I did wonder if we would perhaps cross paths again and . . ."—he shook his head subtly—"well, that is in the past. And I am happy James has found a bride that makes him happy. I hope we can forget about any sort of . . ."

He seemed to struggle to find the words to put to the discomfort both of us clearly felt, and I did not know how to fill them in, either. "There was never any sort of expectation between us, Henry, so there is no reason why things must be uncomfortable."

He let out a quiet breath, appearing relieved. "I am happy to hear you say so. We cannot change the past, but we can determine our future, and I would like to be friends, Felicity."

"I would like that, too, very much."

He gave one distinct nod and smiled. "It is wonderful to have you here, really. Neither of my brothers have read a single book since leaving school, and my mother does not have the time for it. I will be glad to have another bookish mind to speak to on occasion."

With all the newness surrounding me at Chelton, the idea of conversing about books brought immediate comfort. Putting our small past behind us and moving forward was an even greater relief. "That is great news, because I have read *Travels into Several Remote Nations of the World* three times since you lent it to me last summer and have been eager to discuss it with someone. I obtained the second volume from Hatchards once I learned of its existence."

"You liked it, then?"

"Oh, very much. The moment Gulliver finds himself in Lilliput, I knew it was going to be an excellent story."

"Have you read *The Mysteries of Udolpho?*"

"I have not. My mother was convinced it was not proper."

He rubbed his chin in thought. "It could be a tad frightening, I suppose. Perhaps it is better not—"

"No, I would like to read it," I said, reaching forward and resting my hand on his arm. Mama was no longer here to influence my choices, and I was a married woman now. If I wanted to read a gothic novel, that was my choice. "Do you have it here?"

He smiled, chuckling, and his forearm flexed beneath my hand. I pulled away, and Henry stepped back slightly. "It is downstairs in the library. I shall bring it to you later."

"That would be wonderful. Thank you." Though the tension had cleared, the silence between us was thick, as though the things unsaid still wanted to cling to us, reminding us of our past. "I should be going or your mother will be waiting for me."

"Of course. Will you be able to find your way downstairs?"

"I think I can. I should like to try, in any case."

Henry walked away, and I slipped into my room and closed the door behind me. Things were going well with James thus far, and Henry and I had cleared the muddiness between us.

Now I only needed to find a way to gain Lady Edith's approval, and all would be well.

CHAPTER 11

Bakewell was a charming village. Narrow streets lined with stone buildings weaved through the hilly town, and a beautiful church sat above the other buildings, its steeple reaching toward the sky. Lady Edith and I sat in the open barouche, the sun shining down on our bonnets.

"We will begin at the modiste. I should like to buy you a few new gowns, if that is agreeable to you."

I was happy to wear anything Lady Edith approved of, but I could not like the waste. "My mother did her best to provide a trousseau, but we did not have quite as much time as she would have liked. I've yet to embroider most of my linens." A thought occurred to me, for I had yet to gift James something for the wedding. I could embroider something for his particular use, something with his initials. "Could James use a new handkerchief, do you know?"

"Unlikely. It is Benedict who is constantly losing them."

I nodded, watching the shops we passed and admiring the cozy feel of the town. It was a far cry from London, and I enjoyed the lack of coalfire smoke and the stench of the streets.

"And the cards?" I asked.

"I already sent for them, so we needn't stop in the print shop today. We should have the cards Monday."

Five days. That allowed me five days before I would be forced to call upon strangers. The idea drew discomfort through my stomach, and I suppressed the nausea it caused.

"I am certain that, once everyone meets you at church, they will be watching for the notices. It is not a small thing to local Society that a member of the Bradwell family has married—particularly since it was James."

She looked away, but I wondered if it had pained her to miss the ceremony. She had been nothing but polite to me since my arrival, but I couldn't help but feel as though there was a barrier between us—as though she did not like me, but she was determined to stay true to her good breeding and not allow her dislike to show.

"It was kind of you to cede the ceremony to my parents' wishes. They were wed at St. James in London, and it meant a great deal to them for me to do the same."

Lady Edith gave me a tight smile. "Yes, well, it was important for the wedding to take place so you could travel with James to Chelton. I wanted to be there, but I have grown too old for such long rides in the carriage. I fear it makes me ill."

"Oh, I was unaware." But now I understood why she chose the open-air conveyance. I would do the same if I struggled with nausea each time I rode in a carriage.

"While we are at the modiste's we ought to speak to her about the linens for the ball. I had considered a white theme, and since it will be warm, we can open the courtyard for dancing."

Dancing? Ball? I pressed my back against the squabs and did my best to sound unaffected. "I was unaware there were any plans at all to hold a ball."

She looked at me as we rolled to a stop. "We must have a ball. We were not given the opportunity to celebrate the engagement as it was such a rushed affair—so we will celebrate the marriage. Every bride needs a ball, Felicity."

"Even brides who do not enjoy dancing?"

She waved away my concern and allowed the footman to help her down from the carriage. I followed her, but I was not finished. "I truly cannot dance, Lady Edith. Is there not another way we could celebrate? A large dinner party, perhaps?"

I did not do well in any social function, but at least I was unlikely to faint at a dinner.

"We will have a supper during the ball, and of course the dinner before—you will need to give me a list of names so I do not forget to include anyone important to you. You mentioned you had an aunt nearby? Perhaps she would like to come early and stay at Chelton as our guest."

My mind was spinning. The conversation was getting away from me. "She was married recently, and I cannot know if she is presently in Northumberland or at her husband's estate in the south. But in all sincerity, I really do not think a ball necessary—"

Lady Edith stopped and turned to face me. Her eyes were wide, her smile stiff. "My oldest son and the rightful owner of Chelton has been married. In the eyes of Bakewell and its surrounding gentry, that is the most momentous thing to have happened in years. It is a blessing and worthy of celebration to many, Felicity. I do not wish to host a ball because I enjoy parties. We *must* have a ball because it is expected, and James does not shirk his duties."

James did not shirk his duties, *but I did?* I could not ask if that was what she meant, but neither did I need to. She had made herself perfectly clear.

"Do we understand one another?" Lady Edith asked, the barest hint of an edge to her refined tone.

"Yes, of course."

"Wonderful." She turned back to continue walking toward

the modiste's shop, and I walked beside her. "I have been debating the merits of an all white ball, and if we choose to do that, it would be marvelous to have you appear in an exquisite, white gown. What do you think?"

"White would be lovely. But it would be costly and difficult to keep clean."

"You needn't worry about either of those things. It is important, I think, to give Chelton a good showing, and what better than the color that signifies purity."

I missed my footing but managed to right myself without falling. *Purity?* If I wondered before whether or not James had told his mother of the scandal and the gossip surrounding our hasty engagement, I needn't now. She was fully aware of the dark cloud that shamefully followed me around—would continue to follow me for the next six months.

"Do you worry that people would see the white for what it is?"

"And what is it?" Lady Edith asked.

Misdirection. A sorry attempt to prove I was innocent despite what everyone thought of me. Again, *exceedingly* difficult to keep clean.

None of the reasons left my lips, and my mother-in-law simply shook her head. "I may have been away from London for a number of years, but I know well how things are meant to be run *here*, and I hope you will trust my judgment."

"I do trust your judgment."

"Good." Lady Edith smiled, and I believed, for the first time, that it was at least partially genuine. She pointed to the door before us. "Let us design the whitest, grandest gown we can."

The shop was filled with bolts of fabric and spools of ribbons and lace. Lady Edith went directly to speak to a woman with flaming red hair and chalky white skin in the back of the shop, and I perused the silks near the window. A green silk caught my eye that was nearly the color of James's eyes, and I ran my fingers through it, letting the fabric slide over them like water down a stream.

"Felicity, you should be part of this conversation. Madame Rousseau was showing me her new white silk."

I looked up and the women were standing near a table, a bolt of white fabric lying between them. The modiste clapped her hands together. "I have just the thing. The latest Ackermann's arrived, and there is a white dress . . ." She pulled the periodical onto the table and flipped through it. Her thick French accent skipped all of the *h* sounds, and her painted face was slightly garish, but the examples of her talent around the shop gave me hope. "Let me find it. It is simply *magnifique*."

Madame Rousseau scanned the pages as she flipped through them until she paused on one. "Here it is."

She pressed the pages flat, and I leaned closer to Lady Edith to see the fashion plate spread before us. The woman pictured was seated, wearing a white gown with roses appliqued to gathered fabric at the hem and sleeves.

"White silk underdress," Lady Edith said.

Madame Rousseau pointed to the gathered fabric near the hem. "You can see the sheer overlay here. It could be a soft pink—"

"White," Lady Edith said. "I want the entire gown to be white. Even the flowers."

The modiste's gaze flicked to me. "A little color surely will help the young lady to not look pale in the cheeks."

"Perhaps we will employ a bit of rouge for that purpose. If the entire theme of the ball is to be white, it would behoove us to dress our bride in the same flawless color. Can you do that for me, Madame Rousseau?"

"Indeed, I would be happy to."

"Then I needn't tell you that it is my aim to impress the attendees at our ball with an elegant masterpiece, which I know you can provide."

"Of course, Lady Edith."

"And I would like the concept of our gown to be a surprise."

Madame Rousseau looked to me as though seeking confirmation, and I tried to smile. "I am so looking forward to this gown. The design is lovely."

Lady Edith looked at the paper again. "Can we add a train?"

"That could make dancing more difficult," the modiste said.

Which was entirely the last thing I needed.

My mother-in-law looked to me. "I think Mrs. Bradwell is willing to sacrifice a few conveniences in order to make a more striking figure."

"Of course," I said. What other choice did I have? I wanted this woman to like me. "I do not intend to dance very much that evening, anyway." As soon as I stepped onto the dance floor, I would be finished for the night. It was inevitable.

"We could gather more of the fabric here," Madame Rousseau said, pointing to the sweeping fabric beneath the roses at the hem. "If we bring it up higher there will be more fabric to create a train in the back."

The image described resembled the gowns worn by debutantes in the royal drawing rooms. "Are we not concerned I will appear ready to make my bow to the queen?"

"Perhaps," Lady Edith said quietly. "So we must not put a feather in your hair. Maybe a strand of pearls instead."

"Or white flowers to match the appliques on the gown," the modiste suggested.

Lady Edith smiled. "Perfect. I can depend upon you to provide them with the gown?"

"*Oui, madame.* Now, if that is all, we must begin measurements."

Madame Rousseau was thorough in her measuring, and by the time she had finished marking my size from every angle, Lady Edith had amassed a pile of fabrics large enough to supply a dozen gowns.

"Goodness," I breathed. "That is excessive."

Lady Edith ignored my ill-bred remark. "I have gone through Ackermann's and marked the gowns I would like supplied. This ball gown is of the utmost urgency, but the remaining can be made in whatever order you wish."

The sheer number of gowns and some of the selected colors made me feel uneasy. "Shall we review each one—"

Lady Edith ignored me. "I trust your judgment and taste, Madame Rousseau. I am certain Mrs. Bradwell does the same."

Perhaps if I knew the woman well enough to trust her judgment, I would. It was a good deal of money to spend without giving explicit instructions. But what could I say? "I defer to Lady Edith, of course."

My mother-in-law smiled in approval. At least I had done one thing correctly today.

"I will send round a note when the gown is ready for final alterations," she said.

We turned to leave the shop, and I glanced back at the piles of fabric. There was a good deal of green, pink, and yellow, but no blue. Perhaps when I returned for my fitting, I would need to swap out some yellow for blue. It was not a good tone for my complexion, and the pink sometimes clashed with my strawberry-colored hair.

"Should we hold the fabrics near my face, Lady Edith?" I asked, pausing near the door. "I would hate to receive a gown that does not sit well beside the copper in my hair."

She looked from the pile of bolts to me. "I do think I can be trusted to select fabrics that will not make you look awful, Felicity."

"Of course." What else could I say? My mama's modiste had always taken special care to show me the colors that did not work for my skin, but I did not wish to argue today.

Besides, there was still time to change things.

We moved toward the door again when another woman walked in, a younger woman behind her.

Lady Edith stopped, and I paused beside her. "Lady Whitstone, it is so good to see you. It's been an age. And Miss Whitstone, you are looking lovely today. That color of pink suits your complexion very well."

So Lady Edith was aware that *some* colors and complexions did not suit, evidently, if she could notice when they did.

Miss Whitstone curtsied, her cheeks blooming with twin spots of color. "Thank you, Lady Edith."

Lady Whitstone looked pointedly at me, and my mother-in-law seemed to remember my presence. "Oh, of course. Please allow me to introduce James's new bride, Mrs. Bradwell."

Miss Whitstone paled, her blush immediately receding. She looked to her mother, whose lips were suddenly pinched.

"Felicity, this is one of our neighbors and good friends, Lady Whitstone and her daughter, Miss Phillipa Whitstone."

I dipped in a curtsy. "It is a pleasure to make your acquaintance."

"You shall receive an invitation shortly, ladies. We hope to throw a ball at the end of the month."

"So soon?" Lady Whitstone asked. Her daughter had appeared to lose the ability to speak.

"It will take a good deal of preparation, but it is nothing we cannot manage. Once Felicity has made the acquaintance of a few local families, I dare say it will be entirely proper. We must celebrate our bride, you know."

"Chelton has not hosted such an event in an age. I hope you are prepared for a crush. There is not a family in Cumberland who will turn down an invitation to grace its halls."

Lady Edith pressed her lips together. "I do not set such high expectations, of course, but I will be gratified to host regardless of how many people we receive."

"The last ball we hosted was such a crush we were forced to open the back doors and allow people onto the lawn."

"Did you not set out torches for that very purpose?" Lady Edith asked, tilting her head softly in question.

Lady Whitstone's face grew even more rigid. "Yes, well, we were not sure we would need to utilize them. You can understand that I was pleased by the turnout."

"Yes, of course. It was such a lovely ball too." Lady Edith looked to me. "I suppose we should be on our way. So many things to do to prepare."

Each woman curtsied, and we moved to exit when Lady Edith paused by the door. "Would you like to come to Chelton for tea? Perhaps Friday next."

"We should like that very much," Lady Whitstone replied.

Once we stepped outside, Lady Edith came close and lowered her voice. "If there is anyone in this town you need to be wary of, it is that woman, Felicity."

I was surprised by the poison in her tone. "Did you not just invite her to Chelton?"

"Well, of course. We must keep her close so we know what to expect from her. By the time the Whitstones come to tea, many of the invitations for your ball will have been sent out, and she will surely delight in telling me how many of our neighbors plan to attend. It will be a good way to see how our invitations have been initially received."

"I feel I have much to learn," I said quietly.

Lady Edith looked at me with consideration. "All will be well, for I intend to teach you."

CHAPTER 12

That night, following dinner, I waited near the adjoining
door in my bedroom for James to come bid me goodnight.
I wanted to ask about Miss Whitstone and what had given her
reason to pale in my presence. My only thought was that she
was the young woman who had set her cap at James and been
dismissed because, in his words, they had not suited. From my
extremely short acquaintance with the woman, I could only
discern that she was as shy as I was in new company.

The fact that we were altogether similar thus far had not
done my spirits well. It would be a blessed relief to hear that she
had no such connection to my husband.

A brief knock rapped on the main door, and I crossed to open
it. A footman stood in the corridor with a tray. "For you, Mrs.
Bradwell."

I took the book from the silver tray and thanked him before
closing the door. Turning the brown, leather encased book in my
hands, I read the gold embossed title on the spine. *The Mysteries
of Udolpho.*

A folded sheet of paper fell onto the floor from the book's
pages, and I bent to retrieve it.

Felicity—

The book, as requested. Do not fear, for we have the next three volumes in the library when you find yourself in need of them. Though, I recommend you do not read this book at night.

    H.

As a fellow reader and avid supporter of literature, Henry could not truly believe I would have the control to put off opening this book until the light of the morning arrived. I did not possess such great restraint. I commended the man if he did.

A knock sounded on James's door, and I slid Henry's note back into the book and set it on my dressing table.

I opened the adjoining door, and James appeared in much the same state as he had the evening before. His cravat had been discarded along with his coat, and his shirt was open at the neck. This time his boots were missing as well, and he stood before me in his stockings, a casual sight I was not yet used to.

"I am sorry we were unable to go for our ride today," James said. "But perhaps we can do so tomorrow morning following breakfast."

The very idea made my muscles tense. "I was not being modest, James. I am not a talented horsewoman."

"That is a skill that can be taught," he said, raising a shoulder, clearly unconcerned.

But I did not possess a desire to develop that skill. I wasn't fond of horses in general, and they seemed to sense it. "Horses do not care for me, James, nor I for them. I wonder if it would be more pleasant to walk, perhaps? Or take a curricle?"

"We cannot take a curricle to the location I want to take you, and we certainly cannot walk so far. Not on a warm day, which I believe tomorrow will be if today's weather is any indication." His green-brown eyes narrowed slightly. "I do sense that you would prefer not to ride. Is it truly so distasteful to you?"

My heart sped, and I drew in a slow breath, hoping to calm

my nerves. I did not wish to displease James, but I truly did despise riding so. Could I learn to love it as he did? I believed it unlikely, but I could not bear to lower myself in his esteem even further than I likely already had. I had spent so many years in my mother's house not living up to her hopes and dreams for the type of daughter she would have—I could not live my marriage in the same way.

"I can be taught to appreciate it," I said slowly, gauging his reaction.

A smile spread over his lips that made my heart leap, and I decided that it was worth my discomfort to make this effort.

"I promise that you will love it," he said. "Now, tonight I think you should begin with your fact."

"Very well." I had given the prompt some thought at dinner this evening, so I was not unprepared. "I think the most beautiful animal in the world is a tiger, which I was able to see at the royal menagerie a few years ago."

He smiled. "I agree. I saw the animals two years ago, and I was awed by the tiger's beauty."

Two years ago? I'd visited then, as well. "Would it not have been diverting if we had been in the menagerie on the same day?"

"Perhaps, but I know we were not," James said with easy conviction.

I laughed. "However can you possibly know that?"

"Because I would have remembered you."

The dimness in the room and the glowing fire beside me softened James's features, and I looked away, warmth rising to my cheeks.

He must have sensed my discomfort, for he continued. "I have two horses to my name, and they are called Luna and Solis."

"Moon and Sun," I said.

"You know Latin?"

"Not much, but I know some."

"Well, you will have Luna tomorrow. She is more docile. Solis is young and believes himself smarter than his rider."

"How kind of you to consider my preferences," I said. I had not been used to someone doing that. I was usually the person who had to make sacrifices for another's comfort.

He looked over my shoulder and noticed the book on my dressing table. "Have you found the library to your liking, then?"

"I have not visited it yet, actually." My cheeks pinked. "I could not find it earlier."

He indicated the book. "You've brought some of your own, then?"

"No, that was from Henry, actually. He recommended it to me."

James's smile grew tight. "I am glad you have found someone to speak to about your books. I would be a dreadful bore in that conversation, surely."

"You are about as talented at speaking of books as I am at riding?"

He laughed softly. "I suppose, except that riding is a skill that can be taught and perfected. Reading is simply tiresome."

His decree stung, but I did my best not to show it. If he viewed reading that way, did he view me in a similar manner? The thought reminded me of my objective.

"James, I had the fortune of meeting a friend of your mother's while we were shopping in Bakewell today. Lady Whitstone and her daughter, actually."

"Oh? I am not sure I would call them *friends* of my mother, exactly. They had a bit of a falling out last year and things between our families have been tense."

"What was the nature of the disagreement?"

James cleared his throat and looked behind me, gazing at the different things in my room, his attention not resting on any one item for long. When he settled his gaze on me, he looked slightly apologetic. "Me."

As I'd thought. Drat. "Miss Whitstone was the woman who did not suit, then? I wonder, if the relations between your families are so tenuous, why you would believe that she and I would become friends."

"I think Miss Whitstone is a kind enough woman to look past the strife between our mothers, and I believe you would have something in common with her. You remind me of her a little, if I am being completely honest."

"Given that she is blessed with dark hair and looks nothing like me, I can only assume the similarities you see are in temperament."

"Yes," he said, his eyes brightening. "In temperament, indeed. You will surely find a friend in Miss Whitstone."

Or I would perhaps learn what it was about her that was so distasteful James would not marry her—someone who was much like me. Unless . . . "Was it the Whitstones who did not desire the marriage?"

"No, quite the opposite. That is the reason they have gained something of a competitive relationship with my mother. I nearly married the girl only so Mother would not lose her dearest friend, but that is not a strong enough reason to shackle myself to someone for the rest of my life."

Like he did with me.

I could not hold his gaze, not when he spoke so cavalierly about someone so similar to myself. My eyes settled on the contours of his chest visible through his open shirt, watching them rise and fall in conjunction with his breathing. How could James not see that our situation was no different except that he'd been stripped of the ability to choose? I had taken that choice from him when my reputation came under scrutiny and he felt it his duty to save it.

He took a step closer and hooked a finger beneath my chin,

directing my gaze to him. "What is it, Felicity? What did I say to bother you?"

"Nothing." I tried for a bright smile. Speaking the truth now would do nothing useful and would only make me appear as though I pathetically begged for reassurance. He could not reassure me, however, when I had the facts laid out so plainly before me.

No, this was not a problem for James to solve. It was mine. I needed to make myself into a wife he would enjoy, not a wife who would bore him. "I look forward to riding tomorrow."

Not a lie, exactly. I did look forward to spending time with James, just not the aspects relating to horses.

"As do I. I think you will like what I have to show you." He looked beyond me into my room again. "I do not wish to end our evening. I feel our time together is so fleeting."

"That will change," I promised. "Surely, I will not need to spend all my days with your mother."

"Gads, I hope not. I would like to spend some time with you as well. I must be sure to steal you away tomorrow before she is able to." He squinted. "I was not lying when I mentioned that her list of things to teach you is quite long."

"I should get some rest then."

He nodded, then reached for my hand. I gave it to him, and he placed a kiss on the back of my knuckles. "Goodnight, dear Felicity."

My heart flipped over. "Goodnight, James."

I closed the door behind him and leaned against it. Had I done the right thing? I was not being dishonest by keeping my concerns hidden. Indeed, if James had not yet made the connection that I was likely to be just as disappointing a wife as he believed Miss Whitstone could be, then I would not be the person to make that plain to him. Perhaps all I needed was to make Miss Whitstone's acquaintance and learn her character, for then I could determine the components that were unsavory to James and do my best to avoid acting in a similar manner.

The Mysteries of Udolpho beckoned me, and I retrieved the book and wrapped a blanket over my shoulders, sitting close to the hearth so I might use its light instead of wasting a candle.

Surely, Mama only told me to avoid this book because I was too young for it then. Now I had grown and could make my own choices.

If ever I could use an escape, it was now. I turned the page and began to read.

CHAPTER 13

I dressed in my riding habit before making my way downstairs for breakfast. The hunter green costume was nearly pristine, as it had not gotten much use in the last few years since my mama had it commissioned, and I was glad the military style with the high neck and shoulder epaulets was not quite out of fashion yet.

I made it downstairs without issue, but it took a fair amount of time—and help from the butler—to locate the parlor. I was glad to have improved at least a little in my sense of direction.

As I stood at the sideboard filling my plate, Lady Edith paused just outside the parlor door. "I have found you a maid, Felicity. She will arrive by this evening, hopefully in time to manage your hair before dinner."

My hand sought the base of my hair on its own accord, grazing my simple knot beneath my riding hat, and I removed it when I noticed Henry watching me. "I look forward to meeting her."

Lady Edith gave a stiff nod. "I was hoping to beg your assistance in addressing the invitations to the ball, but I can see that you have other things planned."

"James planned a ride, but I would be happy to help with the invitations when I return."

"That should be fine. We have many cards to write." She walked away, and I blew out a breath.

I took my plate to the table and sat near Henry. "I did not heed your advice, and I began the book last night. I perhaps remained awake far longer than I should have."

He looked up from the volume he had open and resting against the edge of the table, his fork suspended over a pile of eggs. "Are you enjoying it thus far?"

"Yes. It is exciting."

"Exciting?" James said, coming into the room. He walked with the confidence of a man who knew his worth but lacked in conceit, and his very presence made my chest warm in anticipation. "May I inquire what has earned that title? Or, no—allow me to guess."

I could not refuse such a gleeful man. "I doubt you will guess it, but you are most welcome to try."

James took a plate and scooped breakfast onto it. "The prospect of riding with me this morning?"

"I am afraid that is not what we were speaking of." Neither was it something I would title *exciting*.

"Blast." He smiled, then paused just before his chair, his gaze sweeping appreciatively over my costume. "You look lovely today, Felicity."

Warmth bled into my cheeks, and I dipped my head. "Thank you, but that is not what we were speaking of, either."

"Hmm." He sat beside me and pulled a napkin onto his lap. "I know it is not the ball, so I imagine my mother's need for assistance is off the list too. Is it the dinner Cook has planned for this evening?"

"Wrong again. What is the dinner planned?"

"I haven't the faintest," James said around a bite of egg.

It occurred to me then that it was *my* responsibility to know the dinner menu. Another thing I would need to ask Lady Edith about. "Shall I tell you what's exciting?"

James looked from me to Henry. "Yes. Clearly I am not going to guess it."

Henry made a grunt that could possibly have also been a laugh.

I cleared my throat, aware of the tension settling around us. "It was the book Henry leant me last night. I remained awake far too long reading it, and it was unwise of me."

"Because you are tired?"

"Because it is a gothic novel, and I am bound to have nightmares if I persist. I should only read it during daylight hours now. Or so I have decided."

Henry laughed. "If you had heeded my advice—"

"Yes, well, I will now." I swung my smile from Henry to James and found that my husband was not laughing. His sober gaze was focused on his breakfast.

He took a roll from his plate and stood. "I am ready, if you are."

I had not yet finished eating, but perhaps that was a good thing. I did not think I would do so well riding on a full stomach. I pushed my plate away and stood as well. "Ready."

The morning air was crisp as the sun had only risen an hour before, and the horses were saddled and awaiting us when we arrived at the stables. It was a grand structure to the side of the house, out of view when one approached via the bridge, but I did not know how such a large building remained hidden. It was tall, with sweeping stone ceilings and an open courtyard in the center. We passed under the opening and our horses stood in the courtyard.

"May I help you into the saddle?" James inquired.

"I think it would be better for me to use a mounting block. I am not skilled enough to achieve the seat with only a hand up."

My neck heated, and I tried to ignore the disappointment flashing over his face.

I walked Luna to the mounting block near the wall and used it to climb clumsily into the saddle, then arranged my skirt over my knees. I was high above the ground, and I took a deep breath to steady my racing heart.

Luna seemed skittish, and I did not blame her. I would not like to carry a woman around on my back, either.

"This way," James called, and I turned Luna away from the wall in order to follow him. He must think me a madwoman. Caught up in my thoughts, surely I had stared for too long at the cream stone.

We left the immediate grounds and turned up the hills behind Chelton, weaving slowly through the thick trees and continuing upward.

"Would you like to go faster?" James asked.

"This speed suits me well," I called back. My hands were sore from gripping the reins with such ferocity, and my legs tired from clenching together around the pommels.

"Truly?" he seemed surprised, and I swallowed my frustration.

I had done my part in joining an activity I did not like. Could he not do his part now to extend some patience and grace?

"Yes, truly. I did try to explain that I am not comfortable on a horse."

James tucked his chin, his brow furrowing. "You mentioned that you were not skilled, I had not realized that it extended—"

"Yes, it does," I said quickly, my heart hammering. Luna could somehow sense my unease, perhaps, because she picked up her speed. "How do I slow her?"

"You need to relax, Felicity. Luna is tense because her rider is tense."

"I am trying," I said, though my voice sounded agitated.

Luna kicked up in speed, and Solis matched her.

"Make her slow, James," I called, unable to do so myself. I pulled on the reins, but it only seemed to frustrate her. She yanked her head to the side, and I pulled again.

"You mustn't do that," James said, trying to guide his horse beside mine. Trees grew thicker and there wasn't enough room for two horses directly side by side. He reached for the reins, but I could not release them. My fingers had closed around the thick leather cord in a vise grip. We went over the top of the rise, disturbing a bird perched on a nearby tree branch. The bird swooped down and passed Luna's face. Startled, she reared back on her hind legs.

I squeezed my knees over the pommels, and a scream tore from my throat.

Luna's front legs hit the ground with a heavy, jarring thud, and she took off, tearing down the other side of the hill and up the next with my scream chasing her.

Wind whipped over my face, and I ducked my head to avoid the branches that hung low and scratched at my hat.

"Stop!" I screamed, though the horse did not obey. I pulled the reins and dug my boots into her side, and by the time we reached the bottom of the next hill, she slowed. She walked toward a bubbling brook, and as soon as she came to a stop, her sides heaving and sweaty from exertion, I slid down the saddle and crumpled to the ground.

Luna walked away to drink from the stream, and I pulled my knees up to my chest and buried my face in them, commanding my breathing to slow and my heart to return to normal. I was on the ground. I was safe. Nothing was going to ever force me onto the back of James's *docile* mare again.

Though now my husband was certain to believe me a foolish lady with little sense after witnessing how badly I handled his horse.

The heavy clopping of hooves indicated that Solis had

arrived. I heard him come to a stop and James's boots hit the ground.

"Are you hurt?" he all but yelled, dropping to the ground beside me.

I lifted my tear-streaked face to find him kneeling before me, his green eyes wide and raking over my body.

"She did not throw me," I managed to say through heaving breaths. It did not matter what I tried, I could not seem to slow my breathing. Panic heightened when I realized that this struggle to breathe was often how I felt before I fainted in a ballroom. The shortness of breath, the alarm coursing through my limbs.

Oh, dear.

I dropped my forehead onto my knees again and squeezed my eyes closed, focusing on maintaining control. I did not wish to grow light-headed enough to faint. Not *now*.

James's arms came around me, and before I realized what had happened, he pulled me onto his lap. I curled against his chest, burying my face in the dip between his shoulder and his neck, and his arms went around my back, his spicy scent engulfing me. He applied enough pressure to make me feel wholly surrounded, and I gasped lightly. The feeling of helplessness seeped away while I was in his arms, and the more pressure he applied, the better I felt.

"Sorry," he said, misunderstanding my gasp and releasing me.

"No, please." I reached for his arms and put them around me again, burying my face once again in his spicy scent. "I need you."

His breath caught, and he wrapped his arms around me tighter. James held me until my breathing returned to normal, and sense filtered back into my mind. By the time I was lucid again, embarrassment had settled upon my skin and in my stomach.

I leaned back, breaking his tight hold. "Forgive me, James. I should not have—"

"No, it is I who must apologize. I did not expect Luna would frighten so easily. She has been so docile and calm for me."

"Yes, but *you* are a skilled rider. I believe I would be better suited to a pony."

He smiled, and his hands rubbed soft circles over my back, soothing my injured pride. "I would not wish for you to ever feel that way again, but I must admit that this is a pleasant way to spend the morning."

I shook my head. "You must think me the most childish creature."

"Far from it, I assure you." His voice was hoarse, and I found myself drawn to his lips.

But I did not want to kiss the man after such an awful experience. How ridiculous it would be for him to always remember that the first time I kissed him was shortly after proving how utterly inept I was at one of his favorite activities.

I tore my attention away from his lips and crawled from his lap. His hands were reluctant to release me, and they slid over my body as I rose. My heart raced again, but this time because of the way James made me feel, and nothing about it was unpleasant.

He stood beside me, much closer than usual, and I had to bend my neck back to look in his eyes. "Thank you."

"The pleasure was entirely mine." He lifted a hand and scrubbed it over his chin. "Do you think you will be able to mount Luna to return home?"

My chest went cold. "I don't think I can."

"It is such a long walk."

"Do you need to return for something in particular?"

"No, but you do. Mother would like to write out the invitations. I believe she has a hundred cards, and that doesn't include addressing the envelopes."

"Drat." I looked to where the horses stood idly side-by-side at the water's edge, their elegant necks bent to the stream. "I do not think I can do it."

"Would you be willing to ride with me?"

"On a horse that . . . how did you phrase it last night?" My lips curved softly. "He believes himself to be smarter than his rider?"

"Yes, he is that, but he will obey me." James shook his head and let out a soft sigh. "You will always be safe with me, Felicity."

I looked from Solis to James and could not deny the earnestness in his gaze. His ardent pleading was enough to tempt me back onto a horse—but only because he would be in control this time. "We can try."

James broke out in a smile that was worth the entire ordeal I'd suffered so far that morning. "I shall mount first, and then you can sit in front of me. I think that is our best course of action to avoid ruining your habit."

"I assure you, I shan't have need of it again."

He looked at me sharply, and I regretted my words. But I did mean them, so I did not attempt to take them back.

James tossed Luna's reins in front of her and tied them to Solis's bridle beneath his throat so she would follow us home. He mounted Solis with the greatest ease, as though it was no effort at all to lift his body and swing his leg over the saddle. He slid back as far as he could and walked Solis to the edge of the stream near a few larger rocks. I climbed up on one of them, though it was awfully angled and not at all like a mounting block, and lifted my foot to slide it into the stirrup.

Using James's help beneath my arms, I jumped up onto his saddle and landed hard. His arms went around my waist, and I turned, seated sideways, so I could hold him around the middle. "I do not like this very much," I said, feeling extremely high up from the ground.

"Would you be vexed if I admitted that I am enjoying it excessively?"

I grinned, burying my head into his shoulder. Perhaps if I did not see the ground so far below, I would not be frightened.

We started back toward the house, and James graciously commanded his horse to walk at a sedate pace. Something about James's arms surrounding me was immensely comforting.

Leaning back slightly, I looked into his steady eyes. "I am sorry we were unable to see whatever you were hoping to show me."

His gaze flicked down to me. "Do not apologize. We can go another time."

I nodded, but I did not see how that would be possible. "Only if you find me a pony."

"I was actually considering a mule. Or perhaps a donkey."

"I would much rather ride a mule. They are far less likely to bite."

"A mule, it is."

I laughed, and James joined me. His chest shook, and I could not help but look up. His face was mere inches from mine. I had not realized that Solis came to a stop until James's hands, free of any hindrance, raised to move the rogue strands of hair out of my face and hook them behind my ears.

"I promised myself I would not kiss you until the agreed upon six months had passed."

"I did not realize kissing was part of that deal," I said breathlessly.

His lips flickered in a smile. "It wasn't, not really. That was my sad attempt to remain a gentleman."

"You cannot think that doing your best to act like a gentleman will ever be in bad taste, James. I commend you, and I am glad to have found myself married to someone so thoughtful."

Something I said unlocked a smile on James's face so wide it took me by surprise, and I nearly loosened my hold around his waist, but my fingers were locked into place. James curved one hand around my cheek. "You constantly surprise me, Felicity."

"With my clear talent at riding?" I asked facetiously.

"With your ability to trust me."

Trust him? I sobered, considering the truth of his words. I *had* trusted him, enough to mount a horse after one of the most frightening equine experiences of my limited experience. But my safety, under James's control, had not been in question—because he was correct, and I trusted him.

It was altogether a heady experience to realize how wholly I did value this man and place my safety so easily in his hands—from the long carriage ride alone between London and Chelton, to the conversations at our bedroom door each night, to riding his horse after nearly being thrown from one, I placed my trust in this man over and over again. It begged the question that had niggled at the back of my mind for the last five weeks since our initial meeting at the Huttons' ball: could I do the same with my heart? Could this be more than a friendship, become a love match?

"I would like to kiss you," James whispered.

My body warmed, and my heart raced, nerves mingling with anticipation. "That is agreeable to me."

He found something funny about what I said, though heaven knew why, and he leaned down and closed the space between us, pressing his smiling lips to mine. My chest exploded with heat, and I clutched the back of his riding coat, gripping the fabric in my fists. James splayed a hand against my back, pressing me closer to him, the other against my cheek to direct my head as he deepened the kiss.

It was no wonder young ladies were ruined for kissing cads. James was no cad—but his kiss was exhilarating, and the longer it continued, the more of him I wanted.

Thundering hooves came toward us, and I pulled away.

James looked over my head and his gaze hardened. "We have company."

I looked over my shoulder to find Henry riding toward us, his face stone. "I was sent to find you," he called, and I felt James stiffen. "Do not shoot the messenger, brother."

"What is it?" James asked, clearly unwelcoming.

I wanted to slide to the ground and walk away. Whatever was occurring between the brothers, I wanted no part in it.

"Cousin Matthew has arrived and requested a private audience with you."

James swore under his breath, then looked apologetically toward me. I pretended not to have heard it.

"We must go," he said quietly. "One cannot expect an earl to wait."

I swallowed hard. Earl? "Of course."

My heart raced as we took off to return to the house, and I had a feeling it would not slow again for some time. I only hoped that I was not so much a disappointment to James. The only thing proving to me otherwise was the lingering feeling of his kiss.

CHAPTER 14

James and I slipped into the house together and found Lady Edith waiting at the door. "You go on and change," she said to her son. "I need to speak with Felicity."

He nodded and obeyed, sending me a glance that I could not quite decipher.

Lady Edith waited until his footsteps had fully retreated before turning her attention on me. "My nephew is here, and it is no secret that he is a stickler for propriety. I can only imagine that he has chosen to visit in order to take your measure and ensure that James has not brought a smudge upon our name."

"The earl does not carry the Bradwell name though, correct?" If I understood the family lines correctly, this earl was the son of Lady Edith's deceased brother.

"No, he does not, but he is connected to our family, and it would be disastrous if he was to revoke his good opinion of us." Lady Edith paced away and paused near the window, moving the curtains in order to see out onto the drive. She looked back at me, as though gauging whether or not she could trust me. "Since his father's death a few years ago, Matthew—or the Earl of Claverley, rather—has made it his aim to prove himself worthy of the title he now holds. I have managed to secure his word that he would assist me with a problem, and I cannot allow him to change his mind."

Lady Edith stepped closer still, her brown eyes intent upon me. "We carry a tenuous relationship, for his father and I were never close. My brother was a difficult man, to say the least, but I *need* to remain in Matthew's good favor, and for that to happen, I need him to approve of you."

Pressure settled on my chest, making it harder to secure a full breath. "What can I do?"

She let out a quiet breath. "You can dress your best, allow my maid to come style your hair, and please do not let his lordship learn that your marriage to James was rushed in any way."

"Does he not already know that we were married within a month of meeting?" I could do my best in this house, but I could not stem the strength of the gossip tide that swept Society across England.

"He has no reason to know. Surely, you can see to it that he believes James and you have an authentic marriage. You needn't prove a love match, merely show Lord Claverley that you did not marry in order to avoid a scandal."

Though that was *precisely* what we'd done. How did my mother-in-law expect me to accomplish this?

"I will do my best."

"It is imperative that you succeed, Felicity. Not that you merely do your best." She closed her eyes and pressed her fingers together in front of her lips. "Lord Claverley has agreed to sponsor my goddaughter for one year to aid her in making a match. She needs his good name—and he needs our money. But it was difficult to navigate an agreement that suited both of us, and one wrong step can surely lead to Lord Claverley retracting from the agreement."

"*You* cannot sponsor your goddaughter?"

"No." Lady Edith's words became clipped. "Even if I could

stomach a voyage to London, I fear I do not hold enough clout to give my goddaughter any real chance of obtaining a good match. I did not marry a title, and mine is old and too distanced from the current earl to be of any real use."

I nodded. Scandal was somehow embroiled in this situation, and Lady Edith did not wish for my connection to topple her precariously stacked house of cards. "James is aware of this necessity?"

"Of course. Now, don your best day dress, and I will send my maid in to see to your hair."

I made my way upstairs and selected my best gown. I washed my face with water from the ewer and slipped on the green muslin dress. Its embroidered sleeves reached my elbow, and while they were beautiful, they were scratchy on my skin, so I hardly ever wore this dress. I tucked a sheer fichu into the bodice, wishing I could tuck a fichu beneath the already itchy sleeves as well.

Lady Edith's maid arrived not too long later, and by the time she was finished putting up my hair, I hardly recognized myself. She'd piled my pale copper hair on the crown of my head, utilizing the curling tongs to place a few ringlets above my temples. It was simple when compared to Lady Edith's hair, but it was far above what I was used to, and the higher hairstyle seemed to draw my face up a little, giving me a brighter, younger appearance.

I hated to admit so to myself, but I rather liked the way I looked when someone else assisted me with my hair. I turned on my seat and thanked Lady Edith's maid. She bobbed a curtsy and left.

Lady Edith awaited me in the drawing room, and I could see from the rigid way she sat with the needlework suspended on her lap that this was of great importance to her. "Come, sit near me," she said absently, and I took the open seat beside her on the sofa, setting my workbasket on the floor near my feet.

The tall ceilings in the drawing room were bright with the midday sun, the gold and burgundy papered walls simple beneath a frescoed ceiling. I had not yet grown accustomed to the majesty of this house, and I doubted I ever would.

"Do you have something to occupy you?" Lady Edith asked.

I bent to retrieve my basket, my itchy sleeves sliding roughly over my skin. I attempted to shift my position to ease the discomfort. "I thought to accomplish a little embroidery."

She nodded. Then, after a moment, asked, "Do you play the pianoforte?"

"Yes, though I'm afraid my skill leaves something to be desired."

"We shan't ask you to play for the earl, then. Do you sing?"

"Not in company."

She gave a light laugh. "Gracious, Felicity. What do you do to impress your guests?"

I did my best not to let the sting of her comment puncture my delicate opinion of myself further. Lady Edith seemed to hold the same great opinion of accomplishments as the rest of the *ton* did, which meant I would pale in comparison to any young debutante of her acquaintance. I swallowed the discomfort of my situation and chose to speak the truth. "My accomplishments are abysmal, Lady Edith. I am often overly nervous in company, and it diminishes the few minor skills I do possess, for I am unable to display them to the best of my abilities."

Lady Edith looked at me with her brow furrowed, but immediately turned her focus to her embroidery when male voices could be heard in the corridor, seemingly coming our direction.

I rubbed a palm over the outside of my sleeves in hopes of removing the itchiness before the men joined us.

A moment later, James stepped into the drawing room, followed by a man similar in age to him but possessed of fair, neatly arranged hair and a round face. I lowered my hand to the embroidery on my lap so as not to be caught scratching. The earl was shorter than James by a head, at least, and one would not imagine them to be related if one was not told of their relationship, for they appeared as different as the sun and the moon.

"Lord Claverley, you will allow me the honor of introducing my wife, Mrs. Bradwell."

I rose for this introduction and curtsied. Lord Claverley bowed over my hand as the remainder of the introduction was performed, then took his seat on the sofa opposite me, James beside him. My sleeve dragged over my skin lightly, and I clenched my teeth to fight the desire to scratch.

Lord Claverley was as foppish as James was elegant and tasteful. His violet coat was bold to the eye and his yellow waistcoat equally bright. He lifted an ornate eyeglass from his pocket and through it he thoroughly inspected me. He put the eyeglass away and turned toward Lady Edith. "James mentioned you intend to give a ball in the bride's honor."

Lady Edith smiled benevolently. "We need to celebrate the glorious union that has blessed our home, of course. Shall I ring for tea?"

"James plied me with both food and drink," Lord Claverley said, then turned his attention on me. "Where does your family reside, Mrs. Bradwell?"

"In London, my lord. Though we spend a good deal of time in Northumberland every summer at Arden Castle, if you know it."

He perked up. "I do. I have the fortune to call Daniel Palmer a friend of mine."

"Daniel is my cousin." I hoped the connection was as positive as his expression seemed to imply. Daniel had the habit of making enemies as swiftly as he did friends.

A wide smile spread over Lord Claverley's lips. "Say, will Palmer be present at your ball?"

"I've yet to extend the invitation, my lord, but I intend to. It is hard to say if we can expect him, however. I believe he is away from Arden Castle more often than he is found at home."

"I should hope to see him." Lord Claverley said, warmth in his tone.

"We look forward to seeing Lady Claverley," Lady Edith said. "I do believe it has been an age since we were graced with her presence at Chelton."

"The dratted business of confinement has made that difficult," the earl said. "Though I am certain my wife will be pleased to visit. She received a letter recently from our Miss Northcott. It appears the young lady will remain at school for the duration of the summer holiday and will come to us in early August."

"Oh?" Lady Edith shifted in her seat. "She has not mentioned it to me."

"She wanted additional time to perfect her accomplishments, or some such thing. I wondered if there was anything amiss, but it would seem that you are no wiser on the matter than I."

Lady Edith seemed to freeze, both body and tongue. It appeared that Lord Claverley had taken her quite by surprise. She'd hoped to warn me against breathing any scandal into his ear, but evidently Lord Claverley came prepared with some of his own. I was unaware of the nature of Lady Edith's agreement with her nephew, only of its importance to her, and I could see that this development was not good.

A quick sweep of the silenced Bradwells present in the room proved that we were at an impasse, and something needed to be done about it. But Lady Edith could not be expected to pull herself from a situation for which she had just admitted to having no knowledge of. The moment of silence stretched and glared over us, and I hurried to fill the gap left by Lady Edith's seemingly tied hands.

"I am deeply looking forward to meeting Miss Northcott," I said, hoping I was not erring in my judgment of the situation.

Lady Edith had not yet stopped me, however, so I smiled and continued as though I did not feel the tense undercurrent flowing in the room. "I have heard nothing but the effusive praises of her talents and her dedication to both the pianoforte and her art. Now to learn that she has chosen to spend additional time on perfecting her accomplishments?" I tried to laugh lightly to soften the self-deprecating blow. "It would appear that I have much to learn from her commitment."

"Do not forget the languages," James added, his twinkling eye cast on me in approval. I was at once relieved that I had not seemed to err too much in his opinion. "She can speak no less than four, and you, my dear, only know a bit of Latin."

I tried to suppress my smile. He had referenced our conversation about Solis and Luna. "Yes, well, my grasp on ancient languages is not to be commended. I suppose my only great skill is reading."

"You are a bluestocking, then?" Lord Claverley asked, his eyes narrowing in interest.

"Oh, of course not," Lady Edith said, laughing gaily. Her knuckles were white where she gripped the edges of her embroidery. "How these two do enjoy their jesting battles. I vow, Lord Claverley, you have yet to meet a couple so contemptible in their joy. It will be a blessed relief for all at Chelton when the honeymoon period has ended."

"Though it *is* true that my wife enjoys a fair bit of reading," James said, smiling at his cousin.

I could have kissed him again for so unashamedly coming to my defense.

"I can see that the honeymoon period is far from over," Lord Claverley said. He pushed up from his seat.

Lady Edith stood as well. "You must stay for dinner, my lord."

"I cannot today, but I thank you for the invitation. I will patiently await the notice for your ball." He crossed over the rug, and I stood, offering my hand. He took it in his thick fingers and bent over it. "You are the picture of poise, Mrs. Bradwell. My wife will be pleased to receive an excellent accounting of James's lovely new wife. Please accept my congratulations on securing the catch of the Season."

James made a brief face at this pronouncement, and Lord Claverley turned to clap him on the back. "You were a tough man to pin down, James. I simply had to see for myself what young flower managed to force a commitment from you."

James looked at me, a soft smile playing on his lips. "Now that you've seen her, I am certain you cannot blame me for swiftly claiming her as my own."

"No. No, indeed."

I did my best to smile prettily, but my scratchy sleeves felt like tiny bugs crawling up and down my arms, and I feared I presented more of a grimace. Catch of the Season? A tough man to pin down? Whatever he meant by that, it was evident I was the only person in the room who did not fully take his meaning.

James led his cousin from the room, and I sat again beside Lady Edith, chafing my arms. She looked at me oddly, and I ceased my scratching. Once the men were outside, far enough away to prove us alone, Lady Edith's shoulders slumped forward, and she dropped her head in her hands.

"That girl will be the death of me," she whispered.

I could only assume she did not mean *me* in this particular circumstance. "Miss Northcott?"

"Yes. She insists on making the whole of our arrangement more difficult than it needs be."

I waited for Lady Edith to explain what the whole of the arrangement was, but she said no more. I understood that she was relying on Lord Claverley to sponsor the girl, but why did Miss Northcott need him at all? She was possessed of both fortune and good name. The scandal demanding their need for Lord Claverley must be grand, indeed—and the money they offered him of equal measure if he was so opposed to any aspersions on his character by association.

The clopping of hooves could be heard through the windows as Lord Claverley's coach carried him away, and James returned to the drawing room only a few minutes later, Henry on his heels. He must have joined James outside to bid their cousin farewell.

"Henry, you must go to Dorothea and ensure that she is well," Lady Edith said.

He nearly missed his footing. "She will find it dashed odd if I do, for I hardly know her. I did not live here when she did, Mother." He lowered himself on the sofa beside his brother. "We are strangers at best. It would be better to send one of the others, for they are at least better associated with the girl. She is more likely to speak to one of them."

"James cannot go," Lady Edith said. "He is needed here."

"And what of Benedict?"

James laughed. "That would be disastrous. The two cannot abide one another."

Lady Edith huffed. "He does not need to *marry* the girl, he need only ensure that all is well."

"Can a letter not suffice?" Henry asked.

"A letter will not verify her wellbeing. She could write anything she wished."

A shadow passed over the mood in the room, and I wanted to offer my assistance, but I did not know in what way I could be of any help. My arms protested my dratted sleeves and I wondered, briefly, if it was too dramatic to burn this gown once I removed it.

"Benedict would perhaps be the best choice," Henry said. "He knows the girl far better than I do. We've only met in passing."

"I will go," James said, casting an irritated look at his brother. "Dorothea knows me, and I imagine she will have no trouble speaking plainly to me. I can leave directly and return no later than Wednesday. Henry can aid you in whatever preparations you need for the ball during that time, Mother."

"I would be happy to help in whatever way I can," Henry confirmed.

My body tensed. James would leave me here alone with his family for nearly a week? After kissing him this morning, I had hoped we would spend more time together under our decision to court. I wanted to grow closer to him, especially now that we'd broken through the physical barrier into a deeper relationship than we claimed before. But that would evidently need to be put off.

"Should Benedict travel with you?" Lady Edith asked. "Perhaps it would give him an opportunity to prove to Dorothea that he is not uncouth and entirely void of manners."

"They bicker like unhappy siblings," Henry explained to me. "Or so I've been told. I haven't been around them much."

"That is the way of things, unfortunately. Benedict cannot be made to see reason around her." Lady Edith sighed. "Forget I mentioned it, James. I do not know if it is wise."

"Perhaps I will not allow Ben the choice." James grinned. "And neither will I allow him to speak in her presence."

"I trust Cousin Matthew has gone?" Benedict asked, his lanky frame leaning in the doorway. "One can only hide in the library for so long." He sent me a wink as he ambled into the room.

"He is gone," their mother confirmed.

Benedict cast a skeptical look at his brothers and paused at the edge of the carpet, crossing his arms over his chest. "Now, who am I not allowed to speak to?"

Henry cast him a look. "Dorothea has written to Cousin Matthew and informed him that she intends to remain at school for the summer holiday."

"Ah," Benedict said, his brow clearing from confusion. "And

our dear mama requires that we ride to York posthaste to ensure ourselves that the little terror is well?"

"*You* were not asked," Lady Edith said primly. "James will go."

"And I think it wise for you to come with me," James said. "You can prove to the chit that you harbor no ill feelings toward her, and she is welcome at Chelton whenever she wishes."

Lady Edith's expression cleared, and she brought her palms together not unlike in prayer. "That is just the thing, James. Why do you not bring Dorothea home with you? If she does not wish to pass the summer with Lord Claverley, perhaps she could do so here. She needn't remain at that school any longer."

"And risk offending our great savior?" Benedict asked, his voice dripping with disdain. "I still do not understand why you must beg help from Cousin Matthew. Why can *you* not chaperone the girl about London?"

"I would need to be in London to do so," she reminded him crisply.

"Ah," Benedict said, a lazy smile crossing his lips as he lowered himself on the chair nearest the fire. "But we have Mrs. Bradwell now, who *can* travel to London without great physical distress."

My stomach flipped over, and I fought every inner desire to scratch my itchy skin, which seemed to worsen alongside this unpleasant conversation. I did not know the first thing about chaperoning a young lady, and given the way James and I were forced to wed quickly, I doubted very much that anyone would trust me as a chaperone either.

"That would not work," Lady Edith said, folding her embroidery and returning it to her work basket. "We depend upon your cousin's name in order to secure a match for Thea."

"Whyever—"

"Please do not press me," she said, closing her eyes. She

appeared inordinately unwell, greatly taxed by the conversation, and I rose.

I could not, perhaps, run a great house like Chelton yet or chaperone her goddaughter around London, but I did know how to assist an overtired mother.

"Lady Edith, you appear as though you could use a hot cup of tea and some rest."

She lifted her gaze to me, a soft line forming between her eyebrows. "That sounds very pleasant, Felicity."

She stood, and I took her by the arm and led her from the room without another word from any of her sons. Their deep voices could be heard in conversation once we left the drawing room, and Lady Edith let out a sigh. "I love my sons, but their obstinance can be trying at times."

"I am certain all mothers could say the same for their children."

Lady Edith smiled. "You are likely correct."

"Would you like a bath as well? I can ring for water to be heated."

"No, a short rest will do just fine."

I walked Lady Edith to her chamber—though in truth, she led me, for I did not know where I was going—and left her outside her door.

"We can begin on the invitations later this afternoon," she promised. "After you remove that uncomfortable gown."

So, my itching hadn't gone unnoticed. A warm blush spread up my neck. "Shall I ring for your tea?"

"I can manage." She paused, her shrewd gaze sweeping over me. "Thank you, Felicity."

There were a small handful of things she could have been thanking me for, and I did not know precisely which it was—the way I spoke about Miss Northcott or presented myself to the earl, or the way I extricated Lady Edith from the drawing room when she appeared to need it. But regardless of the particulars, I felt we had surpassed a pivotal moment in our relationship and determined not to ruin it with a question. I nodded softly and closed the door behind me.

Now, to see if I could find my way downstairs again—*after* I burned this gown.

CHAPTER 15

The new maid Lady Edith had hired for me proved to have a deft hand and a talent for elaborate hairstyles. Since James had left to see after Miss Northcott's wellbeing, two dinners had passed at Chelton, and Fanny had managed to create increasingly intricate coiffures each night. As a person who did not enjoy drawing attention to myself, it had been a test in my comfort to go down to dinner with a tall, braided style, or an abundance of loops. I was certainly not fond of the loops.

I sat at my dressing table, wary of what tonight's design would be. Orange light from the low-burning fire danced over my reflection, and I watched Fanny work with great efficiency. My antsy fingers rubbed gently over the note left behind by James, and I was eager for Fanny to take her leave so I could read it in privacy.

He had taken it upon himself to ensure that I did not miss learning one thing about him each night and penned his facts on folded slips of paper before he left, so I might select and read one each night while he was gone.

I found that I liked to read them before dinner, so I would

have a little of him to take with me when I joined Henry and Lady Edith for the evening.

Not that dinner was the only time of day I spent with my mother-in-law. Nay, the entirety of each day had been consumed by lessons of varying types. How to manage menus and conundrums created by a sudden addition to dinner. How to discipline the maid caught peeking in Benedict's drawer while she was meant to be cleaning his hearth—with firmness and grace, I happily learned. How to receive the caller that arrived unannounced far too early on Saturday morning—with cold dignity and reserve, despite the woman's clear hunt for knowledge about the new addition to Chelton: me.

And lastly, how to elegantly pen dozens of invitations to what was bound to be the ball of the year in all of the lake district.

"I am finished, ma'am," Fanny said, stepping back and holding her hands before her.

I tilted my head to the side and inhaled a soft breath. This was perhaps my favorite design of all. My strawberry blonde hair was curled with hot tongs and gathered high in an uncomplicated but beautiful arrangement. I wore a simple gown of dark green and smoothed my hands down the skirt while I waited for Fanny to leave me. She spent a minute moving the curling tongs to the edge of the hearth to cool and swept my unused hair pins into a pot on my dressing table.

"Thank you, Fanny. Enjoy your dinner."

She bobbed a curtsy and left the room. I pivoted to face the fire and unfolded James's note for today.

As much as I love Chelton, I have never known myself to dread leaving it for a time until today. I fear these five days will be an eternity, and I already look forward to returning to you.

Yours, etc.,

James

I leaned closer to the firelight and read the note over again.

He had written this before embarking on the errand for his mother, and while it was not strictly a fact, I liked it far better than had he chosen to share his favorite horse or preference for beef over pork. My heart surged with affection, and I folded the paper and tucked it into my stays. Strange, perhaps, but I wanted to carry his words with me.

The antechamber for the dining room was dim this evening, and I found Henry alone when I reached it. He stood upon my arrival and helped me to a soft, tufted chair to await his mother.

"Have you finished the second volume yet?" he asked, referencing *The Mysteries of Udolpho*. He sat in a chair near mine and turned his attention fully to me.

I lowered my voice. "I fear your mother's lessons have not permitted me time enough to devote to reading, and I am sorrowfully behind."

"You are learning much, though, about the running of the house?"

I tried to look excited. "Yes. Though, the more I learn, the more it is made plain to me that I am woefully inadequate for the role. It is a blessing to all in this house that Lady Edith yet remains at the helm."

Henry leaned back a little in his chair and regarded me curiously. "She will not do so forever, you know."

"Of course, but for now it is necessary."

"Perhaps. I do wonder though if you only think yourself inadequate because you have not allowed yourself to be otherwise."

I was saved from needing to answer this by Lady Edith's entrance into the antechamber. She crossed toward us and stood near the fireplace—though the warmth of the day meant that the hearth stood empty. "It will be important to introduce you to as many families as we are able to tomorrow after church. That will prevent us from needing to deliver as many cards on Monday."

"Of course, Lady Edith," I said. I was happy with any arrangement that might cut something from our perpetual list of things to accomplish. It was going to be a trial enough simply to navigate the introductions—especially without James at my side. I shifted a little in my seat and searched for the words to explain my social inadequacies so my mother-in-law would be fully prepared for my weaknesses tomorrow.

The door to the dining room opened and dinner was announced, however, placing a necessary halt on my thoughts. I followed Henry and his mother into the room and took the seat to Henry's left.

I felt his gaze on me, but set my focus to the ham on my plate. "Is tomorrow not the day of rest, Mother? Perhaps Felicity might require a break in the schedule as well."

"I do not require her to *work*." Her gaze flicked to me. "I only mentioned that introductions would be better accomplished following the service to save us from being forced to drive all over the county Monday."

"Of course, but—"

"I am equal to the task, Henry. But thank you for your consideration." I speared another bite of ham and pushed it around my plate. He had given me an entrance into this topic, and I needed to take advantage of it. I only hoped my racing heart did not reveal itself in my shaky voice. "It should be known, however, that I get rather nervous in company."

"You performed with excellent decorum before Lord Claverley. And Mrs. Greer, which was an exceptional challenge given the woman's propensity for chasing gossip." Lady Edith added the last bit in a quiet voice, and I bit back a smile.

I could not explain my comfort in the drawing room with Lord Claverley, for I did not know how it came about. "I spoke hardly a word in Mrs. Greer's presence." I snuck the bite of ham into my mouth.

Lady Edith scrunched her nose and searched the painted

ceiling for confirmation to my claim. "Is that true? I dare say *that* is not a challenge to achieve in her presence."

"I think I will quickly prove that it is not a challenge for me in any new acquaintance's presence. I have . . . trouble . . . in new company and grow anxious when surrounded by many strangers. It is a fault I am rather embarrassed by, but I have no recourse for which I can change it."

The silence at the dinner table was excruciating in its purity.

Lady Edith cleared her throat and finally spoke. "I do not fully understand what you mean."

Nerves fluttered in my belly, but I could put this off no longer, especially since I would be called upon to meet members of Society tomorrow. Lady Edith deserved a warning about what type of person her daughter-in-law was. "I cannot be expected to have much to say in company, and I certainly cannot be expected to dance more than one dance at any ball. My nerves simply will not allow it, regardless of how I prepare myself and deeply wish it were otherwise."

Time and again my mother had grown disappointed in me at various social functions or when friends came to call, and I knew it would be no different here. Nay, it would be worse, for the stakes were higher. Mama loved me regardless of how often I let her down—I could not expect the same from people who had only known me for a week.

"We will not force you to do anything you are not comfortable with," Henry said at length.

Lady Edith, I noticed, remained woefully quiet.

The remainder of dinner passed in a discomfiting blend of silence and stilted chatter, of which I played little part, and I was eager to escape to the solitude of my chamber. I missed James's steadying presence, and though I believed I would pass the time well enough with Henry, our comfortable conversational habits from our initial meeting last summer had not transferred as seamlessly as I'd hoped. He was all things good and kind, and when we spoke of books we could get lost in endless discussions on the plot and characters and how they appealed—or didn't—to each of us, but there was something missing now . . . and I believed that something to be whatever James possessed.

The folded paper of my husband's words scratched lightly against my skin, however, and over the course of the uncomfortable dinner, I recalled how deeply James wished to be with me.

And I, him.

Once Lady Edith stood, I followed her from the room and paused at the base of the wide staircase. "I think I shall retire early," I said, already dreaming of continuing the book that I most certainly should not read after dark—but knew I would anyway.

She paused and turned back to face me, her shrewd gaze raking over me. "You are not making it easy for me to ascertain your character, Felicity."

"Pardon?"

She took a deliberate step closer, her eyes wandering over my face. My hands began to shake under her scrutiny, and I clasped them at my sides, clutching my skirt to avoid showing my weakness.

"Each time I believe I have your measure, you do something to take me by surprise." She drew a breath through her nose. "I am not yet sure if I am grateful that you managed to convince James to the altar, or if I should be justifiably indignant on his behalf. I've done my best to put my own reservations aside and welcome you into my home, but you do not make it easy." She closed her eyes and gave her head a small shake before leveling them at me again. "I do not know what your aim is here, but I do hope you realize that I will not give up my son or my role in this house until you have proven yourself worthy of them."

Give up her son? Had she not done so already? My voice failed me, and I tried to swallow against a dry throat. Her vehemence had taken me swiftly by surprise, and I could not understand what I had done to deserve such a sudden change in her opinion of me.

Except, of course, it *wasn't* sudden. Lady Edith had merely reached the point where she could no longer hide her true opinion of me, it seemed. She had remained at arm's length since I arrived at Chelton. She had thanked me for extricating her from the drawing room following her nephew's visit, but every other moment together she had made it clear that she was doing her duty to teach me the ways of being the mistress of Chelton, and nothing more.

Indeed, if Lady Edith did not care so deeply about her home and family, I wondered if she would have bothered to teach me anything at all.

"I hope I have given you something to think on. Goodnight, Felicity." Lady Edith walked toward the drawing room without another word, and I stood at the base of the grand staircase, my feet on the checkerboard tiles, and watched her leave.

My heart raced in the silent, echoing chamber. Turning, I lowered myself onto the bottom step. How was I to accomplish anything now that I understood Lady Edith's true feelings? Without James here to lean upon, I was certain to fail.

Excuses to extricate myself from family time ran through my mind. I could have Fanny tell the family that I suffered from a fever in the morning. But no, for then the doctor would be called. A headache? That could perhaps work, and it would allow me the day to hide away in my room.

But I had three—possibly four—days before James returned, and I could not stretch a headache as long as that without giving cause for great concern. I rubbed the exhaustion from my eyes and swept my gaze over the dim room around me. Paintings covered the top half of the enormous walls and bled onto the fresco covering the ceiling, and marble carvings littered the walls and crawled over the cornices.

This room alone was far more elaborate and elegant than

anything I had ever hoped to call my home, and I allowed myself, in the depths of my current melancholy, to wonder if I would have accepted James's hand had I known the life I was agreeing to.

And furthermore, why, when James was exceedingly aware of the extent of my proclivity for social anxiousness, did he allow me to become the mistress of such an estate with all of the duties that accompanied the role? This was no small country house to quietly manage. This required the work of a productive and capable woman.

I forced myself to stand and turned to move up the stairs, puffing out a defeated breath. There was no changing my situation now, regardless of how deeply my mother-in-law desired it.

CHAPTER 16

It turned out that I was not forced to employ any excuse the following morning, for Lady Edith opted to remain home from church to nurse a terrible headache of her own. Whether it was real or fabricated, I did not know, but I was glad to put off the need to be around her for a little while longer.

Henry drove me to church in a curricle, his skilled hands light with the reins. The noise of the road prevented us from carrying an easy conversation, but I was content with the silence. I was too wrapped up in my concern about the gathered Society at church and what they would make of Chelton's newest occupant.

When we arrived in Bakewell, Henry tied his reins to a post and came around to help me down. "You are not required to speak to anyone you do not wish to meet."

His declaration took me by surprise, and I looked into his steady blue eyes and found compassion there. "Thank you, Henry. Do you think people will find it odd that we have come alone?"

"You are my sister now," he said, an easy smile flickering over his lips. "There is nothing odd about it."

I would do well to remember that. No one was aware of our history, and no one would deem it odd to find a new bride and her brother-in-law riding together. It was completely above reproach.

My cheeks warmed, and I dipped my head, pretending to find an interest in avoiding the mud at my feet. "Of course."

Henry offered me his elbow, and I took it, following him up the hill toward the church. Thick green grass covered the churchyard and surrounded the headstones in the cemetery on one side. Looking down the hill, the tops of the buildings lining the surrounding streets bled out in every direction. Everything about the ancient building held a gothic feel that I loved.

It reminded me of the book I was halfway through reading, and I immediately shoved the fiction from my mind. It did not have a place among the worship today.

Mr. Upshaw, the vicar, welcomed us at the door. His white side whiskers shook as he spoke, but his welcome was warm and inviting. I walked down the central aisle and took a seat beside Henry in what I could only assume was the Bradwell box.

Eyes followed my every movement, and I was glad to have chosen such a wide-brimmed bonnet so I would not be forced to see all of the curious gazes. I leaned close to Henry and spoke quietly. "Are James or Benedict often missing from church, or is it an oddity that they are not here?"

He looked at me, and a soft chuckle escaped his lips. "You are overly concerned, Felicity. I promise you, it is not strange at all that my entire family did not join us. James is often away, and Benedict cannot be depended upon to keep to any sort of predictable schedule."

"And you, Henry, escape to the hunting lodge as often as you are able."

"Indeed," he agreed with a firm nod. "In fact, I should be there now."

"Oh?"

"Yes." He gave me a fleeting smile before turning his attention to where the vicar was now walking to the front of the building. "But I put off my trip for a short while."

My stomach swooped anxiously, and I pressed him quietly. "Why did you put the trip off?"

"Because James asked me to remain. For you."

For me? No, he did not stay for me. He did so for James. He only just said as much. I directed my attention forward and did my best to listen to the sermon, despite the way my mind and stomach both crawled uncomfortably. Henry had tried to get away, to *escape* as he predicted last week he might need to do. It was no wonder that he was so avidly against visiting Miss Northcott himself; he'd already had other plans.

And they had not included tending to me.

How could James have asked this of his brother? My shame only seemed to grow with each new revelation. What was next? Mrs. Prescott would come to me and reveal that she did not intend to give over the management of the menu or the maids to me?

My attitude fell as low as my energy throughout the sermon, and by the time it was finished and I was required to stand and exit the chapel, I had to fight the desire to run before Henry could introduce me to anyone.

"Mother has requested that I help you make the acquaintance of three particular families. I promise it will be over swiftly, and you need not say anything at all beyond a polite greeting."

Henry's voice was serious, and I glanced up quickly, grateful to find his generosity appear quite genuine. I nodded in agreement and slipped my hand over his elbow so he might lead me outside. The sun shone down on us, bringing a layer of heat with it, and perspiration prickled the back of my neck.

"Good day, Mr. Bradwell," a man called as we approached their party.

Henry leaned close. "Two of the families together. I think fortune is smiling upon you."

I could not help the smile that curved my lips.

"Mr. Dodwell, Mrs. Dodwell." Henry nodded to the tall, buxom pair. He shifted his attention to the blonde family beside them. "Mrs. Whaley, Mr. Whaley, Miss Whaley. Please allow me the pleasure to introduce my brother's new wife, Mrs. Bradwell."

I curtsied to the group and nodded to each of the women in turn. "It is a pleasure," I said.

"Oh, Mrs. Bradwell, I have been so eager to make your acquaintance," Mrs. Dodwell said, her eyes brighter than the plethora of yellow and orange flowers adorning her bonnet. "Please tell me Lady Edith intends to host a ball."

"That is her intention," Henry said. "And I expect you will all find invitations in the post shortly. Mrs. Bradwell has been busy writing them herself."

"Oh!" Mrs. Whaley exclaimed, quite impressed by this apparent feat. "How good of you, Mrs. Bradwell."

"I am grateful for Lady Edith's good advice and sacrifice in hosting a ball for me. It is the least I can do to make myself useful."

The women shared a look, and I did not know for certain, but I believed that I had gained their approval.

"Forgive my impertinence," Miss Whaley said, her mousey voice matching her petite figure, "but where is Mr. James Bradwell today?"

"Unfortunately, he and my brother Benedict were called away on a family matter, but they should be returned to Chelton soon."

She appeared disappointed, and I did my best not to search too far into the potential reasons for it.

"If you will excuse us," Henry said, laying his hand over

mine, the one which rested upon his arm. "We must continue the introductions."

"Of course," Mrs. Dodwell said, leaning forward and lowering her voice. "I imagine there is much dawdling today so everyone can have a chance to meet our newest parish member. Welcome to Bakewell, dear."

The sincerity in her warm tone reached into my chest, and I smiled, dipping my head in acknowledgment, while Henry pulled me away.

The following half hour was spent in a similar fashion, meeting members of the local parish and giving excuses for James's and Lady Edith's absences. Henry, for all his dislike of Society and preference for remaining far from it, was adept at navigating the people of Bakewell. He had successfully orchestrated no less than eight different families' introductions and extricated me from each one before I was pulled into a lengthy conversation. We had worked our way toward the street and had nearly made it to the curricle when a woman stepped into our path, her daughter just behind her.

I recognized them immediately from the modiste's shop. "Good day, Lady Whitstone. Miss Whitstone."

"It is such a pleasure to see you again, Mrs. Bradwell. I do hope Lady Edith is not ill?"

Henry stepped in. "She suffers from a headache, ma'am."

Miss Whitstone *tsked*. "And how are you enjoying our little corner of England, Mrs. Bradwell?"

"Immensely. It is lovely, and the people today have proved to be equal to it. I look forward to getting to know both of you better at tea this week." Especially Miss Whitstone. I was determined to learn what about her had seemed so lacking to James.

Lady Whitstone nodded absently, glancing from me to Henry. "Of course. Friday, then."

I dipped a curtsy and stepped around them. Henry retrieved his curricle, and I could not help but feel a little empowered by the accomplishments from the day. Without James's assistance or relying upon Lady Edith, I had managed to meet nine of the leading families in the parish and would now have *nine less* stops to make with Lady Edith in the barouche this week.

Once we had mounted the seat and took off in the direction of Chelton, I turned toward my brother-in-law. I spoke up to be heard over the noise of the road. "I must thank you."

He looked at me briefly before returning his attention to driving. "I did nothing, Felicity. You are a natural."

A laugh tore from my chest. "Indeed, I do think you must be brown-nosing for some purpose. A natural, I am most definitely not."

He did not laugh. "Whatever you would like to title it, I was hardly more than your driver, Felicity. You performed to perfection, and it is my prediction that you will soon have the whole of Bakewell eating out of the palm of your hand."

I thought of the woman in the churchyard with narrowed, eagle eyes. "Well, not the *whole* of Bakewell."

"Believe me, my brother leads the pack."

My body jolted, for I had not been considering James. Though it was true that I would not predict him to be in my pocket quite yet—if ever—I had been thinking of someone else entirely. A person who had lately become Lady Edith's adversary.

"I meant Lady Whitstone."

Henry laughed awkwardly to cover his blunder. "Ah, *touché*, Felicity. It would take a feat of great proportions to accomplish that. But Miss Whitstone appeared to like you well enough."

"I cannot tell."

He smiled. "She is quiet, yes, but very kind. I think you will like her."

"Your brother said the same thing." And I had yet to determine if it was a compliment or a condemnation.

Henry looked at me sharply. "So he told you of Miss

Whitstone?"

"And their brief courting, yes."

"There I was doing my best to avoid the Whitstones, and evidently it was pointless."

We crossed over the stone bridge, Chelton sitting squarely ahead of us, and a large rut in the road jolted me on the bench. I reached for something to grasp on to when Henry's arm jutted out and kept me secured to the seat.

He slowed the horses and turned to me abruptly, removing his arm. "Forgive me, Felicity. That blasted rut has yet to be fixed. I meant to watch for it, but I admit to growing distracted." He ran a hand over his chin.

"All is well."

"Perhaps I ought to begin working on the rut tomorrow. It is far worse than I gave James credit for." He shook his head and continued toward the house. "The man tries me deeply—as brothers are often expected to do—but he knows what he's about."

"I have so far found that to be the case, as well."

Henry stopped the curricle outside of Chelton's enormous stable yard. Green, rolling hills spread up behind it and the river ran before it, slipping beneath the wide, arching bridge, with Chelton to our side. It was idyllic, and I wished I could enjoy the mastery of the sunny scene around me, but my heart was in York, and my nerves were frayed.

"Perhaps when James returns you ought to suggest an outing that would suit you both," Henry said carefully, pulling me from my thoughts. "Not riding, not reading, but something that appeals to both of your preferences."

"That is a splendid idea, Henry. The only trouble . . ."

He waited, but when I did not complete my thought, he bumped me with his shoulder lightly. "What is the trouble, Felicity?"

I bit my lip and spoke the fear that had been plaguing me

since arriving in Cumberland. "I am afraid that does not exist—an activity that appeals to both of us."

He smiled, shaking his head. "If what I came upon during your ride was any indication, there is certainly *one* thing you both enjoy. I am confident you will find others."

My cheeks heated. I knew Henry had found us kissing, but his tactless mention of it was embarrassing.

"After all," he continued, "James does enjoy some things more than riding and sport. He likes you excessively."

I smiled, though I knew Henry could not know this for certain. "James is all things kind and amiable. Even if he does not enjoy reading."

"Well, not all of us can be perfect," Henry said with an affected air of greatness. He sent me a wink and drove through the archway until we came to a stop inside the carriage yard. A man jogged toward us to hold the horses' heads and Henry hopped down from the curricle to help me alight.

If there was one thing James's absence had been good for, it was securing my friendship with Henry. I had long since let go of the idea of any romance between us and had come to count the man as a sibling. I was glad that it appeared he had done the same.

I took his hand and stepped onto the brown gravel drive. "Thank you, sir."

"It was my pleasure." He handed the horse's reins to a stable boy and took my hand to lead me into the house. "Do you have any plans this afternoon, or would you like to meet me in the library for a little reading?"

"That sounds lovely."

CHAPTER 17

S unday was all things pleasant—as it was largely taken up with reading—and it was not until Monday morning that I was forced to face my mother-in-law again. She acted as though no uncomfortable words had passed between us, and I was glad at least to not be compelled to relive the conversation at the staircase again. We delivered cards to a handful of nearby houses before Lady Edith grew too ill from the carriage to continue, and the remainder of the day passed in relative silence while we penned the final invitations to the ball.

Monday evening I sat at my dressing table while Fanny heated the curling tongs in the burgeoning fire. I was debating the merits of begging forgiveness and requesting a tray in my room in lieu of attending the uncomfortable, intimate dinner when a sound in James's chamber alerted me to a presence within. His valet had traveled with him to York, so there was no reason for anyone to be in his room.

Surely, it was not outside the bounds of propriety for a wife to peek into her husband's room when he was meant to be absent from the house. After Mrs. Prescott had found the maid rifling through Benedict's drawers the other day, I felt I had little choice but to ascertain that the person in James's room had just cause to be there.

Fanny approached me from behind, and I spun to face her. "You hear that, yes? Someone in my husband's room?"

She paused, squinting toward the wall. A soft thump sounded, and she nodded. "I do, ma'am. Someone is in there. Is he not meant to be returned until tomorrow?"

"No, he is not. Tomorrow at the earliest, Wednesday more likely." I paused, chewing on my lip. "I should peek inside, yes? To make certain all is well, I mean."

She nodded with widening eyes. "I think it prudent."

The Mysteries of Udolpho was likely to blame, but my wariness heightened as I crept toward our adjoining door. I shook the images of specters and villains from my mind and turned the doorknob, prepared to use a commanding presence to inquire why someone would need to be in the room while James was absent.

It remained unlocked, and I opened the door and swiftly stepped inside to find James standing before his shaving table, void of a shirt and holding a blade to his cheek. He turned to face me, and I lost the power of speech. James's chest belonged to a man who regularly partook in fisticuffs or toiled in fields all day, his broad chest tapering to a narrow waist. A soft gasp escaped my throat, and I tripped over something lying on the carpet before me, falling hard on my knees.

James rushed forward, and I pushed myself into a kneeling position, already feeling the heat bleed into my cheeks. His boot lay discarded to my side, and I righted it.

"Forgive my intrusion," I said, looking up at him. It was a struggle to lift my gaze to his face, but I managed. "I feared an intruder was rifling through your things."

James lifted one eyebrow and reached for me. "Has your gothic novel begun to fill your head with nonsense?"

I placed my hand in his. "No. Well, yes, it has been giving

me cause to feel nervous over every unexplained noise in this house—and James, there are *many*—but this is warranted."

"Is it?" He pulled me up.

"A maid was found looking through Benedict's drawers. I could not allow her to do the same in here."

James tucked his chin and foamy soap clung to his chest when he lifted his neck. "Surely she is not still employed here?"

"Your mother had her relegated to the kitchens and given another chance. I thought it very kind of her to extend such grace."

James tilted his head a little to the side. "You cannot know how much it pleases me that you and my mother have found an accord with one another."

Except that we hadn't. Lady Edith had done a remarkable job fooling me into believing she approved of me during my initial week at Chelton, so surely we could continue the charade. I didn't hold hope that I would change her opinion, but I didn't want to ruin James's good mood so soon. There was time to determine how best to bring up the matter to him.

When my own mama arrived at Chelton, she would know best how to manage things. I was nearly certain anything I said against James's mother would only put him in a defensive mood against me, which was the farthest thing from what I wanted. Not that I blamed James, of course. It was natural to wish to defend one's mother.

His free hand curled a lock of my long hair around his finger, and I was acutely aware of how my hair trailed down my back and in loose waves over my shoulders. I needed to return to Fanny and finish preparing for dinner, but I was not yet ready to leave James's side.

"You have returned early." I attempted to break the silence between us.

"Indeed." His thumb rubbed circles over the back of my

hand, which he still held. "Our business wrapped up swiftly, and we found no reason to delay in York."

"Miss Northcott is well, I assume? Or have you brought her back to Chelton with you?"

His smile grew tight beneath the foam surrounding it. "I would much rather speak of you. Did you find Bakewell Society to be everything you imagined?"

This avoidance of the topic did not bode well. Had it been an easy answer, he would have given it to me.

"Bakewell was far easier to navigate than I anticipated. Henry was a particular help, actually. I could not have made so many acquaintances after the church service without his assistance."

My chest burned slightly on the recollection that James had asked Henry to tend to me, but I suppressed my guilt and irritation over that. I was not an infant in need of a nursemaid, but I could not truly fault James for thinking so after he'd witnessed my less than savory reactions to dancing and riding.

"Remind me to thank him later," he said, tugging on my hand to pull me closer. Heat emanated from his skin, and I lifted my free hand to wipe the sudsy foam from his chest.

"You are making a mess of yourself," I said.

"And now a mess of you." He took my hand and wiped the foamy finger back over his shaved cheek, and my pulse jumped. "I have missed you, Felicity."

I had missed *him*. "You cannot adequately comprehend how pleased I am that you are home."

A look of mild surprise crossed over his face, but I could not credit it.

"Did you think it otherwise?" I asked.

"I do not know what to expect from you. I worried that by kissing you I had ruined whatever friendship we'd begun to form."

"That far from ruined anything, James."

"I am glad to hear it." His foam-covered face prevented me from showing him precisely how I felt, but I wished I could have.

The door opened and James's valet appeared, holding a dinner coat. "I will leave you to finish readying for dinner," I said, taking a step back.

His hand dropped from mine, and it was with herculean effort that I did not give his torso another appreciative sweep—though I did hazard a quick peek. I was only mortal.

Fanny awaited me near the dressing table, and I closed the adjoining door and took my seat. The smile playing at her lips was evidence that she had probably listened to my conversation with my husband, and I felt the rosy hue that appeared on my cheeks in the looking glass.

"I liked what you did with my hair last night," I said. "It was much more to my taste than an excess of loops or plaits."

"Of course, ma'am. Though, might I recommend just one plait? I will keep it small, I vow."

"Very well."

Fanny worked on my hair, and by the time she was finished, I decided I could trust her. The first few days and their intricate designs had likely been her attempts to discern my preferences, for tonight's style was perfection. Much like last night, my hair was gathered high upon my crown with a plait circling the mass of curls. I straightened my gown and paced to the door.

James had not asked me to wait for him, so I determined to go downstairs and await him in the antechamber.

I took the shawl from my bed and slipped it over my shoulders, then raised my head. I would not allow Lady Edith's poor opinions of me to ruin my evening.

Fanny opened the door so she might go down to her own dinner, and I followed her into the corridor and paused. James leaned against the opposite wall, his arms crossed patiently as he waited for me. His head was turned, and the cut of his clean-shaven jaw was shadowed by the light thrown from the candle sconce on the wall beside him. My belly flipped over, and a pleasant sensation ran through my chest.

Was it normal to feel this eager to see one's husband after leaving their side less than an hour before? I wasn't sure. But I had never before felt such a thrill at seeing a man in a white cravat and black dinner coat, and I had seen *that* time and again, so I knew this was different. The way I felt for James was different.

Oh, dear. I was falling in love with my husband.

The realization shook me, and I stopped midway to reaching his side. He pushed away from the wall and offered me his arm, and I swallowed hard before taking it and allowing him to lead me downstairs. We did not speak on our way, which was a blessing, for I did not know if I would be able to say anything of value.

If I allowed myself to love James, it would put me at a disadvantage. It would hurt more when he remained nothing but a friend to me, and I wasn't sure I wanted to live that way.

We reached the antechamber, and the rest of the family was already gathered. Lady Edith looked between Benedict and James with concern, a frown marring her lovely face.

"We are all gathered," she said quietly. "How is Dorothea? What is Benedict not telling me?"

James released me and moved to his mother's side. He leaned forward and kissed her on the cheek. "It is lovely to see you as well, Mother."

She reached for his arm, but he'd already moved away, going to each of the two doors in the small room and closing them. He leaned out of the one that connected to the dining room and spoke softly to the footman likely posted on the other side of the wall.

This must be serious, indeed, and Lady Edith surmised as much by the worry continuing to grow on her brow.

Henry sat in a chair, his hands on the armrests, and unease dipping his mouth into a frown. He must already know what the brothers were going to say. But if he did, why could James not have told me upstairs?

Benedict leaned against the empty hearth, light from the candles on the mantel washing over his curly, chaotic hair. "We went to the school, as requested," he finally said when James had closed both doors. "But Thea was not there."

Lady Edith's displeasure turned to confusion. "Has she gone ahead to Lord Claverley's—"

"The headmistress did not know where she had gone, only that Thea and some of her possessions were missing on Wednesday last."

James reached into his coat and pulled a folded sheet of paper from his pocket. "Thea left this behind."

Lady Edith stepped forward and took the note before moving toward the candles on the bureau. *"Dearest Mrs. Moulton— You have been all things kind and lovely, and I do regret disappearing in such an abhorrent fashion. Indeed, you have taught me better manners than this, but for reasons you cannot understand, please believe I have no choice."*

She lowered the letter and looked at James, a stricken look on her face. The name Mrs. Moulton sounded familiar, but it was such a faint recognition that I could not place where I recalled hearing it.

Lady Edith cleared her throat and continued to read. *"Please do not fret. I am safe where I am going in mind, body, and virtue, and I will see to it that you are notified of my continued safety in one month's time. Please do not discard my trunk. I intend to retrieve it as soon as I am able. Sincerely, Dorothea Northcott."*

She lowered the paper and looked to James. "This must be her ill idea of a prank. Tell me that girl is just now upstairs readying herself for dinner."

"I wish I could." James looked between the door and me.

"Ben and I thought it best to return to you with this information straight away, but we did do a bit of poking around in York before leaving, and I am sorry to report that we did not find any leads to indicate where she might have gone."

"Or *to whom* she might have gone," Benedict added. "Though Mrs. Moulton was convinced Thea did not possess a beau of any type. Surprise, surprise."

"I want none of your witticisms today, Ben," Lady Edith snapped. She crossed to the chair beside Henry and lowered herself in it, looking at the letter as though it held a map to Thea's whereabouts or outlined her reasons for running away.

"Could she have gone to your cousin's house?" I asked, my voice as timid as my feelings.

"No. If that were the case, she would not have felt the need to ask Mrs. Moulton to refrain from searching for her. She would not need to hide what was our original plan." Lady Edith lowered her eyes and pressed her fingers to her temples. "This is my fault. I pressed a Season upon her, and I should have listened when she told me she did not want to stay with Cousin Matthew. I should have invited her here."

"She must know she is always welcome at Chelton," Henry said. "You've been nothing short of a mother to the girl since her own died. How long did she live here before going off to school?"

"More than a year," James said.

Henry lifted an arm as though James had made his point for him. "Exactly. Mother, you cared for and supported Thea as though she were your own daughter."

Lady Edith raised her head to look at Benedict. "Perhaps she was comfortable with me, but I am certain she would not have wished to stay here."

Benedict raised his hands as though surrendering. "I would have been happy to vacate the premises for her. The lodge is mightily tempting this time of year."

"Thea is too gentle a soul to dream of putting you out for her own comfort."

Benedict snorted. "Gentle?"

"Enough, Ben," James admonished in an authoritative tone. "The facts are as follows: Thea has run off. She has not sought refuge at Chelton or with Claverley. She does not have other acquaintances that either we or Mrs. Moulton are familiar with. Can anyone think of anything *useful*"—he speared Benedict with a look—"to add?"

The room remained silent. I considered the poor young woman's situation, and my heart reached out to her. "Perhaps that is not asking the correct question," I said timidly. I waited for permission to continue, for this conversation felt outside of my rights to enter, and I knew I was only included now because I was a member of the family. James nodded at me, and I continued. "If Miss Northcott felt she had no choice but to run away from her school, perhaps the question we should be pondering is not *where* would she go, but *why* would she leave?"

"Cousin Matthew," Henry suggested. "Perhaps she cannot abide him or Lady Claverley. I would not blame her for that opinion."

"Or the husband hunt next Season," James mused, rubbing a hand over his chin. "That was her aim in staying with Claverley, was it not? To find a tolerable match?"

"It was," Lady Edith said. She pressed her fingers to her temples again, and I wondered if her headache Sunday was not fabricated, and if so, did it continue to linger?

I stepped to James's side and indicated his mother. "Should we go in to dinner now and consider the matter privately for a time?"

James released a contented sigh and nodded. "I think Felicity has the right of it. Let us eat and ponder the dilemma. We can reconvene after everyone has had an opportunity to consider what is best to be done."

Then perhaps someone could explain to me exactly why this family had taken on the girl's wellbeing so wholly. I understood the responsibility Lady Edith felt toward her goddaughter, particularly since the poor girl had lost her mother, but where was the rest of her family? Where was her guardian?

James slipped his hand into mine and pulled me toward the door. "Please sit beside me tonight. I do not wish to be parted any longer."

I looked up and found Lady Edith watching us, frowning.

Suppressing my discomfort, I squeezed his fingers. "I would love that above all things."

CHAPTER 18

The sun shone happily down on the sweeping lawn behind Chelton, which was entirely the opposite of how I felt. James had taken the liberty of setting up targets on the long, flat portion of the lawn so we might shoot arrows into them.

Indeed, it was quite as unpleasant as it sounded.

I nocked my arrow exactly as James had shown me and released it, only to watch it fly a measly few yards and flop onto the ground before me.

"I did tell you I am awful at archery," I repeated, moving forward to collect my discarded arrows. "I participated in a competition at Arden Castle last summer and was terribly beaten."

"Yes, but you were also holding the bow incorrectly. Now that I've taught you properly, it shall be an entirely different experience." He tilted his head, squinting against the bright sun. "Tell me it is at least a little more enjoyable when you play against me?"

I bent to pick up an arrow and straightened to find James watching me, waiting for an answer. It was *not* any more enjoyable simply because he was around—but I did enjoy being around him. After the heavy dinner we'd shared with his family the evening before and the confirmation that no one—as of this morning—had determined what was best to be done about Miss Northcott, this small break from the stuffy house was welcome. It would be more welcome if I was not forced to shoot arrows I did not want to shoot.

I tapped one gloved finger against my chin. "Come to think of it, it is far better to lose soundly to you than it is to be beaten by my cousins."

James emitted a sound somewhere between a scoff and a laugh. He took a deliberate step forward, and my body froze. His mischievous smile matched his careful steps, and I found myself moving backward, matching him step for step.

"You do not mean to say that you are *not* having fun, Mrs. Bradwell?" he teased. "That would never do. I must contrive a way to salvage the remainder of our afternoon together."

James picked up his speed, and I squealed—a sound that did not often escape my lips—and turned to run. I hardly made it a yard before James's arm went around my waist and pulled me against him.

I could not allow him to win so easily at everything he did today, so I twisted his hand until he released me, picked up my skirts, and ran for the garden.

James, after a stunned moment, was hot in pursuit. I made it to the thick hedge that lined the garden and jumped behind a tree, narrowly avoiding his hand grabbing at my skirt. I couldn't help but laugh, and he responded in kind. I spun to face him and mirrored his motions, keeping the tree between us.

"You break my heart, Felicity," he said, mocking sadness.

"Well, I must win at *something* today."

James laughed, lunging for me, and I jumped back just in time to avoid his grasp. But my heel snagged on something solid, and before I knew what was happening, I flopped backwards and into a fountain, landing hard on my backside in the shallow pool. Cold water seeped through my gown, shocking the breath from my lungs. I shared a stunned look with James until mirth creeped onto his lips and into the wrinkles surrounding his eyes.

"Yes, laugh," I said, granting permission. I pinched my sodden skirt and lifted it from the water before dropping it again with a splat. My chest rolled with accompanying chuckles, and I pushed up to remove myself from the water feature, but the bottom was slick with a mossy layer of slime, and my hands slipped, dunking me further beneath the water.

"Gads, woman," James said, laughing harder. "Allow me to assist you."

I peeled off my soaked gloves and tossed them on the ground near his feet, then reached for his hand, and he sucked in a breath when our skin met. "That is blasted cold."

My eyebrows lifted.

He chuckled softly. "Here, allow me to—"

"Join me?" I asked, finishing his sentence. I yanked hard and a brief look of horror crossed over his face before he lost his footing and fell down into the fountain beside me. Water splashed around him and soaked my face, and I gasped, wiping the droplets from my eyes.

"Cold!" I exclaimed.

"Serves you right," James muttered, shaking his head like a wet hound. He pushed up onto his knees but must not have anticipated the slickness of the fountain and came down again onto his stomach.

I could not help the rolling laughter that emitted from me. It was quite impossible to stem once it began, and I clutched my wet abdomen and bent forward, laughing at the sorry, wet picture we made.

When I was able to contain my mirth once again, I grinned at James, and he shook his head ruefully. "You look—"

"Like a drowned rat?" I asked, picking up a limp curl that

had broken free from my coiffure and dropping it on my shoulder with a splat.

James, now completely given up and seated in the water beside me, lifted my lock of hair and wound it around his finger. "No, nothing like vermin. You are glowing."

"I believe you mean I am shimmering due to the sun hitting my wet skin."

"No, I meant glowing."

"With my dress ruined and my hair in disarray?" I scoffed. "I am not immune to flattery sir, but I can only tolerate falsehoods when they are at least believable."

He grew serious, tugging softly at my curl to pull me closer. "You can certainly believe me, Felicity. I will never lie to you. Not about this or anything else."

The sincerity in his tone caused a tremor to run through my body—or perhaps that was from the cold. But regardless of its origin, I found myself leaning forward still, seated in the water, my gown floating to the top of the shallow pool. James dropped my curl and slid his damp hand around the back of my neck.

"Have I told you yet how dearly I missed you while I was away?" he murmured.

He had, multiple times. "You mean Benedict was unable to provide you with enough entertainment to keep you occupied during your journey?"

"I find his taste for entertainment and mine do not exactly meld as easily as they once did."

I rested my hand on the wet lapel of his coat and leaned forward still, when the sound of neighing and crunching on gravel alerted me to someone's presence. I leaned back, hoping to see through the trees to who might be arriving at the stable house.

A carriage pulled before it, the yellow lacquered sides bright against the pale stone of the building behind it. "James, who is that?"

He turned his head, lifting it slightly to see. "Blast. It looks like you have callers."

"Why me?"

"Because the Dodwells certainly would not be here for me. And you are the bride. It is a natural conclusion."

"Oh." I wrinkled my nose. "I cannot meet them like this."

James leaned his forehead against mine. "No, I dare say you cannot." He dropped a kiss onto the edge of my nose before shifting to the edge of the shallow pool and climbing out. Once he was securely on the dry ground, he removed his sopping coat, loosened his limp cravat, and reached a hand toward me. "Allow me to help this time, eh?"

"Of course," I said, mocking affront. "I wouldn't dream otherwise." I could not help but watch the muscles in his arms beneath the sheer, wet sleeve, bunch and move as he pulled me effortlessly from the water. Arms were not shaped like that without *some* effort.

"Do you partake in fisticuffs, James?"

"Not often," he said. "Why do you ask?"

"No reason."

He looked at me askance. "Come, let us get you inside."

My heavy skirts pooled water around my ankles, and I bent to retrieve my gloves. I removed my shoes so I could walk easier.

The sound of feminine conversation reached us, and James took my hand, pulling me behind the hedge. Rose bushes fenced us in, the flowers' sweet smell wafting pleasantly over us.

"Why are we hiding?"

His face was only inches above mine. "Unless you would like to be seen as you are, I propose we wait until they are shown into the drawing room before we sneak upstairs."

"Fantastic idea, James. I would rather not attend to them at all, let alone be forced to explain why I look like a drowned—"

"Like a beautiful woman?" He plucked a white rose from the

nearby bush and pinched off the thorn on its short stem. James tucked it behind my ear, and his fingers brushed against the shell of my ear, running a shiver down my neck.

He looked down at me, his voice softening. "If you would rather not meet with the Dodwells, then you needn't go."

"I cannot ignore them simply because I do not wish to sit and talk today." There never would be a day when I *did* wish to sit and talk to strangers.

"You cannot do that *every* time a caller arrives, but you can today. You are sopping wet, Felicity. By the time you are changed and your hair is fixed"—he lifted a wet strand from my shoulder for emphasis, by now there was more hair out of my knot than secured in it—"the Dodwells will surely be on their way again."

His reasoning was sound, but still. "I would not wish for them to perceive my absence as a slight."

"I am positive my mother is, at this very moment, assuring them you are busy with some necessary activity."

"Do you think?" I asked, hopeful.

His wide, bright smile reached me in my core. "Yes, I do. It is her job as the hostess to make certain they do *not* perceive your absence as a slight, and she is adept at navigating excuses when they are necessary. She has had ample practice excusing the behavior of her three sons, so you are an easy addition."

But it was not her obligation to make any excuses for me at all. Uneasiness crept into my chest, and I looked again to the bright yellow carriage that had brought our guests to visit. They did not come for Lady Edith. They came to see me. I shirked my duties by avoiding them and casting my responsibilities onto a woman who had all but challenged me to prove my worth.

This was in no way proving my worth.

"Are you ready to go inside? I think they are in the drawing room now."

I needed to be in there with them. I lifted my skirts a few inches off the ground and water poured in a steady stream from the edge. I chuckled, swaying forward until my shoulder brushed him. "I am ready to change into something warm and dry. But I must be quick, for I plan to join them if I am able. It is my duty to do so, and I hope to take that seriously."

James was no longer laughing. I tipped my head back and looked into his green-brown eyes. His gaze bore into my soul with intensity, and the giddiness of the last quarter hour left me in a rush. A heavy weight fell onto my chest, and I breathed slowly through my nose.

"You are making me nervous, James," I said.

He seemed to shake himself, and an easy smile fell over his lips. "Forgive me. I became lost in thought."

"What about?"

"A few things," he said, lifting his wet shoulder in a simple shrug. "You, most of all. You take up much of my thoughts these days."

"Not in a troubling way, I hope."

"I do not find it troubling, though my woefully long list of things I must do has only grown since we met. You have not been good for my focus."

"My apologies. Shall I take charge of your list? I would not be a good taskmaster, but I can give it my best effort."

"Perhaps I should take advantage of your kind offer. What is my first task?"

"To see me safely inside without running into another living soul."

"I like a good challenge." James took me by the hand and led me toward a small back door. We entered into the servants' corridor, and he pulled me up a narrow, wooden staircase to another small corridor.

"You know your way around here well."

"I have been evading my mother for six and twenty years. I have the practice."

"You are not closer to thirty?" I asked.

James shot a confused glance over his shoulder. "You believed me to be?"

I did. I would not be surprised if he'd admitted to being over thirty years of age. His general bearing was so refined, his knowledge seemingly endless. "You seem so . . . mature."

"You seem mature as well, Felicity. Are you forty?"

I laughed. He had me there. "Two and twenty, I thank you."

We reached our chambers, and James released my hand and bowed dramatically, his waistcoat straining against his wet shirt. "Until tonight."

I dipped into a low curtsy. "Until then." I slipped into my room, my heart racing from the stairs and the man who led me up them.

It was unmistakable. I loved James. And now I needed to hurry and change my gown so I might prove myself worthy of him as well.

CHAPTER 19

Lady Edith held a regal court in her drawing room for the remainder of the week. She was perfectly personable, asked exactly the right questions of her guests to lead them into talking about themselves, and was the picture of poise. I had far to go before I could ever reach the mastery she had achieved as hostess—though I knew I never would. It was outside the realm of possibility for me. My faults so perfectly lined up beside her virtues, each one a matching set.

The tea in my cup shuddered when I carried it to my lips, and I took a long sip of the hot liquid. Miss Whitstone sat beside me on the sofa while her mother was actively engaged in conversation with Lady Edith opposite us, and I focused heavily on my tea while I contrived a way to speak in private with Miss Whitstone.

James had been the picture of perfection all week since returning from York, and the longer he made his affection for me plain, the more deeply I needed to know why he and this quiet, unobtrusive woman did not suit.

She was inordinately reserved, and I did not think she

wanted to be here. Her eyes darted to the door with every sound in the corridor, and I wondered if she was watching for someone in particular. Would she be relieved or disappointed if I offered her a way to leave the house?

"Tell me, Miss Whitstone," I said, setting my cup on the small table before us. "Have you had a chance to walk the gardens recently? The white roses have bloomed, and they are a sight to behold."

"It has been some time since I've walked in Chelton's garden," she said quietly.

A beat of silence passed between us, and she said nothing of the roses. Did that mean she was uninterested? Perhaps I ought to have phrased my question differently. It seemed that a more direct approach would be necessary.

I cleared my throat. "Would you like to see the roses?"

"I do not care much for roses in general, but I would not mind walking in the garden."

Did not care for roses? She had successfully robbed me of an immediate response, and I turned to face my mother-in-law, who I found watching us closely. "I think we will walk outside, if that is agreeable to you?"

"Of course," Lady Edith said.

Lady Whitstone looked at her daughter askance. "Do not forget to tighten your bonnet, dear. I detected a wind when we arrived that was not present down in town."

"Of course, Mama."

I retrieved my bonnet and a shawl to protect me against the wind, and we shortly found ourselves slipping down the pale stone steps toward the lush grass. The brown gravel pathway would lead us past the stable house and up to the gardens, and then we would be completely alone.

Our crunching footsteps carried us toward the garden, and the sun beat down upon our bonnets, but I could think of nothing to say.

What had I been thinking? I could not contrive a way to force this woman to talk, and if I had, she would not find the new wife of the man who rejected her a worthy beneficiary of her opinions. A pair of finches swooped down above our heads and glided toward the branches of a tree ahead, their sweet calls breaking the silence.

It would be better to begin with neutral topics. "If not the rose, what is your favorite flower, Miss Whitstone?"

She did not answer for a moment, and I wondered if she heard my question.

"I am partial to daffodils."

"Those are lovely," I agreed. "I have always thought they resembled tiny trumpets and would be perfect for a small fairy in need of an amplifier."

Miss Whitstone looked at me strangely, and we curved around the path to enter the garden. "Fairies are not real."

"No, of course not. I only meant . . . in an *imaginary* world, they would be perfect for such a thing."

Miss Whitstone did not bother with a response, and I felt inordinately foolish. Her apathy toward roses implied that she was not possessed of an overly romantic heart, and her candid reply to my fairy thoughts led me to believe she had no imagination, so she must not be an avid reader. I hated to so much as think it, but thus far Miss Whitstone had proven herself to be something of a bore.

We trailed along the hedge, and I did not bother to point out the white roses whose blooms scented the air with a faint sweetness, for she would not appreciate them anyway.

Not as I did, anyway. The flower James had tucked behind my ear even now hung from the post of my bed so I could forever keep its sweetness.

I was unsure if I would ever again smell a white rose without thinking of the ridiculous spectacle James and I had made in the fountain.

We walked through the varying shrubs and flowers, circling hedges and skirting finch-adorned trees. The scent lingered, following us, and I could not help but think of my husband. Miss Whitstone walked alongside me through the various interwoven pathways, quietly ignoring the flora on display.

"Have you lived in Bakewell all your life?" I asked, tired of the silence that accompanied our gravel-crunching steps.

"Yes, and my mother has been dear friends with Lady Edith for longer."

She had answered me straight away *and* added a tidbit of her own? I felt like I had been blessed by this woman for so many words when any were rare from her lips. I shook the sarcastic thought away. I needed to focus. I had a mission here.

"From what I witnessed on Sunday, local Society is both large and deeply connected. I would assume the majority of families have been here a long while."

"Most of them, yes. Which has proved both a blessing and a curse."

"In what way?"

Her gaze flicked to me before focusing again on the path we walked. "I do not converse easily with strangers, you see, so the blessing lies in that most of our neighbors are not strangers."

"The curse?"

Her nose wrinkled. "That each neighbor, having claim on such long acquaintances, feels themselves owed a degree of intimacy which I do not easily give to anyone."

I had to admit that I agreed with her regarding the overwhelming nature of such a Society. Since delivering my cards and making Sunday's introductions, I had received an endless number of callers over the course of the week.

This was where Miss Whitstone and I were similar. "I cannot bear to be in social functions when I do not know the people well, and even when I know them well, too great a number will destroy my poor nerves."

Miss Whitstone stopped walking and looked at me. "Truly?"

Had I given the impression otherwise? "Yes. I struggle immensely in any social situation. The crowds themselves do not bother me so much as the attention does. So dancing or anything requiring me to step in front of a group is inordinately challenging."

"That is difficult to believe, Mrs. Bradwell. You comport yourself with such dignity and grace."

A very *un*dignified and *un*graceful laugh tore from my throat. "Only wait until the ball my mother-in-law is holding at the end of the month. If I do not faint by the end of the first set, it will be a miracle. I far prefer reading and drawing to any situation that requires me to put forth physical effort or speak to someone I do not know well."

Miss Whitstone narrowed her gaze above a bland smile. "Perhaps we should have escaped to the library instead of the gardens. Then we could both sit in the silence we clearly prefer."

I tried not to feel the slice of her unintended cut. The honesty of her barb sharpened its point, but it did not feel as though the woman intended to hurt me—only to speak the truth. "You enjoy reading, then?"

"No, but I enjoy the quiet and not being forced into conversation with a stranger."

I had been correct then, and Miss Whitstone lacked both an affection for books and an active imagination. Evidently, she was void of tact as well.

"Perhaps we can circle the garden once more in silence before we return to the drawing room, then?" I suggested.

"That would be pleasant."

We continued down the pathway, and I allowed my shawl to slip down my shoulders and drag low behind my back, the warmth of the sun providing more than enough heat. We passed the shallow fountain in the center of the gardens, and my heart jumped, recalling the escapade from earlier in the week.

James had been nothing but kind and attentive, regardless of how unappealing his idea of courting could be. Since the archery activity, he had taken me for a long ride in his curricle and offered to teach me to shoot, which I politely declined. I was certain he would soon propose a game of cricket or fencing lessons. Henry's advice to find an activity we both enjoyed was becoming increasingly attractive, but less and less likely.

Except, of course, for kissing. An activity I completely enjoyed, but had only partaken in *once*.

I supposed the entire lack of it made our courting feel all the more authentic. For if we were unmarried, we certainly would not kiss.

A shadow passed over the path above us, and I looked up to find Henry striding our direction. Miss Whitstone stopped suddenly, intaking a quiet breath.

"Good day, Felicity. Miss Whitstone," Henry said, bowing to us. He turned his attention on our guest. "I have been sent to fetch you to the drawing room. Your mother is ready to leave."

Miss Whitstone nodded, her cheeks blooming with color that I wagered had nothing to do with the warmth of the day. Did she carry an affection for Henry? Perhaps that explained why James did not believe himself to be the correct match for this quiet woman.

We stood in uncomfortable silence a beat longer before I swept my arm toward Chelton. "Shall we?"

Henry walked by my side, Miss Whitstone on the other, and we made our way quietly toward the house. When we at last reached the drawing room I had never been so glad and relieved to rid myself of a caller—and I hardly ever enjoyed when people came to call.

As the Whitstones were taking their leave, a footman presented me with a letter upon a silver salver. I took it, thanking him, and waited for the women to be escorted away before crossing toward the window to open the missive in the sunlight.

The direction on the front was written in my mother's familiar hand, and I was both anxious and excited for whatever it could hold. I had not been parted from my parents for this length of time in my entire life, and these last few weeks had been something of a challenge in navigating my new roles alone. I needed my mama's guiding hand now more than ever.

Unfolding the sheet of paper, I angled my body away from the window so the sunlight might shine upon the letter.

My darling Lissy—

I do hope you are enjoying your time at Chelton, and I am eager to see the glorious building myself. I have heard it is the most beautiful estate in all of the Lake District from no less than five sources since your marriage occurred, but it is no wonder that you would have such a great house when your husband is possessed of six thousand a year. I can hardly credit it, but the fact remains undisputed. It is a balm to know that you will always be cared for.

I paused and lowered the paper slightly, my brow puckering. That number rang with familiarity. Six thousand a year? I had once claimed that I did not require such an income—and my mother responded that I would prefer books to pounds in that quantity. She was not wrong, and it hit me with a sudden realization that the man Mrs. Overton must have been telling Mama about during the Hutton ball was James. *My* James.

I had declared that I had no interest in that sum of money. Looking about the ornate drawing room now, my opinion held strong. If I had been listening closer to Mrs. Overton's gossip— had I heard James's surname in that conversation—would I have chosen a different outcome after we were found together? Would I have opted for escaping to Jane's house in Scotland unwed and shrouded in scandal?

James was beginning to possess my heart, but his estate and

its requirements of me were far more than I had anticipated, and given the chance to remove myself from this, I did not know what I would do.

I brought the letter into the light again, faintly aware of the voices returning to the drawing room.

It is with the deepest regret that I have written to tell you that your father and I must put off our visit for a little time. Mrs. Hutton has invited us to her house party, and we have decided to attend it on our way to Chelton. It will break up the journey nicely, but it does not begin until the twenty-third of this month, so I am afraid we will not arrive in time for your ball.

You know how dearly your father loves to fish. Mr. Hutton is known to provide a fair bit of game, and the fish in his lake are always plentiful. Surely you can forgive us for indulging in this bit of fun for your father. He has sacrificed so much for us during the Season attending all the functions he did not wish to attend that I cannot refuse him this treat.

You might expect our arrival near the twelfth of July.

All my love,

Your devoted Mama

I lowered the letter again with a sigh. Devoted was perhaps a bit of a stretch. Currently I felt neglect more keenly than devotion. Lady Edith, Henry, and James entered the room, and I faced them.

"Do you have a lake nearby, James? Or any good fishing at all?"

"Yes," he said at once, his eyes brightening.

I realized my mistake and cursed my thoughtless tongue.

"Would you enjoy that pastime?" he asked.

"No, I was only thinking . . . when my father comes, be sure he does not learn of it." My pettiness felt like a thick, discomfiting blanket, and I shoved away the filthiness crawling over my skin. I hurried to amend my words, softening them with a smile. "For he will surely beg to be out there day after day if he knows."

"Consider it noted," James said, though he seemed to realize that there was more to my odd request than I'd let on.

Lady Edith sat in the seat she had previously occupied and had taken up her embroidery, Henry beside her with a book. James crossed toward me, his dark brow wrinkled. "What has happened?"

I shook my head and tried to deliver a smile as though I was not hollowed and made more lonely by my parents' negligence. I hoped they'd missed me enough by now to wish to see me straight away, but it only appeared that they'd been freed of my constraining presence instead. "It is nothing. My parents are postponing their visit by nearly a month. We will be graced with their presence in July."

"I am sorry."

"It is not your doing. It is only that . . ." I gazed into his earnest, green-brown gaze and swallowed my words. I could not admit to this man that the life he'd given me was overwhelming. How could I hurt or offend someone who tried so consistently to please me?

When he'd mildly complained about the ardent misses vying for his attention on the night we met, I'd had no idea that he'd been the object of such gossip and attention for his *money*—I'd assumed the young ladies were after him because he was so handsome. His assumption that I had been attempting to entrap him that evening made perfect sense now, along with his mention that the entire *ton* was bound to believe it of me.

He was a wealthy, handsome gentleman who had attended the Season with the intent to find a wife. I could not, now, tell him how deeply I did not fit into his life or how I'd depended on my mama's guidance to find my way here.

James's concerned gaze seemed to grow more worried, so I settled for a different truth. "I miss my parents."

"Of course you do." He reached for my hand and rubbed his thumb along the back of it, and I wondered if he knew he rubbed my old candle wax burn. Was it a coincidence, or merely the natural location where his thumb fell? I could not help but think of our quiet dance in the dim library each time he touched me in this way, and I wondered if he recalled the same moment.

Mrs. Prescott came into the dining room, stealing our attention.

"Yes?" Lady Edith asked.

"There is some trouble with the maid, ma'am. The one who was found in Master Benedict's room."

"More trouble?" Lady Edith bent to put away her embroidery. "Good heavens."

James gave my hand a squeeze and released it. "Is this not something Felicity should be included in?"

Lady Edith paused and looked up at me, and I could immediately discern the distrust in her gaze. Had it always been there? Had I just been blind before she revealed herself to me?

"I do not think it necessary—"

"Nonsense," James said clearly, his voice ringing through the room with authority. "You are the mistress of Chelton, my dear. It is completely necessary for you to be involved in the trouble that occurs below stairs."

Irritation flashed in my mother-in-law's eyes. I did not know how, but James had likely made the situation worse for me.

I gave Mrs. Prescott—whose worried gaze flicked between me and Lady Edith—a kind smile and a nod. "Can we all attend to it together?"

"Of course, ma'am."

Lady Edith led the way from the room, and I followed her, Mrs. Prescott bringing up the rear. Icy coldness lifted from Lady Edith in waves, and I knew at once I was no closer to proving myself now than I had been before the previous four days of incessant callers. My attempts to appear refined and graceful and kind had fallen flat, and after the strain and toll the effort had taken on me, I was certain I couldn't keep it up forever.

Hope dwindled on its narrow, cheap grasp, and I watched it flutter away into the wind and far from reach like the finches outside, flying away until it disappeared completely.

CHAPTER 20

Mrs. Prescott looked toward her sitting room door with pinched lips. It was dim below stairs, and the lack of light added to the dark mood around us. "I would have dismissed her on the spot, but I thought you would want to manage it yourself, ma'am."

"You were correct," Lady Edith said. She gestured for Mrs. Prescott to open the door for us, and we slipped into the room.

The maid in question was seated at a table, and I followed Lady Edith inside, not for the first time since arriving at Chelton. The dim room was small but well-outfitted, and the window high on the wall was open to allow in some light. The maid's wide eyes flicked between Lady Edith and myself, and I felt for her panic—I too would be terrified to be in her position.

But she'd brought it upon herself.

Lady Edith opened her mouth as though to speak, then turned to me, lifting her eyebrows as if giving me permission to proceed. Drat James and his interference. I would be happy to allow his mother to manage these types of situations. I'd yet to learn from her everything I needed to know. I was being forced to perform with only a cursory glance at the script.

Silence proceeded to hang uncomfortably over us like an awkward tapestry, and I turned to the blonde maid. "Can I hear the situation in your own words, please?"

She looked confused, but quickly stood and delivered a curtsy. "I wasn't rifling through no drawers, I promise."

That was not the report we'd received. "You were seen searching Benedict's drawers twice—"

"Not by Mrs.—"

"Hold your tongue," Mrs. Prescott snapped. "You will not interrupt your betters."

I drew in a breath, certain I was meddling in things high above my abilities. I gave the housekeeper a pert smile and directed my attention back to the maid. "Not by whom?"

She swallowed. "I didn't search Mr. Benedict's drawers, I vow it. Mrs. Prescott didn't see me with her own eyes."

That was an interesting development. "Who was it that saw you?"

"Janet."

I had no earthly idea who that was. I looked to the house-keeper for her input.

"Janet has been a maid here for nearly five years," Lady Edith said, her attention on the maid. "And you have been in our employ for less than one."

"Where is Janet?" I asked.

"I will find her," Mrs. Prescott said, though by the disapproval on her face I could see that she did not like that I'd asked it of her.

Once she left, I returned my attention to the maid. "What is your name?"

"Molly Thompson, ma'am."

"Why would Janet have cause to lie about what she saw?"

"Because she hates me. She thinks I'm trying to catch Mr. Marland's eye, but I'm not. I swear it." She shook her head violently. "I need this job, ma'am. My mother needs the money, and I can't lose it. I would never do anything to risk my place here."

"Mr. Marland?" I looked to Lady Edith.

"The butcher," she supplied.

"Not him. The butcher's *son* is the one Janet fancies." Molly scoffed. "But he doesn't even look at her. It doesn't take smarts to figure that out."

So this could be a case of jealousy. If Janet wanted Molly gone, that would be the easiest way to accomplish it. "Someone did rifle through Benedict's drawers, though?"

"Indeed. His things were strewn about in his drawers," Lady Edith confirmed.

Then *someone* was lying. Mrs. Prescott entered the room again, another maid just behind her. This one I recognized as the girl who had been starting the fires in my room each morning.

"I didn't do anything wrong," Janet said, glaring at Molly. "She hasn't liked me since she arrived last year."

"*Girls,*" Mrs. Prescott admonished. "You will be better mannered than that."

They stood at attention on opposite sides of the room, and I felt unsure. How was I to know which girl to believe? Either story could be accurate.

"What would you like to do?" Mrs. Prescott asked.

Lady Edith stood by, her hands clasped before her, and looked at me expectantly. Her expectant gaze felt like more of a test than an offer of support. It was all too much to place on my shoulders when I knew so little about these situations or how they were typically handled in such a large estate. I had only been privy to the underworkings of a small house—my own mother's.

If my mama were here, she would guide me.

Perhaps that was my answer. What would Mama do in this case? I believed she would not take rash action. She would think carefully and perhaps question other servants until she discovered exactly what was occurring between the ladies. I could never live with myself if I mistakenly dismissed the wrong person.

"I need a day to make a decision."

Lady Edith's gray eyebrows rose on her delicate forehead. "So long?"

"Yes. I need an entire day to ponder. Then I will inform you of my decision."

Lady Edith and Mrs. Prescott both appeared as though they wished to argue, but they had put this decision on my shoulders, and this was how I chose to handle it. If my mother-in-law disapproved of my methods, then I would undoubtedly fall lower in her esteem.

I only hoped I could prove my plan successful. I looked at each of the maids quickly before leaving the room, and their expressions surprised me—for I had not expected *Janet* to be the one to appear relieved by my postponing the verdict, and Molly frustrated.

When I reached the main floor, I found the nearest footman. "Are you familiar with all the maids?"

The footman looked to the side, uncomfortable.

I was quick to reassure him. "I do not mean overly familiar. I only want to know if you are familiar with their characters."

"Yes, I believe I am."

"And who, in your opinion, is the most honorably behaved?"

He narrowed his eyes at the floor. I felt for him—surely he believed he was being tested in some way—but I needed an answer, so I did not relent. I waited patiently.

He cleared his throat. "I suppose that would be Hannah, ma'am."

It would have been much too simple for him to have named

one of the girls in question, of course. "Thank you," I said again, and left. I needed to find Hannah.

Or, better yet, send for her.

The drawing room was empty now, and I wagered that James had escaped with Benedict for that ride. If Lady Edith returned to her embroidery there, though, I did not want for her to find me in the midst of my investigation and intervene or watch too closely. Spinning on my heel, I left for the library. It was a smaller room and would be comfortable and quiet.

And then, perhaps, I could sneak in a little reading when the interview was complete.

I passed Forester, the butler, on my way upstairs. "Could you send Hannah to the library, please?"

"Of course," he said.

The house was silent, my footsteps clipping loudly on the marble floor. I was glad to reach the carpeted library and released a long sigh once I was safely inside.

"I feel obligated to warn you that you are not alone," a deep voice said, disembodied, for I saw no evidence of another person in the long, narrow room.

"Who is speaking?"

A hand raised in the air at the end of the room behind a tufted, wingback chair, and then Henry lifted his head to send me a smile.

I crossed the room but remained standing. Hannah would be here soon. "Drat you Bradwell men and your affinity for being in libraries when I would prefer to be alone."

"I can leave you alone," he offered.

"No, you were here first, and I did not mean to infiltrate your privacy. I asked a maid to meet me here, but once she arrives, I will take her elsewhere."

Henry narrowed his eyes slightly. "Did you choose this room for a particular reason? I do not mind sharing it."

191

"Only to read once my interview is completed. I was hoping no one would find me before dinner."

He laughed. "It appears that we are of the same mind."

Quiet footsteps came toward us, and I gave him a wide-eyed look. "Keep yourself hidden," I whispered.

"I believed I had already done that well," he muttered.

A maid stepped into the doorway and immediately dropped into a curtsy.

"Hannah?" I asked, crossing the room to meet her.

"Yes'm."

"Please, come in." I paused at a grouping of chairs near the back wall and indicated that she be seated. She sat gingerly on the edge of the chair across from me and folded her hands primly in her lap.

"I would like to first set your mind at ease and explain that multiple people are being questioned and you are in no trouble. There is a . . . *situation* which has occurred, and I would like to know what you can tell me about Molly and Janet."

Her eyes widened softly before she shook her head. "They have never been friendly with one another, ma'am. From the first day Molly arrived, they have tried to best one another."

Interesting. "Did Janet have trouble with anyone else before Molly arrived? I am told she has worked here for five years."

"Yes, ma'am. Five years." She paused before continuing. "Janet is not an easy girl to be friends with, but she hasn't had trouble before, not like she does with Molly."

"What kind of trouble does she have with Molly?"

Hannah hesitated. She looked over her shoulder at the door, then back to me. "She was friendly with the blacksmith's son, but he stopped seeing her when Molly arrived. Molly claimed he shifted his affections to her, but she hadn't been here long enough for that, I don't think."

Everything pointed to Molly, except for one thing. Why

would she have gotten herself put in a position to be dismissed if her goal was to dismiss Janet? That would in no way remove Janet from the house.

"Thank you, Hannah. You have been a great help."

She rose at once and bobbed a curtsy before slipping from the room.

"Fancy yourself a detective?" Henry's deep voice called from the end of the library.

I moved down the narrow room to sit in the chair near his seat. "I fear that your mother has placed her trust in the wrong person."

"Is this about the maid searching Benedict's drawers?"

I sat up. "You've heard of it?"

He wrinkled his nose. "Yes, and I wonder if you are asking the right questions but questioning the wrong person."

"I do not know which of the servants are the most trustworthy."

"I did not mean the servants."

"Then who . . . oh. Benedict."

Henry winked and lifted his book again.

That was a good idea. I felt I had already made my decision—Molly seemed the most likely of the two to have erred, but she would not have put herself in the position she was in if her goal was to remove Janet from the house. If Lady Edith had managed the situation, Molly would already be gone without a reference.

Janet could have acted out of jealousy and fabricated Molly's misdeeds. But hadn't she been relieved when I needed extra time, not disappointed that Molly had not been dismissed yet? Had she been the liar, she would have been frustrated that her lie hadn't worked, wouldn't she?

It was too confusing. I wanted to lose myself in a book and consider the matter again later. The fourth and final volume of *The Mysteries of Udolpho* was waiting for me, and I plucked it from the shelf before sitting back down and opening it to the first page.

Henry and I read in companionable silence until it was time to dress for dinner.

"I will see you soon," I said, and left the room, taking the book with me.

CHAPTER 21

Fear was my loyal companion, no thanks to a little late-night reading after dinner. I slunk lower beneath the bedclothes to hide from whatever might lie waiting for me in the dark. My feet hit the wooden footboard of my bed, startling me. A little yelp escaped my dry throat and echoed softly in my large bedroom.

It had been hours since I parted ways with James after dinner, and everyone was certainly asleep by now. The temptation to ring for tea or milk merely so Fanny would come to me was strong, but I resisted. I would not wake my maid merely because I had been foolish enough to read a gothic novel at night and was now terrified of ghosts which were not truly present.

Shadows danced across the wall, cast about from the moonlight through the window, and I squeezed my eyes closed.

Oh, dear. That was worse. I opened them again and looked about for whatever creeping thing could be in my room causing the creaking sound.

There was nothing for it. I simply would not sleep tonight. It was too bad I did not have another book, or even the fire, for I could read to pass the time.

Did James have books in his room? Unlikely. I looked to the door that led from my chamber to his, and an idea struck me. I could go to him. Perhaps if I woke James and told him I heard a creaking sound, he would check my room to ensure I was safe, and then I would be able to fall asleep knowing that he was awake on the other side of the wall.

It was unkind of me, given the hour, but I had no other choice if I wanted any chance of sleep tonight. Then I would finish the book tomorrow in the light of day and read something else to remove it from my mind.

My plan set, I sat up slowly, looking about me for any specters I might have missed a moment ago. The room looked clear of spirits, and I sucked in a deep breath and threw back my blankets, jumping to the floor and padding across it softly in my stockinged feet. When I reached James's door, I opened it slowly, grateful the hinges did not squeak. His room was equally dark, and his soft, heavy breathing could be heard.

The steady sound was at once comforting, chasing away my imagined ghosts, and I knew with sudden surety that I would not be able to wake my husband. How could I? I slipped into the room, soaking in the comfort of knowing he was near, and I could hear him.

My limbs relaxed in his presence, and I slumped against the wall. I had been battling sleep for hours, and my body was exhausted. James lay only a handful of steps away from me, and his bed was so large. I could curl up on the foot of it like a hound, and he would never know I was there.

The idea settled on my chest, and I considered it greater. *Could* I do such a thing? Climb into his bed without his knowledge? I could snatch a few hours of sleep and then return to my own chamber in the morning, and he would never know it.

A creak in my bedroom made me startle, and my elbow hit

the wall. My whole body went cold and still while James turned over, mumbling incoherently. If he was to wake and find me, what would I say in defense of my presence here like a peeping busybody?

Oh goodness. If he was to awake and find me in his bed, what would I say *then*? I could not climb into the man's bed without his permission. That was simply preposterous.

I sucked in a quiet breath and blew it out through puffed cheeks. James had been so kind and attentive. If I woke him to tell him of my fears, surely he would not be angry. Perhaps I would only ask if I could leave the door open between our rooms. He would give his consent, then fall back asleep swiftly.

"James," I whispered, but he did not budge.

I crossed toward the bed and reached for him, pressing my fingers into the bare skin of his shoulder.

Oh, good heavens. The man slept without a shirt? Was that normal?

"Hmm?" he asked, his eyes closed.

"James, I've had a fright."

He sat up swiftly and looked at me through tired eyes, the blanket falling to his waist. "What is it, Liss? What has happened?"

Liss. I liked that. "Nothing has happened. I have only had a fright. I needed to . . . um . . . ask if you would mind—"

"No, not at all." His voice was husky with sleep, and he moved over on the bed.

He was making room for me.

"That isn't necessary," I said quickly.

He looked up again and squinted at me in the darkness. "I will keep to our agreement, Liss. But if you are frightened, you may sleep here. We are married. There is nothing untoward about it."

That certainly sounded better than returning to my creaky,

ghost-infested room alone. "If you are sure it is not an inconvenience."

His low chuckle seeped under my skin. "It is no inconvenience."

No more than being woken in the middle of the night, he was likely thinking.

I slipped under the blanket, the feather mattress warm where James had previously been lying, and pulled the blanket up to my chin. The room was quiet, now void of his deep breathing, and I was extremely aware of every noise and move I made. Did it shake the entire bed? Was I breathing too loudly?

"You may go to sleep now," James whispered.

"That would be ideal, but I cannot relax."

He let out a soft sigh and rubbed a hand over his eyes. "What is it that frightened you? Perhaps if you speak about it, you will be able to put it behind you."

He seemed to entirely miss the point that it was not my fears that now kept me awake, but the man lying beside me. I'd forgotten already what had driven me into his room to begin with.

"Liss?"

"It was the book. *Udolpho*. I read it following dinner, and I should not have done so."

"It put fear into your head?"

I nodded, and he chuckled.

"Every creak was a creature," I whispered, "every shadow a specter."

"Would you like me to light a candle so you can be assured that we are very much alone right now?"

"I assure you, James, I am deeply aware of how alone we are."

He went silent, and I nestled down into the warmth he'd left behind for me.

"I do not know whether to berate my brother for introducing this novel to you, or thank him."

"Whyever would you thank him?"

"Because of this." His low voice rumbled into the darkness and drove prickles of awareness over my skin. "You were frightened, and you came to me. Nothing has made me this happy in days."

"Not even falling into the fountain?"

"That was a close second."

"Not even riding Solis today?"

He was quiet for a moment, and I wondered if he was considering his answer. "No, Felicity. Not even that."

I turned to face him better and I could make out his profile in the moonlight that slipped through his window. "Thank you, James, for being a man I can trust."

He looked at me, his hair disheveled and his jaw shadowed, but just as handsome in disarray as he was when he was composed. Reaching for me, he took my hand in his and closed his fingers around mine. The heat emanating from his skin very much made him feel as though he had recently basked before a fire, and I wanted to be enveloped in his warmth.

"Goodnight, my sweet wife."

"Goodnight," I whispered, and I fell asleep holding James's hand.

I awoke the next morning to a bright room and a missing husband. The door between our chambers sat open, and I could hear the sound of bustling movement within my room. The clock on the mantel was too far to see clearly from this distance, but I was certain James had allowed me to sleep later than I typically did—and I had never slept so well in all my life.

The scent of James's spicy cologne was muted on the pillow,

but it enveloped me in a soft, hazy cloud. Would it be improper to remain in this bed all day?

Fanny's head popped around the corner of the opened door, her wide eyes smiling beneath the white cap she wore. "Oh good, you're awake, ma'am."

My cheeks warmed from being found in James's bed and what my maid was surely thinking now. I cleared my throat. "Is there a reason I should be?" Aside from determining how to manage the maid situation downstairs, there was nothing on my schedule today that I had been made aware of.

"Lady Edith would like to meet you in the drawing room at your earliest convenience. You are to go into Bakewell together."

"Lovely." I slipped out of bed and smoothed the blankets before following Fanny into my room. She dressed me swiftly in a gown of sage green muslin and my half-boots. She took little time securing my hair into a simple style.

I slipped the final volume of *Udolpho* into my reticule and pulled on my gloves. One never did know when one would be presented with time to read, and I hated to be unprepared. Besides, if I had any hope of sleeping in my own bed tonight, I needed to finish this novel during the daylight.

Lady Edith awaited me downstairs, and I could sense her impatience when I stepped into the drawing room. Thankfully Fanny had the foresight to bring a breakfast tray to me while she readied my toilette, and I would not need to ask my mother-in-law to wait longer while I ate. She did not appear to be in a mood for trifles such as breakfast.

"Ah, there she is," Lady Edith said, placing her embroidery in her basket with great forbearance.

"Wait, Mother. There is something I need to speak to Felicity about before you leave."

James stood at the window, his hands clasped casually behind his back, and my heart leapt at the dashing figure he presented. His jaw was freshly shaven, his hair styled as it typically was, and everything in pristine order from the shine of his boots to the knot of his cravat. Had he readied himself while I'd slept? It was such a foreign concept, I could not help but feel my neck heat. I recalled his bare chest lying beside me, and my blush deepened.

Lady Edith stilled, looking from her son to me, then settled her hands in her lap. "Very well."

I approached him at the window, aware of the strength of his gaze as it followed me across the room. "Good morning, James."

He dipped a brief nod. "Were you able to sleep well?" he murmured. I glanced over at his mother, who sat far enough away in the spacious room, her hands occupied with her embroidery. At least the woman gave us privacy.

"Yes. I cannot recall the last time I slumbered so deeply." Proof that he had likely readied himself for the day in his own chamber and I had not heard a peep. "Thank you for your assistance. It was very kind of you."

"Yes, I'm quite the saint," he said, a hint of humor to his tone. "I certainly received nothing from the arrangement."

He spoke with sarcasm, but I did not know why. "Indeed. You suffered a hysterical woman waking you in the middle of the night, broken sleep, and half of your bed."

James ran a hand over his jaw. "None of those were a sacrifice, Felicity. You are welcome anytime."

My pulse jumped at the very thought, and I looked to the window, certain my face would flame if I searched out James's greenish eyes now. "Your mother is waiting for me."

He cleared his throat. "Before you go, I did have something to speak to you about."

I faced him.

"It occurred to me that you might be more comfortable during the ball if you had someone attend who made you comfortable. Since your parents cannot make it—"

Chose not to make it.

"—I wondered if you would like to write to your cousin in Scotland and invite her to stay for a visit?"

"Oh, truly?" I asked, inhaling in my excitement. I'd posted an invitation to my aunt, her new husband, and my cousin Daniel in case they were in residence at Arden Castle, but I hadn't thought to extend the invitation to Jane because of the distance of her house. If she was invited to remain for a visit, that would make the journey to Cumberland worth it for her and Ewan.

"She and her husband are welcome for as long as you wish to have them, of course."

I took James by the shoulders and reached up on tiptoe to kiss his cheek. "Thank you, James."

His eyes sparkled. "You needn't thank me. All I've done is produce the idea."

"I will write to her straight away." I turned to do just that and paused, Lady Edith's frown reaching me from across the room. "I will write to her when we return from town," I amended quietly.

James chuckled softly. He rested a hand against my waist and leaned in, his quiet voice tickling my ear. "Do not let Mother fool you. She is not nearly as frightening as she attempts to appear."

His breath chased a chill down my spine.

"On the contrary. She frightens me exactly as much as she intends."

CHAPTER 22

Madame Rousseau had made a masterpiece out of the white confection Lady Edith dreamed up, and in the gown, standing upon a small dais, I felt as though I was wrapped in an elegant cloud.

"You are stunning, Mrs. Bradwell," the French modiste said, stepping back to admire her handiwork.

"I believe you are the cause of that," I said quietly, though I agreed that the image I could see in the looking glass was much better than I'd expected it to be.

Lady Edith circled me with a discerning eye. "Can you take it in across the shoulders a bit? It looks to be hanging strangely. The gathers are fine at the shoulder blades." She continued to walk, and I found my breathing shallow under her scrutiny. "Is it possible to add more flowers to the hem? It is a little light on the roses."

I looked down, and there appeared to be a tasteful number of flowers to me. "I like the way it looks now," I said meekly.

Madame Rousseau looked from me to Lady Edith. She busied herself adjusting the pins and did not reply.

"We want this gown to shock the attendees at the party by its magnificence, Felicity."

I held her gaze. It was my ball, was it not? "I believe this will accomplish the awe you seek."

She shook her head, looking at me from head to toe. "It is close, but not quite there."

"Just a few more flowers, then?" Madame Rousseau asked. "Not too many."

I was grateful that she seemed willing to compromise between our tastes, but I didn't want any more flowers at all. But peace with my mother-in-law was equally important, and Lady Edith did not appear as though she would retreat from her position. In this particular battle, I was willing to surrender. "A few more, then," I agreed.

"Now that we have that settled, I wondered if you have another ball gown nearly ready? We must attend a ball Tuesday, and I hoped Felicity could wear one of the new ones."

Because evidently my old ball gowns left much to be desired.

"There is the pink, my lady," Madame Rousseau said.

"Shall we have it fitted then?"

"It is not quite ready for that, but I can use the white gown to ensure it is the correct size and send it to you straight away."

Lady Edith nodded her approval. "Are there any other dresses ready to be fitted?"

"One more."

I remained a silent model while Madame Rousseau and Lady Edith analyzed another gown. The style was not exactly to my taste, but I tried to remind myself that, as the mistress of Chelton, I now had a reputation to uphold and an example to set. I supposed I could grow used to more extravagant gowns if it pleased Lady Edith.

By the time we left the modiste's shop an hour later, my arms were weary from holding them out while Madame Rousseau adjusted pins and my legs tired from standing still for such a great length of time. Uncomfortable silence followed us to the barouche and wrapped around us as we pulled out of Bakewell toward home. Lady Edith looked to the pale stone buildings and rolling green hills behind them, her hand pressed to her stomach.

"Who is holding a ball on Tuesday?" I asked.

Lady Edith drew in a breath through her nose. "Lord and Lady Grenville, but I imagine you've yet to make their acquaintance. They do not leave their house often, and they are very selective with who is invited to their soirees."

"A small private ball sounds like a wonderful way to dip my toe into local Society."

Lady Edith's eyes drifted closed. "Do not mistake me, Felicity. This might be a smaller gathering than you are used to in London, but it is no less scrupulous. We must be on our best behavior. Lady Grenville's approval will go a long way in securing your place in local Society."

"In what way? The woman does not go out much, yes?"

"Yes, but her soirees are the peak of local Society. If we find ourselves uninvited to those, we've fallen too far."

I struggled to understand why that would matter much, but it was clear that it was of the utmost importance to Lady Edith.

"I will be on my best behavior."

She nodded but did not open her eyes. Her hands pressed against her midsection tightly, and it occurred to me that her cheeks looked greenish. "Are you feeling unwell?"

"Yes," she said quietly.

"Shall I direct the coachman to stop?"

"No. We are almost home."

"We can pause for just a moment though so you might breathe—"

"No," she snapped. "We are nearly there."

We rode the remainder of the way in silence, and when we reached the stone bridge that spanned the river in front of the house, Lady Edith groaned. I looked at her sharply, concerned to find her face had gone white.

"Stop the carriage!" I called, and we drew to an abrupt halt.

Lady Edith bent over the side of the conveyance and cast up her accounts. I remained motionless, hoping to grant her the privacy she undoubtedly desired, and noticed the servants facing away as well, unruffled. This must not be the first time they had found themselves in this situation.

Footsteps along the gravel road came toward us, and I looked up to see James and Benedict approaching, both in only their shirtsleeves, waistcoats, and pantaloons, and my stomach did a pleasant swoop. Benedict held a shovel, and James pulled a handkerchief from his waistline to dab at the sweat beading his forehead.

Lady Edith sat tall again, and I handed her the handkerchief from my reticule. She took it and dabbed at her brow, then mouth.

"Mother, are you unwell?" Benedict asked.

"I think I shall walk the remainder of the way," she said weakly.

James quickened his step and offered her a hand, which she graciously took. I followed her down from the carriage. She gave the coachman a sweep of her hand, and he took off toward the house.

Lady Edith leaned heavily on James's arm. "To think I had been considering going to York myself in search of Thea." She laughed quietly, without mirth.

Benedict's gaze snapped to her. "You needn't go to the trouble."

"Nay, I *cannot* go to the trouble. I can hardly make it from Bakewell to Chelton."

"Put it from your mind, Mother," James admonished.

"But you know that I cannot," she said quietly, and my heart ached from the acute distress she was under. I understood feeling so helpless—wanting so badly to do something, but my body not permitting it. I wanted, more than anything, to have control over myself when dancing in public, but I could not manage my nerves regardless of how hard I tried.

It was much the same with Lady Edith and her carriage sickness. I understood her suffering.

Benedict remained quiet, watching the interaction with a deeply furrowed brow. When he caught my gaze, he smoothed his forehead and sent me a wink. "I nearly have your road completed, Felicity. That rut will no longer bother you."

James cast me a glance. "I did not know you cared for the rut."

"Henry mentioned that it nearly threw her from the curricle last week after church."

James's expression tightened. "That is more likely due to his driving than this rut." He shifted his attention back to his mother. "Come. Let us get you home."

James and Lady Edith walked ahead of us, and I fell into step beside Benedict. We walked past the rut, fresh dirt and rocks packed into where the scar on the road once ran. "Shall I walk you to the house?"

My lips curved. Now would be the perfect time to ask Benedict about the situation. "Don't be silly. I can walk myself there perfectly fine. But I did hope to question you a little now that I've found you alone."

He ran a hand through his curly hair. "Oh? What about?"

"The maids. Did you find anything missing from your drawers after they were searched?"

"I did not."

"And the maids in question here—Molly and Janet—have you any history or discord with either of them?"

"Not much. Molly approached me once, but"—he looked away sheepishly—"I did not allow it to proceed."

"And she was the woman who was supposedly found in your room."

"What do you intend to do?"

I hesitated. I needed my mother. I needed another's wisdom to lead me. Lady Edith was testing me—not teaching me. I wanted Mama, but maybe I could settle for Jane.

"I intend to tell the housekeeper I need more time. I cannot dismiss the wrong girl. It feels reckless to make a decision before we understand what truly happened."

"You could dismiss them both."

"But one of them is innocent."

Benedict raised an eyebrow. "Are you so certain?"

"The only thing I am currently certain of is my lack of qualifications to be the mistress of Chelton." I drew in a breath, already regretting the directness of my words. Benedict looked as though he meant to argue, but I waved away his efforts. "It will all turn out well. I suppose I need to grow used to these new responsibilities. I will see you at dinner."

I flashed him a smile and turned for the house before he could waylay me. The long walk down the gravel drive would be good for my constitution.

It was unclear whether Lady Edith was refusing her assistance because she wanted to see me fail or because she was genuinely curious to see how I would handle this matter of the maids. The warm afternoon sun shone down on me, and I watched James and his mother reach the house well before I neared it.

James had a talent for making me feel my company was desirable in certain situations, and I could not fault him for hoping to share with me the things he enjoyed doing. I did not press him to read with me in the library, though, and I was glad he'd ceased asking me to ride with him. It was a blessed thing he would be attending the ball on Tuesday, for he already understood why I could not dance. Surely he would help me contrive a reasonable excuse so I would not offend the host and hostess who Lady Edith so esteemed.

When I made it to the house, I immediately went to the drawing room and helped myself to the paper and ink at the writing table set against the wall. My hand stalled before my quill pen touched the paper, and it occurred to me that unless Jane had read the newspapers, she would not know I was a married woman. How was I to adequately explain to my dearest friend what I'd done? The last time she had spoken the name *Mr. Bradwell*, it was to entice me to write to Henry while I returned his book. Jane had been a supporter of that match.

I had much to explain. I dipped my quill again and wrote the briefest of explanations. It would be much easier to tell her what occurred face to face, and I hoped she would agree to come. I finished my letter and sanded the paper before folding and sealing it closed.

Lady Edith walked into the room, the color somewhat returned to her cheeks, but her frown in place. "I intend to lie down until dinner. I expect that the matter with the maids will be dealt with before I awake."

The only sound that followed this edict was the clipping of her heels down the wood planked corridor punctuating her exit. My eyes drifted shut, and I pressed my fingers to my temples. It seemed I would not be granted the opportunity to wait for Jane's wisdom after all.

I did not know what I hated more: that my mother-in-law viewed me as a wanton hussy who convinced James to marry me, or that she believed me wholly inept.

Whenever I needed to discern the right thing to do, in any situation, my mother had always taught me to listen to the innate feelings inside my heart. But as I stood in Mrs. Prescott's sitting room, my heart was telling me nothing. No whispers quietly revealed whether or not I had come to the correct conclusion, no flutterings of confirmation soothed my spirit. Janet sat penitently on the chair, and Molly had fled the moment she was told to return to her tasks in the kitchen.

My reasoning was perhaps flawed, but I did not believe Molly would contrive to get Janet dismissed by placing *herself* in danger of that same thing—especially not when her family relied on her earnings. Surely Janet was angry that Molly had stolen her beau and schemed to get her dismissed so Janet might have his affections returned to her.

I was not sure if I'd made the right call, but it was done. I could not change it now. Mrs. Prescott seemed pleased enough by my decision, which, for some reason, did not give me any further affirmation that I had chosen the right girl.

"If that is all?" I asked Mrs. Prescott, and she gave me a nod. I spun away from the dim sitting room, feeling the frown on my lips drain down and fill my entire being with displeasure.

I found James walking my direction when I reached the corridor that held our bedchambers, and he appeared freshly bathed and free of the dirt from working on the rut in the road. He must have quickly sensed my discouragement, because his smile shifted into concern the nearer I drew to him.

"Felicity, what happened?"

"I dismissed the maid. I'm unsure if I made the correct choice, and I do not like that I had so much control over this poor girl's future with very little information." I stopped and shook my head. "What if I was wrong?"

His mouth opened slightly, but he had nothing to say. He ran a hand over his clean-shaven jaw. "You did not need to—"

"Yes, I did," I snapped. "Your mother allowed me no more time."

He chuckled awkwardly. "Surely if she knew you were unsure, she would have agreed to discuss the matter further."

"That would have been impossible, for we cannot discuss further something we had not discussed at all. This was naught but a test which I failed, *miserably*, as I have many of her other tests." I scoffed lightly, shaking my head. "I am unworthy of you, James. I am unworthy of Chelton. Your mother does not deem me fit to lead or fit to be your wife, and I should not be given authority over these poor maids and their futures."

"Felicity, you cannot mean that," James said, appalled. Though whether he was so disturbed by my outburst or the notion that his mother could think so ill of me, I did not know.

My eyes closed, and I drew in a sustaining breath. "This is not your—"

The words shriveled on my tongue, and I raised my gaze to meet his troubled one. I wanted to tell him it wasn't his fault I was in this predicament, but it was. He had agreed to marry me, he brought me to this house, and he knew the sort of life I was going to be forced into *after* he watched me faint in a ballroom and learned of my flaws.

He reached for my hand, and I took a step back, evading his touch. "I need a moment. I will . . . I will most likely see you at dinner."

James nodded, his concern only seeming to grow. "Of course."

Ever the gentleman, he stepped back and allowed me to pass, uninhibited, into my room. Alone.

CHAPTER 23

Two nights had passed since I dismissed the maid and fled from James in the corridor, and those two nights had crawled by in excruciating slowness. I had taken to avoiding the family as best I could during the day, but darkness brought about the fears that still clung to me in the wake of finishing the gothic novel.

Last night I was nearly certain James had come to the adjoining door and stood for a moment watching me, perhaps to ascertain why I had ignored his earlier knocking. I'd quickly closed my eyes and pretended to be asleep.

Unfair as it might be, it felt like he'd made this choice for me when he convinced me to dance with him at the Huttons' ball. That he'd determined my future, and my bitter feelings toward him were thick and difficult to navigate. I did not wish to hold him in contempt, but I couldn't help but wonder why he had persisted in marrying me when I was wholly unsuitable to the role of Chelton's mistress.

But now, on the third night since the incident, I paced my floor, light from the candles on the mantel casting a glow about and causing me to startle on more than one occasion. My body was exhausted, but my mind was alert, and it would not slow no matter what I did.

The worst part of all, though, was that this was the third night that I did not allow James into my room to share our daily fact. In my anger I had ignored his knocking, mad at him, but also with myself.

I reached up and drew my finger along the dried, white rose hanging from my bed. More than anything, I missed him.

My eyes were sandy from the two previous nights of little sleep, and my body achy. I stared at our adjoining door and inhaled a deep breath. If I did not humble myself before James now, would I ever be able to? Would this discord between us build and grow until it became insurmountable? It was not his fault his mother did not accept me. Her displeasure did not make me any less the mistress of this house.

Perhaps that was where I had erred all along. An idea formed on shaky legs, and I grasped the bedpost as I considered it. The concept bloomed within me, taking root and growing tall. Instead of yielding to each and every thing my mother-in-law required of me in my desperation for her approval, from the excess of white roses on my gown to the menu to the timeline I needed to follow in order to dismiss a maid, I needed to govern my own choices.

If Lady Edith no longer wished to teach me, that was her choice. But her lack of instruction had caused me to retreat in every way, including my power and command in this house. As James's wife, my word trumped hers, but her manipulation had forced me to give her the power I rightfully held.

Tomorrow, I intended to take it back.

Tonight, I would mend the discord in my marriage.

I lifted up on tiptoe and blew out the candles, then ran my fingers through my long hair and braided it into a semblance of order. My bare feet were cold, and I crossed the room before I could lose the gumption to approach James after two days of silence.

The door was hard and cold under my curled fist, and I knocked softly, waiting for James to invite me in. He was most likely awake still—I had heard him in there just a quarter hour earlier.

The quiet seemed to stretch endlessly before the door opened, and I looked up into my husband's enigmatic eyes. Regret curled in my chest, and I briefly wished I hadn't knocked at all. It had been a mistake to think he would welcome me, and I stepped back.

"Wait," he said. "Are you frightened?"

Frightened of ruining the relationship that we'd hardly had time to cultivate? Yes. Frightened of the dark? A little.

But I hadn't come to his door because of fear.

I settled on a half-truth. "Yes."

He stepped back and opened his door widely, then gestured to his bed. "You are always welcome here, Felicity. I hoped I had made myself clear in that regard."

"You did. I was only hoping to avoid becoming a burden."

His mouth ticked into a brief smile, though his eyes remained sad. "You cannot become a burden. Surely you must know that well enough by now."

History had proven just the opposite. My parents were burdened by my troubles, so my husband could feel the same. "I know nothing of the sort."

A chill ran over my skin, and I folded my arms across my waist.

"Come, you're cold." James took my hand and pulled me toward him. He wrapped his arms around me, and I leaned my head against his solid chest, feeling his heart beat into my ear. He was warm and comfortable, his sleeping shirt soft and smelling of him in a way that soothed me to my core.

I found myself leaning against him more, and a yawn breathed from me.

"Tired?"

"Quite. I haven't slept well the last few nights."

"Neither have I." James pressed a kiss to the top of my head and released me. He took my hand and tugged me to the bed and helped me lie down, pulling the blankets up to my chin. I noticed that he'd left the adjoining door open, and I liked that about him—as though he wanted me to remember that I was always welcome.

James climbed into bed beside me and blew out the candle on his table, making the darkness complete. I heard nothing beyond the groans of the old house and the whistle of a light wind outside.

"I've missed your facts, Liss. I feel you owe me at least two now."

"Fact number one: I am not a perfect person. Fact number two: I am sorry for being upset with you."

"You're forgiven, though I do not know what I did to upset you. I understand that my mother—"

"I do not wish to speak of her at this moment," I whispered. Sleep was overcoming me now that I felt both warm and safe, and the last thing I wished to think of before succumbing to that peaceful state was the woman who did not want me in this house. "Though I will, if you so desire it."

"No, we can speak of other things."

"Like *your* facts?"

He chuckled softly. "Fact number one: I missed you last night and the night before."

"Fact two?"

"I fully believe I will be able to sleep easily tonight."

"As will I."

James reached across the space between us and took my hand, his thumb rubbing softly over the back of it, and I nestled further into the feather mattress, inhaling the muted spicy scent.

The cover of darkness and the safety of this bed gave me the courage to ask a question that had been on my mind. "James?"

"Hmm?"

"Why did you agree to marry me? Aside from the obvious, of course. The scandal notwithstanding."

He was quiet for a moment, and I wished to take the question back into the safety of my protection where I could guard and protect that small insecurity.

"Because it was the sensible thing to do."

Sensible. Of course. My eyes drifted closed, and I tried to staunch the sorrow that accompanied that bald truth. James's thumb continued to softly rub my hand, and I was certain in that moment he hadn't meant to wipe the place the candle had burned me. I'd inaccurately assigned meaning to James's gesture —meaning which it did not possess.

Sleep descended on my budding sorrow, taking me under the darkness and away from consciousness. But as I drifted away, I thought I heard James say, "Goodnight, my love."

My love.

CHAPTER 24

A few of the gowns Lady Edith ordered were finished and delivered early Tuesday afternoon, just in time for Lord and Lady Grenvilles' ball. I donned the soft pink gown—the only ball gown in the lot aside from the monstrous white confection —uncertain if the color made my pale red hair appear brash and uncouth. It was a delicate balance at times, and there was no changing my hair color, so I had to be particular about gowns.

"Fanny." I rose, pulling on my elbow-length gloves. "Be honest. Does this gown make me appear pale or discolored?"

She paused near the dressing table, a handful of unused pins clutched in her nervous grip. "You look lovely to me, ma'am."

It was clear that I would not receive an honest answer from my maid. I stepped closer to the firelight and strained to see my reflection in the dressing table's mirror. The only person I could be depended upon in this house to give me the truth of things was undoubtedly my mother-in-law. She cared far too much about Society's opinion to allow me out of the house looking ill in the cheeks.

Which I was nearly certain I did, for my own mama had

never permitted me to order a pink gown before, and with good reason.

I slid on my dancing slippers. *Evelina* sat on my bedside table, and I dropped it into my reticule. It was always best to be prepared. One never knew when one would find an opportunity to read.

Lady Edith stood at the bottom of the grand stairs, her three sons surrounding her, as I descended the steps. I waited for her reaction to my gown, but she did not appear to find fault with my toilette.

Her scrutinous eyes roved over the gown, and she approached me to run the fabric between her fingers. "This is not the pink I selected."

"Are you certain?" I asked.

She nodded. "I chose a silk." She dropped the fabric from her gloved fingers and shook her head. "You look well, in any case. We must not be too frustrated by the mistake."

Well, that certainly explained why she had not yet found fault with my coloring. I could not imagine changing the fabric for the gown was as simple as mistaking one fabric for another —not for a professional. Though, during our first visit to the shop I had mentioned my concerns. Madame Rousseau must have chosen a fabric that would suit my complexion and hair color. She *was* worth the expense, after all.

James offered me his elbow and led me out to the awaiting carriage. My nerves had been so wrapped into the concern for whether or not I looked a fright that I had not yet worried over the dancing that would soon be required of me. I pulled his elbow before stepping into the conveyance, and he looked up.

"What is it?"

"The dancing," I whispered, acutely aware of Henry and Benedict waiting behind us. Their mother was already seated inside. "I cannot do it."

His eyes sparkled from the glowing torches on either end of

the carriage. "Do you think you might perform one? We can choose a waltz so you remain with me for the entirety of the dance."

Could I? I had not considered a waltz with my husband. James had a habit of calming my nerves. Could he do so on the dance floor? "I am not sure."

"Shall we try it?"

"And if I—" I swallowed, unable to bring sound to the worry that plagued me.

"If you begin to feel faint, I will direct you to a chair immediately. You can claim a headache and sit out the remaining dances." He looked at me apologetically. "You are a new bride, Liss. Lord and Lady Grenville will expect you to open the first set."

I shut my eyes and imagined dancing beside James, focusing solely on him, allowing his strength to seep into me.

"Is there trouble?" Lady Edith called from within the carriage.

Yes.

"No," James replied. He helped me inside, and I had a sudden, unnerving thought.

What if the first dance was not a waltz?

Lord and Lady Grenvilles' *small* gathering was anything but small. It appeared that the entirety of the local Society came out in full force, and if Lady Edith imagined this to be a meager representation of the locals, then I could only imagine how massive her ball was bound to be.

My grip tightened on James's hand, and he looked down at me through his clear, green-brown eyes. "The moment you feel faint," he murmured, "I will direct you to a chair."

"Shall we sit now then?" I jested.

His returning smile was laced with concern. I drew in a fortifying breath and allowed James to lead me toward our hosts. They were both shorter than average, plump, and with mouths that seemed to turn down more often than up. It was with displeasure that they each pulled out a looking glass and swept it down my person after James performed the introductions, then shared a look with one another.

Had I proven to be a dowdy, homespun girl? I had not appeared to meet with their approval if their discontented expressions were any clue. It was no wonder this pair did not venture often into Society. They did not seem, to me, a happy sort of couple.

"We ought to be glad Lord Grenville does not dance," James murmured into my ear as he led me away. "Or he would have been your partner during the first set."

A shiver ran over my shoulders. An unpleasant picture, indeed.

Benedict and Henry abandoned us, leaving James to look after both his mother and his wife.

"Shall we begin introductions?" Lady Edith asked. We stood in a line near the entrance to the larger ballroom, and I counted no less than a dozen couples in conversation about the room.

"Have I not met everyone in our local parish already? I am afraid I will not remember anyone else."

Lady Edith seemed to sense the weakness of my excuse. "You must, Felicity. We cannot have you branded as rude."

"She is anything but rude," James said stoutly. "If we want for Felicity to dance, Mother, I think it best to allow her this small respite beforehand."

His thoughtfulness struck me, and I peered up at my handsome husband. His countenance was severe, the playful edge I'd come to adore wholly lacking at present. Something was bothering him as soundly as it was me, but he had appeared unperturbed during our conversation in front of Chelton.

Lady Edith peered at him. "*If* we want her to dance?"

James gave her a tight smile. "Yes. *If.* I have experienced firsthand the depth of Felicity's trouble when she is overcome with nerves, and I will not put her in a position which requires her to tax herself beyond reason. We are here, at your behest, and we will dance. But until the music begins in earnest, I am taking my wife to walk in the conservatory. You are more than welcome to join us."

Lady Edith's face appeared carved from stone. She gave one distinct shake of her head. "I would prefer to greet my friends. One of us must . . . explain."

I did not ask her to describe further what she meant to explain, and she did not feel the need to expound. James dipped his head in deference to his mother and tugged me away, toward the open doors at the far end of the room.

"You needn't have extricated us so fully," I said, completely aware once we reached our destination that we were now alone. Potted trees and flowering bushes lined the glass walls enclosing the small room, and the candlelight reflected on the many windows.

"I thought it wise for you to save your strength."

His consideration touched my heart. But then, it had from the very beginning. His umbrage when we first met in the library at the Huttons' ball had swiftly shifted to concern upon learning that I had burned myself—and then he had even worried over whether or not I was attempting to entrap him. It was simply his nature to consider my wellbeing.

James's mouth tipped into a soft smile, and he bumped my reticule with his elbow softly. "You've a book in there, haven't you?"

My cheeks warmed. "Perhaps."

A small laugh escaped him. "I will never understand you."

That was what I feared. Although he always considered me, he didn't understand me. I searched the crowd for Miss Whitstone, conscious of our similarities more in a ballroom than outside of it.

"It begs the question," I said lightly, "why you would proceed with marrying someone so completely different from you. You had equal opportunity with Miss Whitstone and found your way out of that entanglement before it was too late."

I answered my own question and shame seeped into my chest. *Before it was too late.* He could not have extricated himself from our situation without putting my name through a scandal.

"I did not find myself entangled with Miss Whitstone. We merely spent a little time together."

What foolhardy part of me thought it wise to ask this *now*? My foolish heart, no doubt, was leading the charge untrained and uncontrolled.

Music from the ballroom drifted toward us, and I trained a smile on him. A minuet was announced, and I did my utmost to not allow my smile to falter. Of course the ball would open with a minuet—a sedate, entirely too long, pageant of a dance.

"Shall we?" he asked.

"We haven't a choice."

James led me into position, passing groups of strangers mingled with people I recognized from church or our at-home visits over the previous week. My heart raced in time to the warming violins, and I stood across from James, my feet firmly planted on the painted floor.

"Look at me the entire time, Liss," he whispered. "Only at me."

That would prove difficult when I was led away from him or he from me. I nodded softly, allowing his gaze to hold me captive.

The music began in earnest and the dance alongside it. James's focus was commendable. I could only imagine how deeply he wanted to avoid the need to catch me and carry me from the room. I desired to avoid that very same thing.

My heart kept pace with my concern, ticking up rapidly as we danced. When my gaze strayed from my husband, the beady, watchful eyes of the spectators stabbed me with their persistent ogling. My stomach swooped, twirling alongside my nerves, and my breathing progressed at a faster speed than the dance warranted.

"Liss?" James asked when he neared me for a moment. Had he noticed the green pallor of my cheeks, or was that merely how I felt and not how I appeared? I grew dizzy, my heart pounding so hard it rushed past my ears and blocked most of the music. I turned the wrong direction and stepped on the hem of another lady's gown, and panic gripped me.

It was happening. The black sparkles pricked the edges of my vision and moved inward, my head light and stomach heavy. I searched for James, wishing I would not hit my head if I was to fall. His hand closed around mine and pulled me from the dance floor, making our way swiftly to the smaller parlor that we had yet to visit tonight. We passed groups of people, though I could not focus my eyes enough to recognize any faces.

James led me to a small group of chairs against the far wall and helped me sit. "I will find a glass of lemonade if you think you can remain upright."

"Stay," I said, so quietly I was afraid he had not heard me.

James sat beside me at once, his hand over mine, his fingers unable to remain still on my skin. But his nervous fluttering was soothing. I wanted more than anything for his tight embrace, for his connection to seep the nerves from my limbs as he had during our ride so many weeks ago, but I could not ask it of him in this public place.

I settled for appreciating his touch and allowing my eyes to drift closed until the nausea receded.

"Thank you," I whispered.

James squeezed my fingers in reply. I opened my eyes again to find Lady Edith standing in the open doorway, speaking to another woman, her beady eyes on me. And she did not look well pleased.

CHAPTER 25

The Grenville ball progressed into the evening, and despite the interested glances James sent toward various groups of people chatting, he remained stalwartly at my side.

I only imagined my spectacle served to keep curious gossip-seekers away for fear I might be ill.

"I am perfectly content to remain here if you would like to greet your friends," I said.

He immediately shook his head. "I cannot leave you."

"Do you expect to remain pasted to my side for the duration of our marriage, or am I to be permitted any time alone?"

"You *wish* to be alone?"

No, of course not. But I could not very well be the reason James sat in the corner of a small room all evening when there were undoubtedly friends nearby he wished to speak to. I could feel the energy sloughing from him in waves. He was tired of sitting here, and his desire to be elsewhere was not doing my nerves any good.

"Go on," I continued. "I will walk outside, perhaps, or find Miss Whitstone. I noticed that she walked by the door only a quarter hour ago."

"Allow me to escort you—"

"I am married now, remember?" I said gently. "I do not need a chaperone."

James did not look entirely convinced.

"Honest," I said. "I cannot bear to be treated as an invalid, James. I am perfectly well now. So long as I remain on the fringes of the ballroom, nothing will vex or ruin my peace."

"If you are certain . . ."

I took his hand and squeezed. The sooner he left, the faster I would be able to find a quiet, lit corner to read. "I will walk out of the parlor with you if that helps you to feel better."

James nodded and helped me stand. We moved toward the doorway into the larger ballroom when someone called after him. I sensed his hesitation and gave his fingers a quick squeeze before releasing them and letting myself from the room. He would be required to give my apologies, but I was certain he could come up with a reasonable explanation for my disappearance.

Now, to make it outside of the ballroom before bumping into an acquaintance. Or worse, my mother-in-law. I skirted the throngs of people, the book in my reticule heavy against my wrist. The open conservatory was now filled with people, so I turned the other direction through a set of doors and found a refreshment room.

A footman stood behind the table filling glasses of lemonade, and I accepted one, bringing it to my lips while I analyzed my options. A door sat at the far end of the room and an alcove on the other. "Where might I locate the ladies retiring room?" I asked the footman.

"Through that door and straight ahead."

I followed his directions through the door but turned instead once I reached the empty corridor and let myself into a room just beyond the ladies retiring room. If I found myself somewhere I ought not to be, I could always claim I was lost. It had happened before.

A small fire burned in the hearth of a quaint sitting room, and I noticed at once a chair perfect for my designs. It faced away from the door and would surely hide me were someone to come in, giving me enough time to hide my book before I was found.

Now that I was married, surely there was nothing wrong with being caught alone in a room at a ball.

I uncinched the drawstring on my reticule, making my way over to the small fire. Was there wood nearby? I might need to add a log—

"Oh, dear!" I yelled. *Evelina* flew from my hands and straight at the man seated in the very chair I'd set out to occupy.

Henry dodged my book, and it flew over the back of his tall, wingback chair and clattered on the floor somewhere behind him. "Blast, Felicity. You frightened me half to death." He looked over his shoulder. "What did you mean to do? Hit me with a book?"

"Not intentionally, no." I circled the chair and retrieved my book. The small slip of paper I'd used to mark my place had fluttered to the Aubusson carpet, and I bent to pick it up. It was a note James had written when he left me to go to York, and I shoved it in my reticule.

I circled back to face Henry, and he stood in belated chivalry. "You came to escape the ball?"

"Yes. You as well?"

He lifted the book in his hand. "I had hoped no one would find me here."

A beat of silence passed over us, and in it a wealth of feelings and possibilities. Henry and I had multiple choices ahead of us. I could leave him, pretending I never came upon him at all. We could leave the room together now and return to the ball. Or . . .

we could sit in companionable silence as we often did at Chelton and read.

I did my best to read the expression in his eyes, but I found it difficult to discern. If I was not mistaken, he looked more sorrowful than abashed. If he was disappointed, under the false assumption that I was about to ruin the peace of his evening, he could not be further from the truth.

"I have a proposition, Henry." I lowered myself slowly onto the chair opposite the one he had previously occupied, and he matched me so we might be on equal footing. "The supper dance is not for another hour yet, I assume?"

He looked to the clock on the mantel. "Correct. If not a little longer."

"What say you we remain here and continue to read for that hour? Then we can join the ball again prior to supper so we might not be missed when it matters most."

"Do you not wish to . . . no, of course not." He smiled, a soft chuckle escaping his throat. "You would have preferred to skip the entirety of the evening, I assume, let alone the dancing."

"Yes, but since that is not possible, I will happily settle for skipping one hour."

Henry looked over his shoulder to the door and back to me, uncertainty in his blue eyes. His brown curly hair was mussed, a lock falling over his brow. He usually looked so put together that the disarray seemed strange. For a man so typically neat and tidy, his strong resemblance to Benedict right now was slightly alarming.

"Are you well, Henry?" I asked softly.

"Yes, of course." He cleared his throat and turned his attention to the pages of his book. "I have no desire to dance tonight, that is all."

"I never have a desire to dance," I said lightly.

To think, if Henry had been attending the Huttons' ball at the close of the Season, would he have been the man I found myself alone with in the library? It hardly mattered, but I looked at Henry's troubled eyes and wondered. It did occur to me, however, that he was not the flirt his brother was, and had we discovered ourselves alone then, we likely would have done nothing more than remain on opposite sides of the room and look at books—not been caught in something akin to an embrace.

"What are you reading?"

I lifted the book so he might see the spine. "It is a favorite of mine. I found after the fright *Udolpho* gave me that I wanted to seek the comfort of a familiar story."

"There is nothing like a familiar book to soothe one's troubled soul."

"I will not admit to possessing a troubled soul, but otherwise I wholeheartedly agree."

I found the place where I'd left off reading earlier and turned my attention to the novel in my lap. My eyes had not yet reached the end of the page when I felt the heat of Henry's observation, and I raised my eyebrows. "Is there something else you'd like to discuss?"

Henry cleared his throat and seemed to shake himself. "No. Enjoy your story, Felicity, and let us both hope that no other gentle souls will come in search of a respite."

"Or a place to keep secret assignations," I said with little tact. It received the desired effect in the form of Henry's chuckling, and my attention fell again to my book.

The hour of quiet reading passed uninterrupted, and Henry slid his slim novel into his pocket and offered me his arm.

"Is it time already?" I complained. "Perhaps we ought to feign illness and go home."

"Come, child."

"I am no child."

"No? Your whining was reminiscent of one."

I couldn't help but swat his hand away. "I can be surly as one, too, if you'd like to see."

"I'd rather not." He shot me a smile, and I closed my book and tucked it into my reticule.

We made it to the corridor and back toward the door that led to the refreshment room. Henry seemed to be of the same mind that it would be wise to slip into the small room first instead of going directly to the ballroom. He opened the door and gestured for me to precede him, and I nearly stuttered to a halt when my gaze met James's. He stood at the refreshment table accepting a glass of lemonade, and I watched his eyes lift over my head and harden upon reaching Henry.

I crossed directly to his side.

"Felicity, I wondered where you were," James said. "I should have known you would have found a place to hide."

"I was not hiding from you," I said, hearing the defensive bite to my tone.

The tightening around his mouth and eyes revealed that he was unhappy with my choice, regardless of my motive.

Supper passed in great discomfort. I was not seated anywhere near James, though my table partners, Mr. Dodwell and the vicar, were both polite and did not require much of me in terms of conversation. Lady Edith was placed at the far end of the table, her gaze straying my direction in regular intervals.

On the ride back to Chelton at the end of the night, all in our party were in a sour mood. It was clear that the evening had not gone according to anyone's plan. Benedict, even, was quieter than was typical for him, and I trained my gaze on the moonlit countryside out the window for the duration of the ride. When we reached Chelton, I took myself upstairs before I could be waylaid by anyone wishing to question my actions or provide any instruction.

I had erred, and I knew it well. My guilt was punishment enough for now.

CHAPTER 26

J ames came to the adjoining door, and though my room was exceptionally dark, I could discern the outline of his long sleep shirt and mussed hair, and his presence made my pulse quicken. I had been in my bed for nearly thirty minutes now, long past the time I would have stood at the door and shared a fact with him. In truth, I did not know if he wished to speak to me or only ascertain that I was there and safe. He'd been surly after supper at the Grenville ball and his demeanor unapproachable. My guilt, of course, had not aided us in reconciliation.

"I need my fact," James said, his deep voice penetrating the perfect quiet.

I pushed myself into a seated position.

"And," he continued, when I failed to say anything, "I need you if I am to fall asleep."

My body stilled, the words finding purchase and clinging to me. He needed *me*? Surely he had it in reverse, for it was *I* who needed *him*.

Ah, perhaps that was it. James must have suspected that I would prefer to be in his room and came to me since I'd failed to swallow my own pride and approach him. But how could I do so when relations between us were tenuous? We had found a strange balance between friends and lovers where we did not so much as kiss regularly, but I knew I could wholly rely on him— all while sharing in the intimacy of sleeping in the same bed. That very habit had broken a barrier between us in one regard, forcing a familiarity between us before we had an opportunity to grow acquainted with one another's minds.

Had we moved too quickly in one area, or too slowly in the other? Even now we spoke like tentative acquaintances yet stood in naught but our sleeping clothes.

"Liss?"

I'd spent too long considering the state of our relationship. Regardless of how much a stranger I felt to this man in some ways, I also knew he and I were inseparably bonded. We'd exchanged vows, and that set us apart from any other relationship in my life.

My hair fell down around my shoulders, and I swept it back. The room was dark, the summer warmth causing little need for a fire outside of heating the curling tongs or burning off the crisp chill in the early hours of the morning.

"My fact," I said, climbing from the bed and crossing the room. "I do not like feeling as though we are not in accord with one another."

"Can that be my fact as well?"

"I'm sorry, but no. You must contrive something original."

His gleaming smile was clear in the dim room. "I already have this evening."

"Oh?"

"Yes. It has become a fact about me that I need you if I am to fall asleep."

My heart leapt, despite my reservations. "How is it that we can seem so ill-suited in the light of day, but darkness seems to hide our differences?"

"Do you not need me?" he asked. His gaze was steady, the dark pools shining in the moonlight.

"I do," I whispered. "I need you."

James's strong hand slid under my jaw and around my cheek, and I leaned into it. "Where did you go tonight during the ball?"

My body stilled. Did that bother him so dearly that he needed an answer now? I straightened, unable to think clearly with his skin on mine. "I wanted a break from the mass of people, so I found a small room with a fire and the intention to read."

"Henry—"

"He was in the room first, doing the same thing I intended to do." My body swayed away from him, though I did not do so intentionally, and his hand dropped. I did not like the tone of his voice or the direction of the conversation. It almost felt as though he did not trust me. Though I owned that the thought was ludicrous. I had proven myself anything but untrustworthy, had I not? It was James who'd asked his brother to remain while he was gone and look after me.

"Reading?"

"Yes. I found Henry in there, and we decided to spend an hour reading quietly before returning for supper. It was not so very odd, James. I was doing the very same thing when we met."

"But as my wife, I rather expected you to remain in the ballroom for the evening. You are a new bride, and certain privileges are afforded you for this period in your life. If you are missing for a great length of time, it is noticed." He ran a hand over his face. "If someone else was to see you return with Henry, rumors could have begun. We are already on unsteady footing as it is."

Why would anyone believe nefarious things about a new bride and her brother-in-law? And furthermore, had we not put the scandal to rest when we sacrificed ourselves in matrimony?

James seemed to think we were on unsteady footing even now. "What do you mean by that?"

"The scandal surrounding our engagement," he said. "Surely you realize that marrying did not snuff that fire entirely."

"It certainly seemed to work when we made our announcement and every woman who had snubbed me instantly welcomed me again."

He stared at me. "Yes, they accepted you, but that does not mean they did not talk about you when you left the room. The very reason we are not . . . that we have not . . . it is *because* you were made aware of the gossip." He scoffed lightly and dragged a hand over his face. "You realize it is a struggle for me to stay away from you, yes? It is a difficulty I am bearing for the good of our names and your own opinion of yourself that I do not kiss you at every opportunity available to me. It is torment having you so near, and yet, such a great distance from me still. I agreed to a six month period of abstinence for *us*. For our children. For the Bradwell name."

Elation and fury swept together like a raging storm and twisted in my stomach. I had thought James agreed to wait for *me*, so I might prove my good character, so I could live with myself. After residing in Chelton for weeks and enduring Lady Edith's unending strictures on upholding the Bradwell name, it should have been more clear to me that James would be concerned for that as well. It was a blow to realize that he did not sacrifice wholly for me.

I stepped back, speaking with an icy accent that plagued my body as well as my words. "I had not realized that, no. Please accept my apologies."

"You are offended."

I turned away. "I am enlightened, rather."

"No, do not do this." He reached for my hand, but I did not allow him to take it. I would not permit him to ruin one of my most favorite things by dragging it into this distressing moment.

"I rather think I need to try and sleep, James."

"What did I say to so wholly offend you?"

"It is not what you said. It is what I have discovered." I walked back toward my bed.

He followed me. "If you do not tell me, I cannot know what I did. Speak to me, Liss. Do not run away."

"I am not running—" But, I was. I closed my eyes and clenched my hands into fists. "My expectations for marriage were entirely wrong in every regard, James. Each of the things I had anticipated for my future turned out to be the opposite of what I anticipated. I pride myself on the deftness with which I have accepted each of these alterations and made the best of it, but I can only be expected to do so much before I need to remove myself from the situation for a time and breathe."

"Remove yourself from which situation?" He paused. "Our marriage?"

"No, James, of course not. Remove myself from the presence of an overwhelming ball, for instance." Remove myself from his mother. Remove myself from his bedroom.

I reached my bed and felt the gap between us lengthen, both physically and emotionally. I wanted to turn back and fall into his arms, but how could I do so after he professed his difficulty with that?

"Please do not turn away from me," he pleaded.

"I do not see how we can sleep now, not after this discomfort." I moved my hand between us to indicate the thick air so heavy with things unsaid and things laid bare.

"Please?" he asked. "I am afraid if you do not come tonight, that you will break the habit. We can work through the things that we disagree on, but we must always work together. We must make the conscious choice to not allow our disagreements to burden us. I do not want to be estranged from you, Liss."

"I do not want that, either," I whispered. But my mind was muddled. Through the fog and the insecurities plaguing me, I knew two things to be undeniable: I loved James, and he at least cared for me.

I lifted my hand toward him, and he crossed the space between us in three rapid steps. He took my hand and pulled me against him, healing some of the contention and fear that had begun to tear at my heart. My arms went around his back, and I leaned close, inhaling the spicy scent that was only his. James breathed deeply, pressing his cheek into the top of my head.

My body relaxed in his arms, my nerves loosening until my tightly wound fears unraveled like a spool of thread onto the carpeted floor.

"No plait tonight?" he asked, his fingers playing with the ends of my long hair.

"No plait."

"I do like when your hair is let down."

"I like when your cravat is missing."

"I like how small your bare feet are."

"I like the shape of your arms."

James leaned back and looked at me, his eyebrow raised. "That is interesting."

A blush warmed my cheeks, widening my smile. "In what way?"

"My arms, eh? Is that why you asked if I partake in fisticuffs? Because you would like to see me go a round?"

"No, that sounds appalling. I only wondered if that was how you managed to build any sort of muscle."

"Well, it has nothing to do with bravely fighting my brothers, unfortunately. I have spent a good deal of time in the last few years managing and working on different parts of the house. I enjoy the exertion, and riding or hunting does not provide enough for me."

Ah, like the rut in the road. I hadn't even questioned why James and Benedict did the labor themselves instead of requesting it of the servants, but I realized now how odd that was.

"I am not complaining," I said softly.

"You might when I grow old and have less time for these pursuits. Softening is part of aging."

"I won't mind if you soften, James." I pressed my hand against his heart, heat seeping through the shirt and warming my palm. "This is my favorite part of you."

"My manly chest?"

I couldn't help but chuckle. "Your heart."

He laid a palm over my hand. "Good, because it belongs to you."

My breath caught, and I looked up sharply to find him looking seriously down at me. His gaze flicked to my lips, and the heated conversation we shared only a few minutes ago was fresh in my mind. *It is torment having you so near, and yet, such a great distance from me still.* That distance was important, and I would not sacrifice the reparations to my name—indeed, to *his* family name—for the sake of a kiss.

James swayed toward me, but I turned my face away, avoiding the kiss I so desperately wanted. "We've five months yet to go," I said softly.

"An eternity," he mumbled.

I could not agree more.

CHAPTER 27

The next week passed with excruciating slowness. I wanted to count the days until my cousin's arrival, but we had not yet heard word from her, so I could only hope she was on her way now. She would need to be in order to make it to Chelton before the ball, for the event was set to take place in four days.

No word had yet reached Lady Edith about Miss Northcott and her whereabouts. She dispatched a handful of letters to various people who knew Miss Northcott before her mother died and she traveled to Chelton to live, but so far no one had yet responded.

James and I had found a peculiar sense of harmony over the previous week. I spent the days assisting his mother in preparing for the ball or attending to at-home visits, and he spent them riding or out with his brothers. And each night, we spoke to one another about our day and shared our facts. I was glad he had fought for me last week, that he had not accepted my decree that we were better off in our own bedchambers.

I wanted to know James's mind, and we were accomplishing that with our nightly conversations. By the end of a year

243

together, I would know more than three hundred things about him.

Lady Edith, however, had grown increasingly distant as the days wore on. She sat across from me now at the breakfast table, papers spread between us containing all of the details regarding the ball. The dinner guests, ball guests, both the dinner and supper menus, the dance order, and the house guests had all been combed through with excruciating detail. We'd now moved on to the decor, and Lady Edith had a list of flowers, candles, and mirrors to rival the great parties of the *ton* in London.

"We'll need torches in the courtyard, and we can move the potted shrubs and trees to that area to give it more of an earthy appearance."

"What of the white flowers?" I asked. It had been a strong theme Lady Edith was clutching tightly.

"Roses on the fountain. We can tuck them into the sculpture. Perhaps Athena can appear to be holding a bouquet."

"And flowers *in* the fountain," I added. "Floating in the water with the stems snipped off."

"Perhaps. If we have any spare roses."

My spine straightened. This was my ball, was it not? I had determined not long ago that I'd taken the wrong approach with my mother-in-law, but each time I attempted to hold any power at all, she closed the door on my idea immediately. It was a terrible juxtaposition, for if I wanted her to find me capable, I needed to prove it. Only, she would not allow me that opportunity. I needed to take the authority that was mine by rights in order to show her that I could be trusted. That I was worthy.

"I would like floating roses in the fountain," I said again, this time stronger. I found it symbolic in a way she would not understand, because I would not share the story with her of the day James and I had fallen into the fountain in the garden. He had tucked a white rose behind my ear and made me feel special. If this ball was meant to celebrate our marriage, that seemed a very subtle, private way to pay homage to our union.

"Perhaps," she repeated.

My pulse raced, blood rushing past my ears with alarming speed. "There have been many things about this ball that I have ceded to you, Lady Edith. I am asking for this one, small thing. I am exceedingly grateful for all you've done, and I do not wish to cause any strife. But I do expect, as the mistress of Chelton, to have *some* authority over my own ball."

Lady Edith's cheeks colored, and her lips pinched. She picked up the quill and dipped it in the ink before marking a notation about flowers in the fountain. But it was a hollow win. Somehow the success of my endeavor did not make me feel any better. The discord between us tainted all of our time together.

She kept her focus on the paper as she spoke. "Do you also expect, as the mistress of Chelton, to escape each ball we attend and hide away with a book? Or will you accept *all* the responsibilities of this role along with the benefits?"

If words could slap, I was certain hers would have left a mark. "I have tried to explain that large gatherings—particularly those with strangers—will send me into a fit of nerves when I find attention is drawn to me. It is not a choice, Lady Edith. I do not wish to be so overcome."

"What you describe as a fit of nerves, others see as a woman who does not wish to be there."

"It is the truth of things," I said calmly.

"Which reflects poorly on our—"

"Good name? Yes. I do believe I am quite aware of how important that good name is."

Lady Edith opened her mouth in umbrage, but Forester came to the door and cut our conversation to a close. "You've a visitor, madam."

It was exceedingly frustrating that I could not tell who he was speaking to between the two of us.

Lady Edith, evidently, felt the same. "Which of us has a visitor?"

He looked between us then, uncertainty clouding his aged eyes. "It is Mrs. Moulton."

Lady Edith sucked in a quick breath. "Show her into the drawing room straight away."

Forester delivered a curt bow and turned to do her bidding. Lady Edith closed her eyes for a moment. When she directed them at me again, they were clouded with concern. "Can we resume our plans at another time? I must question Mrs. Moulton."

Still Miss Northcott's headmistress's name rang a bell of familiarity, though I could not place it. Perhaps that was due to my aunt writing about the town she passed through by the name of Melton . . . though that was quite some time ago, and not, what I believed, to be owed this familiarity. It was unimportant, though it bothered me that I could not place it.

I nodded to my mother-in-law. "You hope she can provide insight into Miss Northcott's whereabouts."

"She is the only person I can think of with that potential, yes. I cannot . . . it is odd to say aloud, but I cannot shake the feeling that Thea is in some sort of distress, that I have failed—" She ceased speaking and cleared her throat, leveling me with a plain look. It appeared that she recalled to whom she was speaking and chose not to continue to confide in me.

It stung. I wanted to be a member of this family in every way. This was far too similar to my experiences with my own mother growing up, not being the social daughter she desired, only getting in the way or forcing her to end her engagements at an earlier time than she wished. I'd hoped marriage would be the end of those feelings—that I would no longer find myself unable to come up to snuff.

"I do not want to burden you further," she said.

"It is no burden—"

Lady Edith stood. "We can resume at another time."

"Would you like me to come with you to visit Mrs. Moulton?"

"Only if you wish. It is your house, Felicity. I will not tell you what to do."

I clenched my teeth and waited for her to leave the breakfast room. One small comment about the role I rightfully carried, and I was subjected to barbs. Would I forever be in her shadow?

The chairs on the far side of the room held pillows, and I crossed the room, picked up one of the pillows, and screamed into it as loud as I could. The sound was extremely muffled, and I was certain no one outside of this room would hear me, so I took another breath, raised the pillow, and screamed again.

Pent up frustration slipped from me, releasing through the exertion of my scream until I was hollow and leaving behind a tingling sensation in my stomach. I was glad to expel my vexation so fully. I lowered the cushion, my chest heaving with the dregs of my outburst.

"Might I ask if all is well?" a deep voice called to me.

I turned toward the sound, fully aware that no blush threatened my pale cheeks. I was not ashamed of my outburst. Benedict stood in the doorway, watching me with mild concern.

"I needed to release some of my anger," I said calmly, setting the cushion back on the chair.

"Is this James's doing? I am not above challenging my own brother to a bit of fencing in order to humble the man."

My mouth curved into a smile. "No, not at all. It was nothing to do with James, and now I feel much better." I patted the pillow for emphasis.

"Poor pillow."

"No harm has come to it." I looked to the stodgy cushion, and it was no worse for the wear.

Benedict came into the room and eyed the papers on the table, amusement faintly trailing him. "Ah. The ball." Concern lit his dark eyes. "You've heard, then? For what it is worth, I suggested we remove them from the guestlist."

"Remove who?"

"The Whitstones, of course." He glanced up quickly, seeming to read my confusion. "You did not know, then."

"Apparently not."

Benedict laughed awkwardly, tapping his finger on what must be the guest list. "I now have no choice but to tell you, then, yes?"

"That would be best," I confirmed. "If you do not tell me, I will have to ask James."

He nodded. "That just might be better—"

"Benedict, please do not make me wait. What occurred? Have I committed atrocious offense?"

"Gads, no. It was them who did the offending."

"Out with it, please."

"Lady Whitstone asked Mother if the babe caused you to flee the dance floor at Lady Grenville's ball. It would seem that the rumors have reached Cumberland."

I turned and sat hard on the cushion which had just received a brutal vocal beating. If I had conceived a child after my wedding, it would be too soon to grow ill at the Grenville ball. "The rumors have reached Bakewell."

Benedict looked apologetic, but to his credit, not uncomfortable. He crossed to sit on the bench beside me. "If it means anything, I was present when Lady Whitstone voiced her question, and James gave her a mighty set down. It might be unnecessary to remove her from the guest list. I wonder if she would dare show her face, for I'm certain she could very well sense how deeply James would not want her present."

"James?" I could not wrap my mind around the scenario Benedict described. "This all happened at the Grenville ball?"

James had stalwartly risen to my defense while I had been

hiding in the sitting room with Henry. I did not voice what we were both likely thinking.

"Yes, but you needn't fear, young maiden. Your knight hath rescued your good name from the evil clutches of the sorceress."

I looked up at him, confused.

"It is a metaphor," Benedict explained. His brow drew together. "Do you not like to read?"

Laughter bubbled up from my chest, and I nodded. "I do, indeed. It was a lovely metaphor."

"Thank you." He gave an elaborate, foppish bow from his seated position beside me. "Now, do you mind telling me where my mother has gone? I expected to find her here with you."

"You might not expect that any longer. I do think I've upset her."

"She is quick to forgive."

I eyed him from the side. "Even when someone dares to claim the title of mistress of Chelton?"

He sucked a quick breath through clenched teeth. "Perhaps it will take an extra day or so for her to regulate her feelings. Though it should not, I suppose. It is well within your rights to claim the title."

"Within my rights, perhaps, but that does not make it easy when your mother has refused to willingly pass the responsibilities to me. She has not found me worthy yet," I explained.

"Does she need to?"

I sat up, considering the question. "If I want her to approve of me or give me assistance while I learn what is expected of me, then yes."

"But *worth?*" His eyes narrowed in thought. "That is not for my mother, or anyone else, to determine. That is something you find here." He tapped the location of his heart with two of his fingers.

I felt his rapping as though a phantom leaned over and touched my heart as well, and it overwhelmed me with sudden longing. Tears welled in my eyes, and I blinked them away before any could fall. How *did* I see myself? How could I expect Lady Edith or James or anyone to believe me capable when I did not necessarily perceive that ability in myself?

My mama's frustrations with my social failures had caused me to become excruciatingly aware of where I lacked. I feared it also created a standard by which I judged my value. If I chose to see myself the way James looked at me, unadulterated and without motivation to change me, I did not believe I would find myself so lacking.

"Have I said too much?" he questioned.

"No, you said precisely the right thing." I laughed awkwardly and dashed away a stray tear. "Your mother is in the drawing room with Mrs. Moulton."

"Moulton?" he asked, sitting up. "From York?"

"The headmistress, yes. Lady Edith sent for the woman in order to question her fully. She is determined to locate Miss Northcott."

Benedict ran a hand through his mussed curls. "As am I. I cannot wait to find the chit so I can wring her scrawny neck."

I swallowed. "Perhaps do not say as much before your mother."

He gave me an amused smile. "I will not. I do not truly mean it, you know."

"Not entirely, perhaps?"

"No, not *entirely*. Thea has caused Mother a great deal of stress, and she will be forced to compensate us accordingly."

"I cannot tell sometimes when you speak of Miss Northcott whether I will like her a great deal or despise her."

"You will adore her," he said sullenly. "Everyone does, heaven knows why."

Benedict stood and offered me a hand. "Would you like to come with me? I should like to hear what Mrs. Moulton has to say."

"No, but I thank you for the offer. I will continue to work on the plans for the ball."

Benedict paused and looked at me appraisingly. "I would not take it personally that Mother has prioritized her hunt for the girl over the preparations for your ball. She has been the only parent Thea knows since both of her parents have died, and Thea is left with no other family to depend upon. Mrs. Northcott was Mother's dearest friend, and I know she feels a deep sense of responsibility toward her daughter, even though there is no legal requirement for her actions."

I was not offended by her choice. Indeed, I found the timing of Mrs. Moulton's appearance to be fortuitous. Lady Edith's actions—alongside the devotion shown to her by her sons—proved that she possessed a caring, loyal heart. I hoped someday to be a recipient of that great affection as well.

Benedict bowed before leaving the room. He was surprisingly wise, and I took his advice to heart. But it was all for naught when I remembered Lady Whitstone's comment at the ball. It was made alarmingly clear to me that James had been so bothered following the event because the scandal had been mentioned. If it had reached Bakewell, which truly had only been a matter of time, then it was still being bandied about that we married swiftly because we had been intimate.

My resolve to prove that I was not with child had only grown.

CHAPTER 28

James found me the following morning in the library, wearing a look of mischief so broad I was equal parts alarmed and entertained.

"What have you schemed this morning, sir?" I questioned, setting *Evelina* on my lap.

"I've found the components needed for a certain activity which I am certain will bring both of us joy."

"Oh?" I could not, for the life of me, figure what it could be. But the way James stood before me grinning, his hands behind his back as he rocked on his heels, it was clear he was feeling mightily proud of his idea. I did not wish to dampen his enthusiasm.

"So long as it does not involve horses, I am prepared to enjoy whatever you've come up with." I set the slip of paper inside the book and closed it, but not before James noticed what I'd used to mark my place.

"That was one of the notes I wrote when I left for York, was it not?"

"Yes, I use it as a marker."

"Can you believe that was only last month? It certainly feels much longer since that occurred."

I took his hand. "Much, much longer."

He looked at me from the side, taking my arm to lead me from the room. "You must have liked the little notes I left if you kept them."

"They were decent, I suppose."

He glanced over sharply, and I smiled broadly.

"You little tease," he muttered, his low voice diving directly to my belly.

"I'm learning from the best."

James directed me to the door which led to the lawn in the back garden of the estate, and I was surprised to find a small table set out containing a pair of battledores and a shuttlecock. I had played this game as a child with my cousins at their annual house party and disliked it excessively then. I imagined the years since had not altered me enough to enjoy it any more now.

But James was too proud of his idea, too convinced—heaven knew why—that I'd *enjoy* the game, for me to do much else but pretend.

"Battledore and shuttlecock," I said. "I have not played since I was a girl."

"I realize it is often a children's game, but I do not know why that is the case. My brothers and I pull out our old battledores on occasion still, and it is great fun. The bird is not too difficult to hit at least a handful of times."

For some, perhaps. He obviously believed he had hit upon an activity that was so easy, anyone could master it. I was about to show him how truly inept a woman could be when it came to sporty pursuits of any kind, at any level.

We each took up a battledore and separated on the lawn. James tossed the bird into the air, its feathers glinting in the sunlight, and whacked it in my direction.

I ducked. In my defense, the thing was coming directly toward me.

"You are meant to try and hit it back to me, Liss."

"Oh, is that how it's played?" I bent to retrieve the bird and puffed a breath from my cheeks. I tossed the shuttlecock into the air and spun my battledore, but missed it completely, and it plopped on the ground.

"Give it another go, darling."

Darling. I could quite get used to that. I picked up the bird again and tried to hit it with much the same result.

"Again?" James called. His dubious tone betrayed his uncertainty. "Perhaps if I move closer?"

As though that would help me to hit the bird *I* was tossing in the air. He was sweet in his unrelenting optimism. I tried to smile. "I am sure that will help."

James moved closer still. I tossed the bird into the air and swung my battledore as hard as I could, connecting the netting with the shuttlecock. It flew straight and fast, landing squarely on James's face.

He shouted in surprise and tossed his battledore to the ground, lifting his hand to cover his eye.

I dropped my battledore and ran to him. "Oh, dear. I am sorry, James! I am not to be trusted with battledores and shuttlecocks!"

"You did not say so." His voice was partially muffled by the hand which still covered his eye.

"I believed you would surmise as much when I was very clear that I am no good at games or sports of *any* kind." Though I should have said something this morning. This could have been avoided if I'd been honest—but I had not wanted to ruin his fun.

He gave an exasperated chuckle and turned toward the house. "I cannot open my eye."

"Oh, James!" I gasped. "It hit your eye?" I'd assumed the bird had made contact with his eye*lid*.

"With the hard tip of the feather, I believe. It does not feel so good."

For a man in such pain—or so I assumed—he sounded remarkably calm. "Shall I call for the doctor?"

"That would be wise, yes."

His ready acquiescence could not be good. I took him by the elbow, fearful that he would hurt himself by attempting to walk straight with only the one eye to see by, and directed him into the house. We walked along the corridor, and I had a thought. I led him to the drawing room. "Wait here."

He looked at me, his one visible eye widening. A cold compress was just the thing. I left him behind and made my way to the kitchens to locate a cloth and water, when a sound in James's study caught my attention. Perhaps someone was inside, and I could send them for the doctor.

I opened the door and froze, unsure that I wanted to see what was before me. Molly stood at the desk, her body bent over the open drawers she was currently rifling through. She glanced up, caught my eye, and the color bled from her cheeks.

Drat. I had clearly made the wrong call in regard to the maids.

"Mrs. Bradwell, I can expl—"

"Hush. I do not wish to hear another word. Ring that bell, please."

She seemed frozen.

"Ring the bell!"

Molly jumped, then moved toward the hearth and tugged on the bell rope. I went to James's desk, the contents of his drawers now in utter disarray. Foolish, foolish girl.

"Did you expect that he would not notice his things all moved about?"

"I planned to put them back in order," she said quietly, her gaze trained on the floor. A hardness edged her words, and I felt the animosity snaking from her in waves. "You do not know what it's like to be hungry, to not have nice things. You have so many nice things, you aren't even aware when something goes missing."

"You've taken other things, then?"

She seemed to sense her mistake and shook her head, her eyes widening.

"It hardly matters whether or not the Bradwells appreciate their wealth, Molly. It is theirs. If you were in true need, you should have gone to Mrs. Prescott, not taken it upon yourself to correct the perceived imbalances. Stealing is always wrong."

Molly kept her gaze lowered, her eyebrows pinched in anger. I was the first to admit that the level of wealth at Chelton was far above what I was accustomed to, but that did not make it right to rifle through drawers and secret away small trinkets.

I shuffled the items in James's drawer into a semblance of order and paused when something in the back corner caught my eye. I pulled the drawer open until I could read the full title and confirmed what I'd believed it to be.

James was reading *The Mysteries of Udolpho*. Either that, or he was hiding it so I would not further frighten myself by reading it again.

It was much more likely to be the former. My heart fluttered. Had he done so for me? Though I could not see how or why his reading a novel would benefit me, it warmed my chest all the same. For a man so opposed to reading for enjoyment, finding a book in his possession was a mystery I wanted answered.

Another time, though, after his poor eye and this ridiculous maid had both been dealt with.

A footman entered the room, and I shut the drawer. "I need a basin of cool water and a clean cloth sent to the drawing room quickly. There has been an injury."

"Right away, ma'am." He turned to go.

"Wait, please," I called.

He paused.

"I also need Mrs. Prescott to the drawing room straight away and someone needs to fetch the doctor."

"Yes, ma'am. Of course." He paused, seemingly unsure if he was released or not.

"Yes, you may go."

He left, and I turned to Molly. "Come with me."

She bobbed a curtsy and trailed behind me toward the drawing room. I was worried for a brief moment that she would run, but she stayed right behind me. James was seated on the sofa, his head leaning back and his hand still covering his eye.

I pointed to a ladder back chair set against the wall. "Sit," I commanded, and Molly obeyed.

James looked up quickly, his one visible eyebrow raised in alarm.

"Not you," I said. He was already sitting.

He looked over to Molly, and his confusion seemed to grow.

Mrs. Prescott entered the room then, holding a cloth, Hannah trailing her with a basin of water.

"On the table just there," I said, pointing to the low table set before the sofa where James waited. She obeyed immediately, then left the room.

The clack of horse hooves on the gravel drive alerted me to a rider leaving the property, and I crossed to the window to find a bewigged footman taking off at a rapid clip. He knew no more about the situation than that an injury occurred, so I hoped he did not incite too much fear in the doctor.

Spinning toward Mrs. Prescott, I clasped my hands in front of me and stepped forward. "Do you have contact information for Janet? The maid?"

"I do," she said.

"Good." What an inordinate relief. "Please write to her and

ask her to return. She deserves an apology and her position, if she wants it."

Mrs. Prescott's face pinched.

"Molly was found today rifling through more drawers. She is dismissed"—I looked to Molly to punctuate my words—"immediately. I made a mistake and asked the wrong maid to leave."

The housekeeper's shock was understandable.

"Now I need to attend to my husband. Will you please search Molly's things before she is permitted to leave this house?"

"Of course, ma'am."

Mrs. Prescott motioned to Molly to leave and followed her from the room, dipping in a curtsy to my mother-in-law as she passed her in the doorway.

My cheeks flamed, and I turned my attention to James on the sofa. I moved the bowl of water closer and sat beside him. How long had Lady Edith been standing there? What had she overheard?

"What is this?" she asked, crossing toward us. "James?"

"An injury to his eye," I explained. "I've sent for the doctor, and I have a cold cloth here."

"And Molly?"

"She was caught searching the drawers in the study, then raved to me about the injustice of having nothing when this house is filled with opulence. She has been dismissed, and Mrs. Prescott will send word to Janet that her position is available if she should choose to return."

Lady Edith said nothing.

I folded the cloth and dipped it in the water, then rang it out. "Would you like to press this to your eye, James?"

He watched me closely through his one visible eye. "Yes, you may."

I may? "Tell me if it hurts," I said softly. He removed his hand from his closed eyelid, which was red and slightly swollen.

Guilt gripped my stomach and twisted, and I pressed the cloth gently.

Lady Edith took the seat across from us. Quiet settled in the room.

"Does it hurt?" Lady Edith asked.

James smiled. "A little."

"I cannot apologize enough, James. Will you forgive me?"

"In time, I suppose."

His response startled me, but the slight curve of his lips revealed his teasing.

"If my presence is so distressing, I can send for Mrs. Prescott to continue in my stead."

He blindly reached for my hand and circled my wrist with his fingers. "I think I could be persuaded to tolerate your ministrations a while longer."

"How very magnanimous of you," I said drolly.

Lady Edith cleared her throat, and I jumped. My hand pressed into the cloth on James's eye, and he winced, leaning away from me.

"Forgive me," I said, removing the cloth.

"It was nothing."

"Is it helping?"

"The pressure hurts, but the coolness feels good."

I dipped the cloth again and wrung the water out before pressing it into his hand. He lifted it to his eye and held it there —a safer option, evidently.

"Can you see through your eye?" Lady Edith asked.

"Yes, but the images blur."

Oh, dear. What had I done? What if my foolish attempt to play a wretched game with James had forever ruined his eyesight? It hardly mattered that the game was his idea. I was fully aware of my own ineptness.

Footsteps warned us of someone's impending arrival, and

Benedict appeared in the doorway, a roll of folded news sheets tucked beneath one arm. "What's this, then?"

"My lovely wife assaulted my eye."

I scoffed. "I believe you mean to say that the bird assaulted your eye."

"Bird?" Lady Edith all but screeched.

"Shuttlecock," James corrected. "And a very powerful hit."

Benedict slapped his rolled-up news sheets against his thigh, his grin wide. "Well done, Felicity."

"*Ben,*" his mother scolded.

He raised his hands in surrender. "Not that I'm glad she hurt you, chap. But it must have been a powerful strike. Tell me, James, did you teach her to attack the bird from above or below?"

James's one good eye shot to his brother. "Below, of course." He looked up in consideration, then to me. "You did swing your battledore from below, yes?"

"My recollection of the moment is a little fuddled, but I do recall my focus being driven on hitting the bird, and not entirely on *how* to do so. My previous failed attempts were motivating."

"Quite." Benedict's grin widened. "I should have liked to see this."

"I can safely promise you will never have another chance to witness my wife play battledore and shuttlecock," James said wryly.

I was in wholehearted agreement.

Motion sounded in front of the house, and I rose and crossed to the window. "I believe the doctor has arrived."

Lady Edith released a relieved breath. "One never does know if Dr. Settle will be in town or not."

The doctor was soon after let into the room, and I kept my distance, watching the man set his leather bag on the floor near James. "Does the patient wish for privacy?" he asked, looking to Lady Edith.

"My wife may remain," James said.

Lady Edith and Benedict rose to leave, and I stood my ground near the window, watching my mother-in-law analyze me as she left. Her stony mask was impeccable, and I could not tell whether she was angry with me or suspicious. I put it from my mind.

I had done nothing wrong.

Well, except for hitting my husband in the eye with a feathered ball.

The doctor appeared similar in age to my father, his brown hair liberally sprinkled with gray and white. He requested that James lie back on the sofa and knelt at his side, asking all manner of questions about the event which led to his injury and how his sight had been impacted.

"When do you feel pain?"

"When I apply pressure," James said. "Though the coolness of the cloth was a minor relief."

"Mmm."

"And I can see through the eye, but it is blurred."

"That could be a result of the pressure and the cloth. We will not know if your vision is impacted permanently until you remove it for a length of time."

Impacted permanently. My fears were being realized. It had been a relief to pass jokes with James, but the situation was potentially as dire as I'd feared, and that drained the humor from me at once.

"Remove the cloth and tell me how it feels," Dr. Settle requested.

"As though sand is in my eye."

Dr. Settle continued his examination, first flushing James's eye and then inspecting it with a large magnifying glass. I paced behind them, some distance away so as to remain out of the way.

My anxious steps had apparently grown too much for the

doctor, for he raised his head and looked to me. "Your husband's sight will likely recover, madam. Would you like me to call for a servant? It seems to me your nerves could benefit from a dram of sherry."

I had never before used alcohol to calm my racing nerves, and I did not wish to begin now. The idea of having *less* control or awareness over myself did nothing but further fray my delicate nerves.

"I do not require anything of that nature, but I can send for tea if you would like, Dr. Settle." I remembered Mrs. Hutton offering James brandy after we were discovered in the library at her ball. "Or something stronger, if James would like?"

"No, but I thank you, ma'am. Mr. Bradwell?"

The weight of James's stare was no less powerful for being reduced by one eye. "Remain, please. I need nothing else."

"Of course." I sat on the chair opposite them and funneled my focus into stilling my anxious feet and appearing the picture of poise.

The remainder of the examination passed quickly until the moment Dr. Settle looked up, held my gaze, and asked, "Mrs. Bradwell, how adept are you at sewing?"

CHAPTER 29

S ewing a patch to cover James's injured eye had only taken a quarter hour. It was quick work to hem in the edges of a piece of Mrs. Prescott's scrap fabric and attach a string for James to tie around his head. Dr. Settle was long since gone when I returned to the drawing room, black fabric patch in tow.

Lady Edith stood near the window upon my entrance, Benedict and Henry seated on the couch, and Mrs. Moulton—her trip extended a few days for recuperation after being summoned from York, as was proper—sipping tea on a plush seat beside the cold hearth. James, however, was absent.

Henry glanced up. "He has gone to rest upstairs," he explained, correctly assuming who I was searching the room for. "Dr. Settle does not want him to exert his eye more than necessary today."

Benedict snorted. "How *does* one exert their eye, exactly? Rolling it in exasperation too frequently?"

"Unless you wish for your brother to sport a patch at the ball in *three* days, I expect more support from you in this time of healing."

"He might wish to wear it anyway, Mother. Is it not dashing?" Benedict looked to me. "Perhaps I can request one as well?"

I shook my head at him, but my smile came unbidden.

"Mind yourself," Lady Edith requested, "or you will give Mrs. Moulton the worst opinion of us."

Benedict grinned to the headmistress, who was only now glancing up from her tea, her cheeks pinking. "Mrs. Moulton is too agreeable to think ill of you, Mother, based on my behavior, I am sure."

"All too right," the headmistress replied.

Henry watched me linger in the doorway. "Will you take the patch to him?" he asked.

"I should." Though I'd been distracted by Benedict.

"Have you forgotten your way?" Benedict asked, nothing but false concern.

I shot him a wry smile. "No. In fact, I do believe I have only gotten lost twice this week."

"Progress, indeed," he said stoutly.

Lady Edith did not seem to find humor in any of these exchanges and crossed the room toward me. "I will accompany you part of the way. I wish to speak to Mrs. Prescott."

I waited near the door, and we left together. It was not until we were a good distance away from the drawing room when she spoke again. "James's eye, it will heal?"

Had he not told his mother the details of the doctor's visit? "Dr. Settle believes so. Though, the extent of the damage will not be made known until tomorrow."

She let out a sigh. "What a relief. Tomorrow cannot arrive soon enough."

"Indeed."

The quiet stretched between us, and I wondered if she wanted me to bring up the topic of the maids, or if she preferred to pretend it had not happened. I could not do so, however— pretending something did not occur would not actually erase it from existence—and when we reached the top of the grand staircase, I turned to her. "Has Molly left the house already?"

"Yes. Actually, Mrs. Prescott informed me shortly after the doctor's departure that there were two small trinkets found among the things in her trunk. One of Benedict's jeweled snuff boxes, and a small figurine from my chamber."

"If only I'd thought to have their trunks searched from the beginning, we could have avoided the hassle of dismissing the wrong girl."

Lady Edith was quiet for a moment. She looked away. "If I had not placed the burden of the situation entirely on your shoulders, I might have suggested that very thing instead of watching you manage it poorly. My pride had taken a hit, and I hope you will forgive the thoughtless way I left you to handle things."

Sweet vindication soared through my chest, humility quickly at its heels. I would not boast this win, for I could see that it took a great deal of humbling for my mother-in-law to admit her mistake.

I, too, carried some blame. "If I would only have asked for help instead of needing to prove my worthiness, we could have worked together to find the best solution."

"I do not pretend to be perfect," Lady Edith said.

I did my best to hide my astonishment at that, for I was certain all she had done since my arrival at Chelton was do her best to portray perfection, both inside and outside the home.

"But I can admit when I have erred." She drew in a shaky breath, and I could see how difficult this was for her. "I should not have told you to prove yourself, Felicity. It was not my place to say whether or not you were worthy of the callings you already held. That of mistress in this house, and that of James's wife."

"Thank you."

"I allowed the nature of your entrance into my family to taint the way I viewed you, and I have since learned the value of forgiveness and contrition. You've impressed me in the last week or so. I observed the way you managed things today with the maid and James's injury, and it was precisely how I would have done myself."

The compliment she spoke was overshadowed by the two words I could not remove from my mind. Forgiveness and contrition? On whose part? She had nothing to forgive me for, since I had done nothing wrong in marrying her son.

Unless she was under the impression that the wedding was a product of my design—that I had been after his money or position or some such thing.

"Forgive my confusion, Lady Edith, but do you mean to say that you believe I somehow *convinced* James to marry me?"

She blinked in surprise. "Well, of course."

Shock rippled through me like the curl of a wave crashing over the shore. Lady Edith not only knew of the rumors surrounding our engagement, she *believed* them. My good character had not so far proved my innocence?

"I'll let you take that to James," she said, nodding to the patch clutched tightly in my hands.

"No."

Lady Edith startled. "What do you mean?"

"I will not accept that slight against my character. I've done nothing to earn it, so it cannot go uncontested."

She gave an uneasy laugh. "Surely you see that I am not as easily convinced as others."

"Convinced of my good character?" She drove the knife deeper with each new revelation. My hands shook, but my voice remained steady, sustained no doubt by my righteous indignation. "I have not made any attempts to dupe anyone, least of all this family. I have been incredibly straightforward and sincere since the beginning."

Her eyes were hard. "I might not have been in London, but I

have known James for the entirety of his life. My son would not have rashly married anyone unless she convinced him to. He had no reason otherwise to agree to the union. He is a man of prestige, a good name, a fortune—what cause would he have to marry a penniless girl of no real social standing if not for some persuasion or coercion on her part?"

I froze, doing my best to keep from trembling in my anger. Her opinions and beliefs were made abundantly clear. "You believe I seduced your son."

She did not grace my crudeness with a reply.

I scoffed, unable to believe what I was hearing. The nature of her disdain was now clear, but not the depth for which she held onto it. It was one thing for the whole of London—veritable strangers—to believe ill of me. But *this* woman? After I spent weeks living in her home and proving myself?

"It might interest you to know that our predicament was a product of your son's attempts to help me to overcome the nerves which accompany all social functions for me. The kindness he showed me was entirely without blame and wholly misinterpreted by those who discovered us. It was *not* my design to entrap him."

Her skepticism was nearly palpable in the wrinkling of her nose and the downturn of her lips, and it raised my hackles.

"If anyone is to blame, Lady Edith, it is yourself," I said. "Your son persisted in his desire to marry me on his own accord, without any persuasion. When I asked him why he insisted on going through with it, he explained that he had made a promise to his mother long ago, and he could never live with himself now if he did not do his part to save our reputations."

"Promise?" Her lips pinched. "That promise was derived in a moment of desperation, when Thea was turned away from her father's brother and delivered to our doorstep, hungry and scared. I requested that none of my sons ever ill-treat a woman in need, and they swore they would not. This situation hardly compares."

Never to ill-treat a woman in need. James must have believed that if he walked away from me and left me to the mercy of the *ton*, he would be abandoning me. I could not change that now, but I was glad to understand it. The root of his motivations were chivalrous, much as I'd suspected.

Lady Edith, however, did not seem to agree. She watched me with the displeasure one reserved for a particularly foul odor. I swallowed the hurt that spread through my chest. "While you have been busy looking for someone to blame, I have been making the best of this difficult situation. We cannot change it now, Lady Edith, so I suggest you find a way to come to terms with the way things have come about."

I turned away before my tongue could escape me further, my heart beating out of my chest, but she did not allow me to leave yet.

"How can you expect me to believe that you are not over-joyed to find yourself the mistress of Chelton? That you did not know what you were marrying into?"

I would not pop her inflated opinion of her family name by explaining that I had never before heard of her grand estate before James spoke of it, or that I was unaware of his income. I faced her. "It should be extremely clear by now that I cannot manage easily in social situations. I did not leave in the middle of the dance at Lady Grenville's ball because I am ill from a child. I left because the overwhelming attention in the room nearly caused me to faint."

"Faint?"

"Yes. I am no more able to control my physical discomfort in situations where large groups of people are watching me than you are your uneasy stomach in a carriage. When you remove the prejudices you have so liberally placed upon me, you might see that I am anything *but* a fortune or husband hunter."

"You cannot claim innocence when you admitted you were acquainted with Henry just last summer."

My mouth fell open, and I shook my head. "Henry did not tell me the name of his estate or his brothers. He did not speak of his immense wealth, and I did not surmise its depth from the little time I spent in your hunting box. Good heavens, Lady Edith." I laughed mirthlessly. "You may ask him yourself, for you clearly do not believe me, but surely you can trust that Henry's nature is not a boastful one. I did not even learn James's surname until *after* we were engaged."

Still, she did not seem to believe me, and I turned away. There was no use in arguing my innocence further, not when it was not to be believed.

My heart raced by the time I reached James's door, and I let myself in without knocking. He lay in the bed, his arm slung over his forehead. The room was darkened, the drapes pulled closed, and the bed cast in further shadows by the bed hangings drawn on all but one side.

"You've brought my patch?" he asked.

"Indeed." My clipped answer seemed to have alerted him to my foul mood.

"What happened to vex you?"

"Nothing. I . . . your . . ." I shook my head. How did I reveal such an awful picture as Lady Edith painted? I sat on the edge of his bed, facing where he lay against the pillows in its center. "James, when we initially spoke of our engagement, you mentioned that you had made a promise to your mother and you could not live with yourself if you did not see it through. She told me of it tonight, that after Miss Northcott arrived, she asked you to vow—"

"That is not the promise to which I referred." He looked at me for a long moment, his good eye seeming to analyze my face. "Though I can see why she might have thought that."

"Will you tell me what it was, then?"

He waited a beat before speaking, then pushed himself up to a seated position. "Yes. When I left for Eton as a lad, my mother took me aside and explained the importance of duty and doing right by one's family. She preached about the particular obligation I held as the oldest son and heir, and she had me promise I would do nothing to besmirch the Bradwell name, that I would respect and protect it for the rest of my life."

Realization hit me like a mad horse, jarring in its swiftness. I had thought James's need to keep his promise had something to do with me, but I'd been wrong. It was about upholding his own honor. "Your mother holds your name in esteem the way one would their title."

"Yes, precisely. It has not earned us a place in Lords, of course, but it is no less important to us."

"But why? Why does the Bradwell name come before you, before your brothers and their happiness? You chose a wife who was a veritable stranger to you for the sake of a name?"

"That was only a small part—"

"But it was part."

"Of course it was," he said swiftly. His eyes were unbending, as though he wanted me to understand. "What of your parents, Liss? You mean to say they had no bearing on your willingness to agree to our union?"

They'd had a large influence on my decision. James took the wind out of my pretentious sails by pointing that out. "My parents did influence my decision. I could not take away the one thing they live for, James."

"What is that?"

"Their social calendar."

He reached across the blanket and took my hand, and I immediately felt better for being connected to him in a small way. "It is no wonder you were hurt when they postponed their arrival date. Is this a common occurrence?"

"I have spent my life in the shadows of social situations. The only one I truly enjoyed was the house party we attended every year at Arden Castle, for I was able to spend that time with my cousin Jane. But my parents both thrive on being surrounded by their friends and going to balls and soirees or hosting dinners and card parties. When I came of age and was expected to join them, we all quickly realized that I was a crutch in their system, that I held them back. My nervous fits were a hindrance, and as much as my mama loves me, she could never understand why I went to such great lengths to remove myself from dancing."

"As though you fainted by design."

I looked at him wryly, aware of his thumb drawing lazy circles around my old burn. "You were the first person to accept my anxious fits and the fainting for what they were, and to not put more expectations on me than I could endure."

He scoffed lightly. "I've done nothing but add to your expectations since our marriage."

"The problem, I think, is that I did not know what I was agreeing to when I married you."

"And I did not realize it would be a problem. It never occurred to me that you would find Chelton a burden." He looked at me earnestly, but it was hard to take him seriously with one swollen eye closed.

I lifted my gift. "Shall we tie the patch on now?"

"I suppose," he said, somewhat sullenly.

James sat forward, and I knelt beside him, gently placing the patch over his injured eye and drawing the strings around the back of his head. I bent forward to tie it in place, and when I sat back on my heels, he was watching me closely with his good eye. The bed was dim, the curtains pulled tight around all but one side, and my breath caught at the intensity of his expression.

"I have wondered multiple times since bringing you to Chelton if I made a mistake," he said quietly. "If, perhaps, you had married the wrong Bradwell brother."

273

I froze. What did he know about my time in the hunting box last year? Had I inadvertently given my little *tendre* away? No. I could not have. It left me the moment James carried me from the Pickering ballroom.

"Do not take my meaning the wrong way," he said quickly. "I do not *wish* you had married another man. Indeed, I only wonder if you would have been happier married to someone who understood you better. A man who did not require you to ride horses you disliked or play games with him on the lawn."

"You are the one who suffered most in that particular situation."

"True." He looked away, his hand falling from mine. "Dr. Settle recommended I try to sleep, and I think it wise if I heed his advice."

I could have jolted for the shock this provided me. He needed to sleep, and he did not wish for me to be here by the way he looked at the door. "You would like me to leave?"

His mouth curved into a sad smile. "Like it? No. But I think it would be best."

CHAPTER 30

The day before the ball dawned overcast, and Lady Edith was a ball of nerves. If we had rain, her plans to open the courtyard were dashed and the ballroom was bound to become too much a squeeze. If it did not rain, all would be well. She and I had not spoken of our argument since it occurred two days before, and I had hardly seen James.

He'd not come to my room in the last two evenings, and I wasn't sure I could attend such a large ball without his steadfast support. But as it was to be given in my honor, I had little choice in the matter. I'd rolled his words about my mind over and over again since they left his mouth and could not reconcile the truth with his concerns. I'd given James no cause to believe that I preferred his brother—a simple truth, since I did *not* prefer anyone to my husband.

I descended the main staircase, a flurry of activity going on around me in preparation for the ball, and a footman approached when I reached the checkered floor.

"Yes?"

"You've visitors, ma'am, in the drawing room."

This was exactly the last thing I needed. If it was the Whit-

stones hoping to gain my favor again after their rudeness at the Grenville ball, I would feign a headache. I did not care if it was rude.

"Who are they?" I asked.

"Mr. and Mrs. Lennox, ma'am."

Jane. My heart leapt clear to my throat. I could have collapsed on the floor in relief. "Thank you," I said calmly, though inside my heart raced, and I went directly to the drawing room.

Jane stood near the hearth, admiring the painting above the mantel, her tall husband beside her. She looked a picture of poise, her raven hair styled neatly and her green traveling gown without a crease. Ewan looked ever the gentleman, his dark hair swept to the side, and it was never obvious until he spoke with a thick brogue exactly how Scottish he was. Though there was a tanness about his face that suited him well.

"Jane, Ewan," I said, entering the room.

Jane turned, and we both crossed the room swiftly, embracing upon impact. She gripped me by the elbows and leaned back. "Felicity, this *house*! It hardly warrants the name."

"It is much to take in, I know it well."

Ewan stepped forward and took my hand, placing a chaste kiss over the knuckles. "Aye, what we saw of the grounds were bonny when we drove up. I canna wait to see more of yer fishing pond."

His hint was easily understood. "I am certain my husband will be more than pleased with any excuse to fish."

"Indeed," James agreed, coming into the room. His dark eye patch still wrapped around his head, but his smile was not dimmed. "I take great pleasure in escaping for a quiet afternoon at the pond."

Jane leaned close to me and whispered, "Are all the brothers so handsome?"

I nudged her with my elbow to quiet her. "James, come meet my cousin Jane and her husband Ewan Lennox."

The appropriate bows and curtsies were exchanged. James came to my side, and I had not realized how greatly the space between us these last two days had affected me until he stood so near. I ached to reach for his hand but feared his rebuff.

"The ball is tomorrow evening," I said. "You received my invitation?"

"Shortly after your letter, yes. I came prepared with a ball gown."

I clasped my hands before me. "I wrote to invite your mother and Lord Moorington to the ball, but as I did not receive any word back, I can only assume they are not at Arden Castle presently?"

"No, they are spending some time in Brighton just now. But I am certain Mother would have attended your ball had she been home."

"It is to be a crush," I said. "Or so I'm told."

"In this large of a house? I do wonder how that shall be managed."

James smiled. "My mother does not entertain often, so she invites everyone she knows when she does."

"That is kind of her. I'm certain it shall be great fun."

"So long as I dinna have to dance with anyone but ye, I will be pleasantly occupied," Ewan said, his brogue thick.

Jane blushed prettily and swatted her husband playfully on the arm. "You will sound uncouth if you are not careful."

"I am a Scot, after all. Is it not expected?"

James looked at me briefly. "You sound nothing but relatable to my ears, Mr. Lennox."

I crossed to the fireplace and pulled the bell rope to summon the housekeeper. I would have shown them to their room myself, but I wouldn't know which one it was.

"I cannot wait to look in the gardens," Jane said.

James cleared his throat. "Are you hungry? Perhaps after you've had the opportunity to settle in your room, we can meet in the parlor for refreshment. I would be happy to show Mr. Lennox the pond afterwards."

"That sounds lovely," Jane said.

Mrs. Prescott appeared in the doorway a moment later.

"Mr. and Mrs. Lennox have arrived," I said. "Is their room prepared?"

"Yes, ma'am. We've had it ready a few days yet."

Jane looked at me with impressed eyes. "You are quite the hostess, Lissy."

Her usage of my family's pet name squeezed my chest in a bittersweet way. I missed my parents all the more, but I was glad to have Jane. "I did not know when or if to expect you, so I had a room prepared in case you were able to come."

"If you'd like to come with me," Mrs. Prescott said, and Jane and Ewan followed her from the room.

When their footsteps receded, I turned to James. Things were tenuous between us, like a thin string ran from his heart to mine, taut and breakable. "Is it wise to go away for the afternoon when there is much to do to prepare for the ball?"

He smiled kindly. "Mother has things well in hand. She never requires my assistance for these things until the event begins. I do promise to be standing there in my best clothes at the appointed hour tomorrow."

"If you are certain."

"I've lived in this house a long while. There is nothing she wants from me today, I assure you." He stepped closer but kept his hands behind his back. "I assume there is nothing for you to see to, either. You might be mistress of Chelton, but Mother is hosting the ball in your honor. She would wish for you to spend time with your cousin today."

That sounded more like an excuse for Lady Edith's desire to be rid of my presence. "How will I learn what needs doing unless she teaches me? I will be wholly unprepared for the day I need to host a gathering."

"Surely Mother will help you then." He smiled as he spoke, but the words did a weird spin in my head, refusing to settle.

Until they dropped one by one into place with alarming clarity. Of course she would help me when the time came, because *she would always be here.*

"What is it?" James asked softly, coming to my side. He looked between my eyes, his brow puckering.

"Lady Edith is incapable of leaving Chelton. She will live here with us always."

"I assume so. Travel is difficult for her, as you know." He paused, the air between us growing thicker. "Will that be a problem?"

"Only if your mother continues to hate me."

He reared back as though he'd been slapped. "You should not speak so."

It was a comfort at least to know Lady Edith had not gone so far as to share her ill opinions of me with James. Or perhaps she was allowing me that privilege, which would only make me appear unsavory.

"It is the truth," I finally said.

"It cannot be. My mother does not hate a living soul. She even cares for Lady Whitstone still, and they fell out terribly."

"I've heard it from her lips, James," I said, my voice tired. Though hate might have been too strong a word, the sentiments were close. "She believes I trapped you into marriage, that I had an eye on your fortune and this grand estate." I scoffed lightly. "As though I would *want* to be placed in charge of such a grand house."

His face tightened, and he rubbed a hand over his jaw. "Did she say these things the other night when you brought me the eye patch?" His ready acceptance did not make me feel any better.

"Yes. I defended myself, but it was all for naught. It appears her opinion is unchangeable."

"We will change it."

"How?"

"I will tell her the truth," he said simply.

"She will not believe you. I am a harpy, did you not know it?" Bitterness slipped from my tongue, and it was not an attractive sound. I didn't like the way I felt or the things I was saying. I closed my eyes and ran my fingers over my eyelids, pushing away the oncoming headache. "Forgive my loose tongue, James. I am nervous for the dancing tomorrow, and it is causing me to say things I shouldn't."

"You needn't apologize to me. It seems there is a conversation I must have with my mother after all."

"No," I said, grabbing his forearm. "Please do not. Things are uncomfortable enough as it is between us, and I do not think it will matter what you say to her. Her mind is made up on the matter."

"But you are innocent of what she accuses you." His voice held more fire than I expected, and his defense of my character was a boon to my spirits.

"Indeed, but you and I both know that, so what does it matter?" I sucked in a quick breath and looked at him sharply, the truth of my words ringing through me with ferocity. I believed them to be true, and that surprised me most of all.

He looked down at me, his one visible eye darting between mine. "That is not what you said at our wedding breakfast."

He was correct. I'd told him during the breakfast that it mattered dearly to me to prove to the *ton* that I was blameless, that my heart and intentions were pure. "No, I did not. I did not feel this way then. I think I have grown a little in the time since we left London."

"Or perhaps the distance has shown you something I have known all along?"

"What is that?"

He stepped forward and trailed a finger up my cheek and behind my ear, sending a volley of shivers down my neck. "It matters not what others think of us. What matters is how we view ourselves. My good name is intact, and we can sleep knowing we've done nothing great to besmirch it. We can hold our heads up with pride and integrity, knowing we've done nothing wrong."

"Well, we did one thing wrong," I corrected. "Two, perhaps."

"Oh?"

"Yes. We escaped the ballroom when we should have remained, and we danced alone."

His green-brown eyes bore into me, and the fierceness of his words rang through his calm, deep voice. "I have thought of that night often in the last few months, and I cannot say I regret any of it."

"Even the dancing?"

"Especially the dancing," he confirmed. "If we had not shared that waltz, I might not ever have known of your graceful talent."

An unladylike guffaw ripped from my throat. "I am anything but graceful. My nerves make that so."

He looked at me still, the back of his knuckles running over my cheekbone. "In company, yes, you are jittery. Alone? When no one is watching? You are a swan, my love."

I froze beneath his fingers, my eyes widening like saucers. *My love.* Had he meant it?

He seemed to react in a similar manner, his knuckles going still. "Liss—"

"Goodness!" Jane said, entering the room with her tall, Scottish husband behind her. "The room you assigned us is lovely, Lissy. I cannot believe this is your home."

James did not seem to hear them, his gaze remaining locked

on mine. I pasted a smile on my face and stepped away, and his hand fell to his side.

"I did warn you of it in my letter," I said brightly.

Jane's eyes widened. "I believe you called it a beautiful estate and once mentioned that it was large. I had no idea it was *this* grand."

Ewan slid an arm around his wife's waist. "We didna ken where to find the parlor, so we returned here."

"If you are anything like me, you will become lost many times before you locate any of the rooms you seek."

Jane's cheeks pinked. "Yes, we already have."

"What is it? You are blushing."

Her eyes darted to James and back to me. Good heavens, she needn't be fearful of speaking before him.

"Would you like to show them to the parlor?" James asked me softly. He must have sensed her hesitancy as well. "I will send someone for refreshments."

I agreed and slipped my arm around Jane's, pulling her from the room, Ewan just behind us. "What is it?" I asked when we left.

"We walked into a private conversation when looking for the drawing room again, and I fear I have caused great offense."

"In what way?"

She glanced over her shoulder at her husband, then continued. "I knew the woman—Mrs. Moulton, you'll recall? I attended her school in York for a few years—and I was happy to see her so unexpectedly. I rudely interrupted, and the man who was speaking to her looked exceedingly vexed."

That was why the name had always sounded familiar to me. Jane had written to me during her time at school and must have mentioned her headmistress by name. Glad to finally have that mystery solved, I returned my attention to Jane's mild distress. "A man was speaking to her? Did you learn his name?"

"No, but he looks similar to your James, only possessed of curly hair."

"Benedict, the youngest of the brothers." She'd already met Henry last summer, so it was easy to puzzle out.

She bared her teeth in distress. "Do you think I've caused great offense? I fear Scotland's casualness has begun to change me a little." She added an arch look toward Ewan, who merely ignored the comment. I couldn't help but assume it was a playful jest between them.

"I would be shocked beyond all things if you have. Benedict is possessed of the easiest of characters and not at all to be taken seriously."

"He appeared in the depths of a serious conversation with Mrs. Moulton, and quite frustrated, besides."

"I can attest to it," Ewan added.

Odd, that. "I would not think on it another moment. But I will speak to him and be certain he understands that your interruption was the product of a great surprise at finding your old headmistress here."

We reached the door of the parlor, the sounds of ball preparations reaching us from down the corridor.

"Thank you, Lissy." Jane squeezed my hand, and looked into my eyes. Her own narrowed slightly. "Something about you has altered, but I cannot place exactly what it is."

"Perhaps it is that I am married now, away from my parents, and living in an enormous museum?"

She laughed. "Yes, all those things. But there is something more. I will ruminate on it until I determine exactly what it is."

I shook my head indulgently and pulled her into the parlor. It was so very good to have my friend here.

CHAPTER 31

The large, white gown spread out over my bed like a stretch of freshly fallen snow. Fanny had insisted on doing my hair before helping me to dress in order to avoid sitting too long and creasing the gown, and I watched the mass of white fabric through the looking glass, equally mesmerized and appalled by it. Shades of flowers, painted designs on the floor, and special wall hangings all conveyed Lady Edith's intended message: innocence.

She failed to believe me innocent, however, so I wondered at the point of the farce. If my own mother-in-law could not accept the truth from my lips, how would she expect Bakewell society to do so from all this pageantry?

A knock sounded at the adjoining door, and Fanny moved to answer it. She spoke softly then stepped back and opened the door.

James stepped into my room but lingered in the doorway, and I shifted on my seat to better see him. His black coat and breeches were impeccable, his black waistcoat and white cravat crisp and starched. He looked the perfect, handsome rogue, due to his eyepatch, and I liked the look excessively.

If he found my staring odd, he did not comment on it. "There is something I wanted to show you before the ball begins, if you think you can spare a minute?"

"Of course." I had not slept beside James in days, and I missed him. His voice, his handsome face, had haunted my fitful sleep, and I hated that he was so close but felt so out of my reach.

He gave a brisk nod to me, then to Fanny, and returned to his chamber.

"We're nearly finished," Fanny said, bustling back to my side. "We've only to add these flowers." She pointed to the ridiculous pile on my dressing table that Madame Rousseau provided for my hair.

"We needn't add them all," I said with conviction. I'd been tempted to don the pink ball gown again just to spite my mother-in-law, but even I had more control than that. "Perhaps one or two?"

"I *did* think so many flowers wasn't in your taste, ma'am, if I can be so bold. Your hair would be more white than copper if I was to add them all."

Fanny made quick work of pinning a few flowers into my hair and helping me into my gown. When the enormous dress was on, I smoothed my hands down the gauzy overskirt. It had a flattering empire waist that flowed slimly down to an enormous train. The sheer overlay bunched at the hem with an inordinate amount of clustered flowers. It would have been perfectly tasteful if it boasted half as many roses—exactly as it had during the fitting.

I gritted my teeth and crossed the room, the weight of the gown making movement more difficult. I wanted to glide, not drag. I blew out a frustrated breath and knocked on the adjoining door. James opened it so quickly I could only assume he'd been waiting nearby.

His gaze swept over me, his eyes widening in appreciation.

He let out a low, soft whistle, almost as though by accident, then cleared his throat. "You are a vision, Liss."

"Thank you." I gave a low curtsy, more in jest than otherwise. "You can thank your mother for the design. She wanted me to splash white wherever I go tonight."

"Inventive."

Manipulative.

"Shall we?" he asked, offering his arm. I slipped my gloved hand over his bent elbow and followed him from the room. We turned away from the main stairs and James led me through corridors and up a set of stairs that were vaguely familiar. I was certain I'd found myself lost here a time or two, but I did not know where we were.

We reached a long, open corridor lined with lit sconces and windows open to the enclosed courtyard below. The wall opposite the windows was bestrewn with gilded frames and portraits of every size.

"Have you been here before? This is our gallery wall."

"I haven't." I stepped away from him so I could better see the paintings.

The large one on the end was a tall man with brown, curly hair and James's eyes. He wore his regimentals, the red coat striking and bold, his medals gleaming.

"That is my father," James said, though I had surmised as much.

"He was very handsome."

"And brave," he added. He stepped to the side, pausing before another painting of a man in a long, white wig and frilly cravat. "This is my grandfather."

We spent the better part of a half hour walking the length of the corridor and discussing James's ancestors and all they'd achieved or the various aspects of the estate they had personally developed. England's history was steeped in Bradwell military accomplishments until the last, and I could not help the surge of pride James's anecdotes built in my chest. This strong line held the ancestors of my future children. The name passed from one father to the next, building on duties and responsibilities that had not suffocated or snuffed each man, but given them a reason to fight.

The Bradwell pride was a living thing, and I had looked at it in entirely the wrong way.

"For such a militant family, it surprises me that none of you . . ." I stopped, aware that I had begun asking an extremely personal question. I didn't wish for James to believe I cast judgment on his decision not to follow his father's footsteps to join the army.

He sent me a brief smile. "Henry did, actually. He joined up freshly out of Eton and followed my father across the pond to fight Napoleon."

Henry? Quiet, bookish Henry? "I had no idea."

"He does not like to speak of it. He sold out shortly after bringing my father home from Waterloo so we could bury him here in the family cemetery. I do not know if Henry never intended to be a career soldier, if losing my father changed his mind, or if he'd always meant to sell out when the trouble on the Continent was resolved. We do not discuss it."

"He was there," I said reverently, the facts clicking into place. Henry was present at the battle that killed his father.

James nodded, his mouth pressed in a firm line.

"I cannot believe I did not know." Though so many things made sense to me now. Henry had not been familiar with Miss Northcott—a development in the Bradwell household which must have occurred while he was away. He was reserved by nature, yes, but the sorrow in his being was undoubtedly a result of the things he'd experienced.

"I have spent a long time feeling as though I owe something to Henry," James said, his hands behind his back and his gaze on the portrait of his third-times great-grandfather. "I wanted to purchase a set of colors, but my father would not allow it. He'd trained me my entire life to take over as heir of Chelton, and he could not go away to war without the assurance that I would remain to care for my mother. It was a blow to my young pride, but I accepted the responsibility and watched Henry take on the role I desired."

"He did not relish it, I suppose?"

"No. He wanted to study at University but put it off when soldiers were needed in order to do what he believed was his duty as the second son. Ben wanted to join him, but Father asked him to complete his studies first."

"Henry *never* went to university then?"

"Never. Ironic, is it not? He is the only one of us who cared to." James ran a hand over his jaw. "After we married and came to Chelton, when I struggled to find an accord with you, it was a direct blow to watch how easily you and Henry found companionship. I am ashamed to say how deeply it offended my pride, how jealous I grew."

"I do not love him," I said quietly.

James looked to me, his visible eye gleaming in the candlelight. "It is painful to watch your easy camaraderie with him. An inordinate beast of jealousy has grown within me ever since we came to Chelton. I want to be the man you desire, the one who can sit beside you in the quiet or hide away with you at a ball. I want to be the man you choose."

The man you choose. My heart stuttered at the words. I wanted the same thing, to be the woman James chose every day, forever.

"Henry is such a private man," James continued, unaware of how deeply his words had pierced me. "He had the first claim on your acquaintance. I fear I have stolen you from a better life with him, that if it had been him in that ballroom, you would have been happier situated with a man who understood you fully."

The man you *choose*. It repeated in my mind over and over, heavy and jarring like a battering ram.

I stepped back, needing to clear my head, and James took the distance for something else, hurt splashing over his face. "Liss—"

"No, listen." I shook my head and raised a gloved hand. "I have spent the last two months fearing the same thing, fearing that I took the role of mistress of Chelton from a far more deserving woman, that there was a lady out there who would relish these responsibilities and duties and not shy away in the face of social niceties. I have ridden horses and played ridiculous games and attended social functions all in an effort to be a wife you would not be ashamed of. But more than that, I wanted to be a wife you would *want*."

"Want?" He ran a hand through his hair, messing its perfect order. "Can you not see how deeply I have *wanted* you from the very beginning? I could have stepped back and allowed you to leave that library easily at the Huttons' ball, but you'd wholly captured my interest, and I did not wish for our time together to end. I cajoled you into that wretched *dance*, for heaven's sake."

His vehemence startled me, and I could not reconcile the truth in his words. "You cannot expect me to believe that my quiet, bookish—"

"Believe it." James took my hand and turned it over, running his finger over the place on my glove I'd burned that night so long ago, the mark long since healed. "My belief that you meant to entrap me that night died swiftly upon the realization that you were sincere in your efforts to escape the crowded ballroom for your own reasons. I was in London to find a wife, and every young chit who threw herself in my path was nothing but artifice and deceit or a blasted fortune hunter. Yours was the first conversation I'd held all Season that lacked deception. You were genuinely yourself, darling, and you stole my heart that very night."

"But we've *nothing* in common."

"We do share one thing. Or, I hope we do at least. We cannot fall asleep without the other there, and that has daily given me hope."

The man you choose.

My heart surged with affection, and I stepped forward, sliding my hands around his waist and pressing my nose into the hollow between his shoulder and his neck, inhaling the muted spicy scent embedded in his lapel. James's arms came around me, holding me tightly to him, and all the anxious flutterings dissipated slowly until calmness seeped into my limbs and infiltrated my entire being.

I turned my head to speak but remained tightly in his arms. "I've loved you since the moment you carried me from the Pickerings' ballroom, James. You are the first person to accept my nervous fits for what they are and to never try to change that about me."

"You are not upset that I forced you into a life that is outside the bounds of your comfort?"

"I was, initially. I could not understand why you would marry me and bring me to this monstrous house when you knew how I struggled." I leaned back to look into his face, hoping he would understand the sincerity in my heart. "Perhaps Henry and I, had we pursued any sort of acquaintance, would have one day found an accord with one another, but that possibility is deep in the past, and I have left it there. What matters now is that I love you, James. I choose you, and I will continue to do so for the rest of my life. We do not need to share the same opinions or the same interests to love one another, and I believe it is through the sacrifices we make that we share an even greater regard."

"Sacrifices?" His hands rubbed my back, making it hard for me to focus.

"Yes. I sacrifice comfort to join you in your outdoor pursuits or at balls or dinners, and *you* sacrificed as well. You do not press me to dance or attend at-homes when I do not wish to, you made an effort to find a pastime that would suit both of us. And, best of all, you tried to read a book that did not interest you in the slightest. Or, at least I believe you did."

The tips of his ears went red, and he looked away. "You found that, then? I wondered if you'd seen *Udolpho* after you mentioned discovering the maid rummaging through drawers in the study. I only wanted to know what it was you found so interesting in it."

"Did you?"

He grinned. "I have not yet discovered the appeal, but I do intend to give it my best efforts."

"I think, so long as we are both doing that, we will be happy together."

"Choosing one another?"

I nodded.

His grin widened. "I have chosen you since the Hutton's ball, Liss, and I will continue to choose you every day."

James leaned down and pressed his lips gently to mine. He kissed me slowly, with all the affection we'd held back and suppressed over the last month finally erupting in our shared tenderness for one another. Time slipped away and nothing mattered outside of this moment and this man. His fingers slid around my neck and curled up so his finger rested gently on my ear. He tilted my head and deepened the kiss, and I knew I could lose myself in him completely.

James leaned back and rested his forehead lightly against mine. He blew out a soft breath, a chuckle whispering on it. "Fact: you are my favorite person in England."

"Only in England?"

"Fine, in the whole world."

"Better." I reached up to kiss him again, then pulled back. "Fact: you are *my* favorite person in the whole world."

"You must come up with something original. I believe you gave me that very same rule one night."

I shot him a wry smile. "Very well. Fact: I did not realize I could feel this happy."

He grinned and took my lips again, this time with more fervor but no less tenderness.

When he released me, I stepped away and smoothed down my gown. "Time to face the crowd."

He kissed my temple. "I will be at your side the entire time."

CHAPTER 32

Lady Edith stared at me with barely concealed frustration when James and I finally made it downstairs. We'd spent too long in the gallery hall learning of his ancestors, and I returned to my chamber afterward to remove half of the white roses adorning my hem. Madame Rousseau had left the ones on my bodice to a tasteful amount, but the number of roses on my hem were nothing short of ridiculous.

Once I'd carefully snipped half the roses off my hem, it felt much lighter and dragged far less. I moved more comfortably, but Lady Edith appeared to notice, and she did not seem pleased.

"You are late," she said. "The dinner is about to begin. Lord and Lady Claverley are here already, and I need help if I am to navigate any conversations that have to do with Thea's absence."

James leaned in to kiss her cheek. "Sorry, Mother. I did not mean to cause you distress. Felicity and I needed to discuss something and time escaped us."

I looked over her shoulder at the crowd mingling in the ballroom, and my pulse increased. Lord Claverley stood beside a regal woman whose feather-endowed hair was styled abnormally high. Neither of them smiled, though they carried a regality that made their status clear. My sight fell upon Jane and Ewan standing against the wall together not far behind the earl and countess, and I inhaled a deep breath. I was not alone here. I could do this.

"There is another matter I wanted to settle before the majority of our guests arrive," James said.

"The majority of them *have* arrived," Lady Edith said. But she seemed to sense that James would not be put off. "Can you be quick about it?"

"Yes." His gaze flicked to me, then back to his mother. "Felicity will not be required to dance."

I sucked in a quiet, surprised breath.

"I beg your pardon?" his mother said.

"It is ridiculous to ask it of her when it is bound to end in a fit of nerves and a fainting spell."

Lady Edith looked from her son to me. "He is in earnest?"

"It would appear so." I had never felt so wholly loved in my life.

"This ball is to celebrate the both of you and your union. You realize—" She looked behind her, then walked into the drawing room and we followed. She closed the doors behind us, her face a tight expression of irritation, red mottling her cheeks. "If Felicity does not dance, it will only confirm the rumors that she is with child and that your union is a product of that very child."

"That could not be further from the truth," James said.

"But that is what you face, all the same."

Lady Edith was correct. Something about seeing the ancestors that built the foundation for the life I was able to give my future children had unlocked an appreciation in me for this family and all that it represented. It gave me the desire to further investigate my own heritage—another time—and it gave me a desire to protect the Bradwell name in whatever way I could.

"I can dance."

"No," James said, taking my hand. "I will not spend another dance watching you for signs of distress. I cannot do it. I refuse to carry your limp body from the dance floor again, not when it can be helped by so simple a thing as avoiding dancing."

Love shined in his eyes and reached my heart, warming my spirit and giving me confidence. "I can dance with you, James. I truly think I can do it, so long as it is a waltz."

"A waltz?"

"Yes. I can dance with you and only you. In a waltz, you can hold me, and I will not be passed off to another partner. I will be well."

"And if you are *not* well?"

I lifted one shoulder in a small shrug. "Then I suppose we've learned our lesson. But I do believe I am capable."

He took up my other hand and squeezed both of them. "I know you are capable, though it makes me nervous all the same."

I turned to Lady Edith. "We will open the ball with a waltz. Surely it will not be frowned upon. It was approved in Almack's last year, if you want to share that bit of information with any of the sticklers."

She gave me an odd expression, a faint line forming between her eyebrows. "It is true, then? You will actually faint?"

"I have never lied to you," I replied, hoping she understood my greater meaning. Everything I shared with her was true.

"Our first public dance was at the Pickering ball, and before we took to the floor Felicity's mother warned me to try and catch her should the need arise."

"Good heavens." Lady Edith's hand fluttered to her heart. "Have you hurt yourself?"

"I've had headaches on occasion." A defensiveness rose

within my breast from the appalled look on her face. I could see that she was likely wondering why my mother allowed me to dance knowing what came of it. "My mama does love me. She just does not . . . understand. She believes I could control my nerves, should I wish to."

Lady Edith's gaze flicked to the floor, then back to me. "You cannot master it any better than I can control becoming ill in a carriage." She spoke softly, reiterating what I once told her. She cleared her throat, and her cheeks were red, her neck mottling with a blush. She learned she was wrong about her initial assumptions regarding me, and it likely embarrassed her. "I owe you an apology, Felicity. I did not believe you, and I"—her gaze darted to James and back to me—"should not have assumed that you coerced my son into a wedding. I hope you can forgive me."

"I do," I said immediately. "If you'll forgive that I removed half of the roses from my gown. It was too much for me."

She gave me a strained smile. "I do forgive you."

When we entered the ballroom some time later, I crossed the floor immediately toward Jane and Ewan. "Forgive me. I am a terrible hostess."

"I was only just thinking quite the opposite," Jane said. "Your letter implied that you were under a great deal of stress, and I have to admit that I expected to find you in an awful situation here at Chelton, but the opposite is true. You are glowing, Lissy. You look to be thriving in your new role."

I smiled, aware that the glow was a result of acceptance. My own acceptance that I did not need to change who I was in order to be a good mistress of Chelton or a good wife to James, and acceptance from James and—somewhat tenuously—Lady Edith into their family.

"Your bearing has altered slightly, and the way you command

your servants is kind but firm. It is plain that you are finding your place here." Jane's mouth bent into a slight frown. "Though I suppose it would be much better if your mother-in-law treated you differently."

"I believe that is about to change," I confided. I had explained the situation last night to Jane's sympathetic ears. "Lady Edith and I shared a brief moment of understanding, and she is not too angry that I altered her design for my gown a little."

"That sounds like good progress."

"It is."

The waltz was announced, and Jane raised her eyebrows at me in interest. "Your local country folk are this accepting?"

"I am not sure," I said honestly. "But I hope so."

James appeared at my elbow, proffering his arm. "I believe this dance is mine."

Jane grinned widely, and I knew she was happy that I had found joy. Everyone deserved to have someone like Jane in their life, an uplifting friend, glad purely for the sake of my success.

James and I moved to the center of the ballroom and took our positions, waiting for the other couples before we began the promenade.

Miss Whitstone joined the circle of couples waiting for the dance to begin on the arm of a gentleman I did not know, and I tensed.

"What is it?" James asked.

"It is only the Whitstones. It appears that they've decided to attend anyway."

"They no doubt intend to pretend as though nothing happened."

"Your mother will accept that?"

"She and Lady Whitstone have been friends for a long time. They'll manage, somehow," he grumbled. "Though I would prefer to cut the acquaintance, I can see why Mother prefers to keep the peace. There is no hostess in the greater area of Bakewell that will not invite both of the women to any event they hold. It is easier this way, I imagine."

I nodded, understanding the need to keep peace with one's neighbors. The violin began in earnest, and the rest of the musicians joined in. James pressed his hand against mine softly and we began the promenade. "When I showed Miss Whitstone the garden, Henry met us outside, and she immediately blushed scarlet. Do you think she has a *tendre* for him?"

James laughed. Heads turned our way, and my stomach flipped from the attention. I focused on the man holding my hand and leading me about the circle.

"Perhaps, but I doubt it," he said. "That is merely her way. She cannot speak to a man without being red in the cheeks for the entirety of the conversation."

My heart went out to her. "We have much in common."

"You think that, but you could not be more different."

"I am inordinately shy as well, James. You cannot deny that."

"No, I am well aware of it, but when you are in the company of few, or surrounded by those you know well, you are not as reserved or anxious. You can hold conversations. Dash it, Liss, the night we met I was a stranger and still you spoke comfortably to me."

I had, hadn't I? It was a truth I had not considered before now. "Hmm. I wonder why that was."

"Because I was so dashing you could not help yourself," he said simply. The sparkle in his one visible eye reached my heart. "In all seriousness, I imagine it was because you felt comfortable with me."

"I suppose that would make the most sense." I agreed. I had felt comfortable with James then, though I hadn't made the connection until now. "So, you did not come to the conclusion that you and Miss Whitstone would not suit simply because she was shy?"

"Not at all. I am not opposed to a quiet woman." He winked at me. "But she could not carry any conversation at all. It was nothing but silence between us, always. I would, at least, prefer a wife who speaks to me."

"That is understandable. There is a gentleman somewhere who will make Miss Whitstone equally comfortable, I am sure."

He eyed me warily. "For her sake, I do hope you are correct."

We moved from the promenade into the dance, and the further the song progressed, the more at ease I felt in James's arms. We danced the same figures we had danced in the Huttons' library, though this time to real music, and I did not once avert my eyes from his. His strong arms and sweet smile made me feel safe and loved, and when the song came to an end, I stood before him, grinning widely.

"I've done it," I said triumphantly.

"I knew you could," he murmured, placing a kiss on my temple near my ear.

CHAPTER 33

Sun streamed through James's open windows and spread over the navy rug like shafts of bright fire. I shifted on the feather mattress, and James's arm slipped from its position around my waist, freeing me from his sleepy hold. He made a low guttural sound and rolled to face the other direction, and I slid quietly from the blankets and tiptoed across the cold floor. Shivers ran up my bare legs, and I closed the adjoining door between our rooms softly before sliding my dressing gown over my shift.

Fanny had not yet been in to light the morning fire—a task which had fallen to her while the maids were being dismissed and shifted around. I tugged the bell rope and sat at my dressing table, where I'd placed a white rose that James had given me the night before.

You are part of Chelton now, darling. You even look the part.

It had been a jest about how closely I resembled the flowers that filled the gardens, and I intended to dry this rose as well and press the petals between the pages of a book so I might keep them always.

Fanny arrived and helped me dress, and I was down in the

breakfast room before too long, pouring myself a hot cup of steaming chocolate and buttering a slice of toasted bread. Jane had intended to meet me down here for breakfast before anyone else awoke, but she'd not yet arrived.

Heavy boot tread traveled down the corridor, and Benedict tore into the room at a fast clip, halting in his surprise upon setting his gaze on me. "You startled me, Felicity. Why are you awake so early?"

"I'm meeting Jane." I swallowed another sip of chocolate. "Are you going somewhere?"

He wore his riding boots and coat over pantaloons, gloves and hat in hand. He set them on the table and moved to fill a plate at the sideboard. "Yes, actually. I had not intended to tell anyone, however, so you are putting me in an odd spot."

"You needn't confide in me, but I do hope you at least told your mother you intended to go *somewhere*."

He shot me a guilty look, and I set my cup on the saucer. "Benedict," I scolded. "She will worry herself ill were she to awake and find her son missing."

"It would not be the first time."

"*That* is meant to make you sound better?"

He sighed, carrying his plate to the table. "You are sounding more and more like the mistress of Chelton every day, you know."

"Like I have authority?"

"No," he deadpanned. "Like my mother."

I grinned. I knew he meant it kindly. "Perhaps you ought to heed my advice and at least leave a note. Do you know how long you shall be gone?"

"I haven't the slightest."

I took a bite of my toast and swallowed it, allowing him time to confide in me. When he remained quiet, I decided to speak my mind. He had no compunction in doing the same with me, after all. We were siblings now. "You recall how overset she became when she learned of Miss Northcott's disappearance?"

He looked sullenly at me.

I wanted to straighten the curl that flopped over his forehead, but refrained. "Perhaps it would be similar were this to happen with her child."

He chewed for a long while before swallowing and leaning back in his seat. "She is why I am leaving."

"Your mother?"

"Thea. Miss Northcott." He looked down at his plate and toyed with the roll there, ripping small pieces from it and littering his plate with crumbs. "I feel a little of the responsibility for her disappearance. I know my mother does not place that blame on me, but I also know that if I was not in residence, Thea would likely have approached Mother for help instead of whatever it is she's done."

This I had not expected. It had become increasingly plain that Benedict felt some level of guilt over Miss Northcott's absence, but to seek her himself? "Where do you plan to go?"

"York, again. I will begin there. I'm certain one of the servants knows more than they're letting on. A little coin should provide me some answers."

"Miss Dorothea Northcott is missing?" Jane asked from the doorway.

We both startled and looked toward her. Drat. How long had she been listening?

Jane glided into the parlor, the picture of grace and poise, even at so early an hour. "I went to school with Thea. We had something of a friendship, actually, though we were not very close. Is she in trouble?"

"I hope not," Benedict said. "Not that I care for her wellbeing in particular, but I do feel a modicum of responsibility."

I fought a smile. It was more than a modicum if the man was leaving on a journey to find her. His disdain for the woman seemed exaggerated at times. "That is why you do not wish for your mother to know your goal," I said, the point occurring to me then. "You do not want to give her false hope?"

"Exactly."

"Perhaps I will tell her, then, that I saw you this morning and you mentioned going to visit . . ."

"A friend in London," he said decisively. "That should buy me enough time to discover Thea's whereabouts before I need to write again. It will not be a lie, either. I have a feeling I shall end up in London."

"But is she a friend?" I questioned, my tone facetious.

Benedict shook his head, his eyebrows raised. "The farthest thing from it." He reached into his pocket and retrieved a small, oval miniature in a gold-painted frame. The young woman pictured had dark hair and a heart-shaped face, her smile playful as though she possessed a secret. "This is the little minx."

I leaned over and analyzed the playful face. "I think you are correct, Benedict. She looks as though I will like her excessively."

"I did already tell you, most people do."

"She is a lark," Jane agreed. "Though I didn't have much time to know her better."

"Yes, a lark," Benedict said with no feeling. "Running to hide from the one woman who has sacrificed greatly in order to provide for her is quite hilarious, is it not?"

He did not appear to be the least bit amused. Thea's antics had offended him. I only hoped she had good reason to defend her choices.

Benedict slipped the miniature in his coat pocket and patted the outside. "I hope this will help me locate her. James and I hadn't taken it with us to York the first time, but we hadn't realized we'd need it then."

"I wish you a safe journey and all the luck in locating her," I said, reaching for his arm and giving it a gentle squeeze.

Jane filled her plate and brought it to the table, and Benedict rose. "Thank you, Felicity. I shall need it. Good day then, ladies." He bent in a bow, picked up his gloves and hat, and sauntered from the room.

"I wish him good luck," Jane whispered. "How awful for poor Thea."

"She did mention in the letter she left behind that she would be safe where she was going."

Jane looked uncomfortable. "The need she felt to leave, though, and to promise she is safe does not make her situation sound good." She took a bite of her roll.

"I suppose we must wait for Benedict to send word. There is nothing else for us to do." I offered a smile as comforting as I could muster.

Jane's worried frown shifted to a soft smile. "Now, Felicity, I want to hear everything about your lovely married life."

"I want to first hear from you," I countered. "You've been married far longer and thus have more to share."

"Well, I do have more to share," she said in a singsongy voice.

I sipped my drink and waited. Jane looked at me a long while, a slow smile spreading over her lips, and I knew at once what she meant to imply by her impish grin. A small gasp slipped from my throat. "You are with child?"

"Yes."

I squealed quietly and pulled her into an embrace. "Oh, that is the best of news. Is Ewan excited to become a father?"

"Inordinately. And he will be a very good one, I think."

"Undoubtedly."

She sat back and appraised me. "You could give my babe a friend, if you wanted to."

My cheeks warmed. I wanted to do just that, eventually.

"Who would have known last summer when we met Mr.

Bradwell that this is how your life would turn out," Jane said in a little awe.

I finished off my chocolate and sat back, content. "I do believe everything has turned out for the best."

Jane grinned. "Indeed."

CHAPTER 34

A week had passed since the night of our ball, and I awoke to find James leaning on his elbow in the bed beside me, his shadow-darkened eyes trained on me.

"It is somewhat alarming to wake to a set of wide eyes staring at you," I said, remaining perfectly still while I raked my gaze greedily over his sleepy morning face.

"Not romantic?"

"Perhaps if I knew to expect you, it might be." I fought the smile threatening my lips and widened my eyes for impact. "Otherwise it is just shocking."

"What is shocking is how you've yet to comment on my lack of an eyepatch this morning."

"Oh, James!" I sat up swiftly and knelt before him, sliding my hand over his cheek. I ran my finger beneath his injured eye which was now watching me closely. "Can you see clearly? Does it hurt?"

He chuckled softly, and I felt the rumbling of his chest through the feather mattress. "It does not hurt today—though in fairness, it no longer hurt last night really, either—and my vision is perfectly clear."

"What a relief. I worried I'd maimed you. What an awful way to begin a marriage that would be."

"The beginning of our marriage has been anything but awful."

I slid my hand further over his cheek, losing my fingers in his mussed hair. His jaw was a little scratchy from the overnight beard growth, his smile lazy, and he was so handsome my heart squeezed in affection.

"Perhaps I will become injured more often if this is the sort of treatment I receive," he murmured. "I could grow used to your tender ministrations."

"That is a little dramatic."

"Oh, my head aches. I believe I need a cool compress."

"Your poor head," I said. "I ought to leave you then. A headache is best healed in darkness and solitude."

I pulled my hand away from his face, and he caught me by the wrist. "I meant my hand, not my head. It is tired from all the writing I've endured this week."

"Your poor hand." James had received word from Benedict that he was no closer to achieving his goal in locating Miss Northcott, and James sent out a variety of letters to the girl's old acquaintances in the hope that someone would know something useful. "You are doing a good thing in helping to locate Thea."

His face fell from facetious to serious. "Perhaps, but I worry that we will incite a scandal if we are not more circumspect. Thus far we've only written and spoken with servants, really, or families who knew Thea's mother and father but don't attend Society functions. It is only a matter of time before her antics are discovered and all the work Mother did to prepare her for a Season and a husband are for naught."

"It cannot be as bad as that, surely? If Benedict is able to find the girl before the summer is over, Lord and Lady Claverley need never know that she disappeared at all."

James gave a lopsided smile. "That is the hope, of course. We shall see if it is so easily accomplished. Now, enough of Thea. I have a surprise for you today."

I slumped into a seated position and leaned away from James. "The last time you planned a surprise, you ended up with an eyepatch."

"Did I not tell you moments ago how I planned to remain injured always so you could nurse me back to health?"

"That is not equally humorous on subsequent repetitions, James."

"Very well." He pushed himself into a seated position, the blankets falling down around his waist and revealing his bare chest. "Forgive my ill attempts at humor. This surprise will hurt neither you nor me, I promise."

"I am certain you felt confident that you could promise the very same safety for a round of battledore and shuttlecock, and look where that led us."

James chuckled. "Trust me, darling."

"Oh, I do," I said easily. I let my head fall back against my pillow and closed my eyes. Why could he not find more interest in sitting around safely inside a drawing room or walking sedately through the garden? Neither of those activities required enormous, powerful animals or balls stuffed with feathers. I shifted my head to look at him. "It is trusting *myself* that I have more difficulty with."

He moved to lean over me, his face hovering just above mine. "In this case, I think you have nothing to fear."

"Easy to *say*, of course, but I am certain I can prove you wr—"

James lowered his lips to mine and cut me off with a kiss. His mouth moved over mine in a rhythm that had become both familiar and exciting. Warmth hummed through me, and I was quite positive that I had never expected to love or be loved so fully as I was now.

He leaned back, breaking the kiss, and turned his head away

to blow a breath through puffed cheeks. "Enough distractions, young lady. I need to see to your surprise. Meet me at the bottom of the stairs in one hour?"

"I will be there."

Lady Edith had seemed embarrassed on the night of our ball when James had finally told her the truth of the nature of our relationship, and I had hoped the bit of healing we found together would lead to a more comfortable relationship between us. In the last week, however, I'd found myself sorely disappointed. I suppose it was too difficult to correct her wrong opinion of me so quickly, but I had hoped it would not be such a chore.

I dressed swiftly and had half an hour before I was meant to meet James downstairs, so I'd gone to the drawing room but pulled up short when Lady Edith appeared to be the only person already in the room.

She glanced up and found me in the doorway, and it was now too late to disappear.

Drat.

"Good morning, Felicity," she said cordially as I made my way into the room.

I lowered myself on the sofa opposite her. "Good morning, Lady Edith. I trust you slept well?"

"I did, thank you."

My teeth grated against the discomfort floating between us. It was stuffy and uncomfortable, the air thick with each of the emotions that had colored our recent past.

"The Whitstones have invited us to tea," she said mildly, her focus remaining on her embroidery. "Though you have every reason to refuse, should you wish it."

It was bound to be uncomfortable, but not attending could

only make matters worse. If I wanted to prove I wasn't yet with child, maintaining social appointments was one way to do so. Then when I did have news to share, it would be extremely clear that the timing took place *after* the wedding.

"I will not refuse," I said at length.

"Miss Whitstone does become more agreeable over time."

I nodded my understanding.

Lady Edith set her embroidery on her lap. "And I suppose the same could be said for me as well."

"What do you mean?"

She closed her eyes and pressed her fingers to her temples as though gathering her strength. "I have not treated you as I ought to have since you've come to us, and after James made the nature of your engagement perfectly clear, I've felt at a loss for how to proceed."

"I've forgiven you—"

"Yes, I realize that. But we did not begin comfortably, and I do not know how to fix the discomfort between us unless I leave Chelton." She leveled her gaze at me. "I've given it some thought, and I think it best if I were to move into the dower house. You've seen it, perhaps? On the south lawn?"

"I haven't."

"It will need a bit of repair before it is livable, but I imagine it could feasibly be made ready by the end of the summer."

She held my gaze, and my argument with James when I had desired space and he had fought to remain together came freshly to mind. Even in our discord, we chose to sleep side by side, and that choice had a healing power that separation would not have lent us. I desired the same healing with Lady Edith, and I knew it could only take place if we both made that active choice. Her willingness to move into the dower house only proved—in my mind, at least—that she was prepared to work and that she desired peace and accord for our relationship.

"I do not think that will be necessary, Lady Edith."

She blinked at me. "No, not necessary, but perhaps it is important."

"There is plenty of room in Chelton for both of us—"

"I am not sure there is room enough for two mistresses."

"No, I agree with that." I drew in a sustaining breath. It was the way of things for me as James's wife to take my rightful place as mistress, and I did not want to cede that honor to her when it was mine to bear. "But I cannot do it alone. I need your wisdom and guidance, and I know the servants and the household will run more smoothly if you were to teach me all that you know."

She was silent for a beat, her hands unmoving. "You wish for me to remain, and for me to teach you?"

"Yes." I crossed to the other sofa and sat beside Lady Edith. "I would like to forget our uncomfortable beginning and start anew, if it is agreeable to you. I think we can sometimes feel bound by our past mistakes, but we have the choice to move forward with a fresh perspective, and I choose to be the best mistress of Chelton I can. I would like your help in order to accomplish that."

Lady Edith looked at me a long while, her cheeks pink, likely from the discomfort of the current conversation. "Yes, Felicity. I would like that very much."

"I am glad."

"When I told you last week that I was impressed with the way you handled Molly's indiscretion and James's injury, I meant it. You have the makings of a wonderful leader"—she swallowed—"and we are very lucky to have you."

My chest warmed from her praise. "I am certain to make many mistakes."

"As did I, in the beginning," she said in a confiding tone. "It takes time to master this house and the army of servants who run it. But you will learn, in time, and I will be here to help you." She reached over and took my hand, squeezing it once before dropping it.

I stood, brushing the front of my gown to avoid the sheen that suspiciously lingered in her eyes and would undoubtedly be reflected in my own soon. "I must go to meet James now."

"Oh yes, the surprise."

I looked up, startled. "You know of it?"

"I do."

"Will I hate it very much?" I asked.

She smiled. "No, I don't believe you will."

That was a little comforting. I left to find James in the great hall, and he was waiting for me at the bottom of the stairs. His jacket was tight over broad shoulders and his smile trained on me. "Ready?"

"I suppose so."

James laughed, sliding his hand into mine. "I promise, it has nothing to do with birds or arrows or shooting or fishing."

He led me through the front door, and we stood at the top of the split staircase, the wind blowing against my face. A small horse and cart waited for us at the base of the stairs.

No, it wasn't a small horse, though its body resembled one. It had long, pointed ears like a donkey. "You've bought me a mule?" I asked, a laugh tearing from my throat.

James grinned. "Yes, and I thought we could call her Stella."

CHAPTER 35

S tella's small cart wasn't too difficult to manage, and after a week of lessons and a new pair of driving gloves were delivered, I was somewhat adept at taking my mule and cart about Chelton's small lanes. James met me at the stablehouse while the early morning fog still clung to the hilltops, a glint in his eye that spoke to something he had planned. My parents were set to arrive soon, and I was glad Lady Edith and I had found an agreeable rhythm with one another prior to their appearance. I was eager to show my parents the comfortable life I'd found at Chelton and within my new marriage.

"Where are we off to today?" I asked, taking the reins and settling myself on the driver's seat of the cart. James and I had fallen into a routine over the previous week that suited both of us. In the mornings we went driving together, but we'd taken to playing chess in the evenings or I would read aloud while James listened on. He found he enjoyed stories, just not reading. Every day we made sacrifices for one another and found a way to choose our marriage and prioritize one another in small ways.

"Do you recall the day you rode Luna?" he asked.

"How could I forget?"

"Yes, well, I had wanted to show you something I thought you would appreciate. It is too far to reach on foot, and riding horses is out of the question, so I thought this would be the way to accomplish it."

It took a moment for his meaning to settle. "You bought me a mule and cart and spent a week teaching me to manage them just so you could show me the thing you wanted to take me to when I first came to Chelton?"

"Yes."

I leaned over and kissed him on the lips. "That was extremely sweet of you, James."

"Save your praise until you've seen the surprise. You could be disappointed and this will all be for naught."

I highly doubted that would be the case, but I quieted. James directed me where to go and we left the stableyard and slipped onto a narrow lane that ran up toward the hills behind Chelton. The house shrank further away when we left the road for the rugged countryside, and I recognized the hills we climbed and the stream we passed from our first terrifying ride.

Birds sang above our heads and dove through the misty trees, but Stella was unruffled by them. She was sedate, steady, and strong, and I loved her excessively.

After we crested another hill, James sucked in an eager breath. Sunlight bore down on us, melting away the lingering fog, and the curves of the countryside were making themselves clear. "Just over there," he said, pointing. "Toward that copse of trees."

I directed Stella toward the thick crop of trees at the base of another hill and we navigated around grazing sheep dotting the grass, their long, fuzzy tails flicking occasionally.

When we reached the trees, a white stone building came into view, its pillars tall and shadowed by the doming ceiling above them.

"It is a folly," James explained. "My grandfather had it built for my grandmother as something of an escape. She loved to paint, and she could often be found out here while her horse grazed the field. I thought you could find the same peace here that my grandmother seemed to."

I pulled Stella to a halt before the beautiful folly and secured her reins. "It's lovely, James."

"You like it?" he asked hopefully.

"I do."

He helped me down, and we walked toward the stone structure, mounting the steps until we stood on the platform. Chelton's rolling hills and lush, green lawns spread out in every direction, dotted with sheep and trees and the faint sparkle of the river in the distance. Warm light touched the tips of the trees and edges of the hills, laying an orange glow over the varying shades of green, and I could see how a painter would long to spend hours here replicating the natural beauty.

"It is magical," I said reverently. "But the best thing about it, I think, is how thoughtful it was of you to bring me here."

"It was nothing, really," he protested. "You drove the cart yourself."

"But you bought me the mule and the cart, and you taught me to drive it. I have an escape now, and a way to bring myself here without being dependent upon another soul." I wrapped my arms around his waist and leaned my head against his chest, gazing out at the expanse of luscious land while I inhaled his spicy scent. "I do not deserve you."

James scoffed. "The opposite is true."

I leaned back to see into his eyes. "You jest."

"No, I mean it. I cannot fathom how I was so fortunate to become your husband, Liss. I love you, dearly."

"Heaven knows why."

His arms tightened around me. "I've loved you, I think, since the moment you argued with your father in his study and begged him to allow us to test the waters of Society before entering into an official engagement."

Love on the second day of our acquaintance? Impossible. "You hardly knew me."

"But you'd piqued my interest in the library, as you well know, and when I asked Mrs. Hutton for a character reference, she assured me that you came from the best of families and were possessed of a good character. I saw the truth of that character and your claims that you had not been trying to trap me for my money when you fought the engagement. I had gone to your house to do the respectable thing and protect my family name and your own, and I left the meeting with the confirmation that you were someone I *wanted* to marry."

Words fled me, and I tried to make sense of the great compliment he was paying me. He had not loved me then, but he had realized its potential. The choices he had made each day since that moment were what led to his robust, sensitive love.

"I piqued your interest and then I fainted."

"And I realized that you were honest from the start, never turning a phrase to make your faults seem more palatable. It was a point that allowed me to fight my jealousy regarding Henry. You have never lied to me, Liss, and our marriage—though perhaps off to a rocky beginning—has been sturdy and strong. It will only grow stronger, I hope."

I nestled against his chest, warm tears filling my eyes and spilling onto his jacket.

"Don't cry, darling," he said.

How could I not? I'd been blessed with the kindest, most generous husband. "I do not deserve you."

He scoffed. "I feel the same. Perhaps that humility will aid us forever. We will always be grateful for the love we've found."

"I am most assuredly grateful for it." I leaned up and kissed him while the sun grew warmer and the fog melted to nothing. Stella remained nearby, steady and calm, and I could not imagine anything in the world would ruin the happiness that I'd found with James. My sweet, darling husband.

"We will not, perhaps, have a perfect marriage."

"No," I agreed. "But I think we can count on having a happy one."

EPILOGUE
EIGHT MONTHS LATER

M y heart raced as we mounted the steps to our first ball of the London Season. Mr. and Mrs. Hutton stood in the doorway of their ballroom to welcome their guests, and I glanced over my shoulder to ensure that Thea and Benedict were behaving. I hadn't relished the idea of acting as the girl's chaperone for the Season—for that meant attending numerous balls and soirees—but I'd wanted to return to London to visit my parents, and it was the least we could do to bring Thea with us.

Lord Claverley had not been well pleased by the change of circumstances, but it was unavoidable.

"Are you ready to prove to the *ton* that you are happily without child?" James asked, leaning so close I could barely hear his whisper in my ear.

My heart gave a little pang. "I would be happy to be with child by now," I reminded him. So long as it was obvious that we had not been together before our marriage, I wanted nothing more than to know a little one was on the way. But so far, no such luck.

And besides, I would like to think my character had grown

enough over the duration of our marriage to the point that it was no longer a priority to prove my worth to Society. James and I knew we had been innocent that night so long ago in the Huttons' library, and that was all that mattered to me now. Through the love and acceptance from my husband and myself, I grew less dependent on the acceptance of others. I could return to Town with my head held high.

Lady Edith believed as much, too, or she would not have asked me to chaperone her goddaughter.

"Good evening, James, Mrs. Bradwell," Mrs. Hutton said, curtseying politely. We greeted her and Mr. Hutton.

"Allow me to introduce Miss Dorothea Northcott," I said, pulling Thea's arm so she stood beside me. "And thank you for allowing us to bring her with us."

"It is no trouble at all," Mrs. Hutton said, an odd tinge in her tone. She almost sounded as though she was fighting emotion. "Miss Northcott, it is so good to see you, dear."

"The pleasure is mine," Thea said politely, dipping in a curtsy.

Benedict stood behind her, fidgeting with his cuffs as though he could not be removed from this ballroom fast enough, and we'd yet to even step into it. Strange, for his presence was never required. He *chose* to attend with us, though he acted much like a small boy who was dragged in front of his mother's guests to display his good manners.

Once the introductions and welcoming had completed, we moved into the half-filled ballroom and found a place to stand along the back wall.

Thea nestled to my side. "I know you will not dance, but you do intend to provide introductions for me, yes?"

"I will aid you in whatever way I can, Thea, as promised."

She sagged a bit in relief. "I should like first to meet Lord Keene, and then Lord Hampton, if it can be managed."

Lords? Was that not a bit lofty for her? I swallowed my

remark. I was in no place to judge. "Who are these people? How do you know their names?"

She gave a little, unrefined shrug. "I have my methods."

"Oh, heavens, Thea. I wanted to help you make a match, but please promise me you will be wise. After what happened last year—"

She looked from me to James. "That worked to your benefit, did it not?"

I clenched my jaw. I truly liked Thea, but sometimes I wanted to press understanding into her where it seemed to lack. "It did, but I was fortunate that it was *James* who I was found with and not a cad. It could just as easily have been my ruin."

She laughed a little, the sound hollow. "I intend to remain above reproach in all my behavior, Felicity. I promise. I do want to secure a good husband."

I believed her. She had a good heart, that much I knew even from our somewhat short acquaintance.

"Quite impossible to promise a thing such as that, isn't it, Miss Northcott?" Benedict said dryly. I wanted to swat him with my fan.

She blinked innocently up at him. "You mean to say you don't believe I am capable of good behavior, Mr. Bradwell? How shocking of you. I had thought we were friends."

Something between a laugh and a guffaw tore from his throat. "Is there anything to drink here?"

I happened to know that Mr. Hutton kept his brandy in the library. James opened his mouth, and I gave him a quelling look so he would not reveal as much to his brother. The last thing we needed was for another Bradwell man to find himself in a compromising situation in the Huttons' library during a ball.

I took both Benedict and Thea by the sleeves and forced them to look at me. "Whatever you do, promise me you will both remain in the ballroom all evening until it is time to leave. Promise me."

They each gazed at me with widened, mildly disturbed eyes, but did me the courtesy of promising.

"Thank you."

Mrs. Ormiston approached and greeted us fondly. I removed from my mind the memory of her snubbing my mother briefly last year. These social activities were, perhaps, going to be more difficult than I expected. I pasted a smile on my face and promised to find her once my mother arrived.

"We ought to find a few gentlemen to introduce you to," I said to Thea. "James will know who is best."

"Lord Keene or Lord Hampton would be fine," she said again.

Benedict struggled to suppress his obvious frustration. "Neither of those men would suit our purposes here very much."

"Because I am not worthy of a title?" Thea snapped.

"Because neither of them are in the market for a *wife*," he said.

Thea looked to the ceiling as though it would grant her serenity and patience. "Perhaps I could be the woman to change their mind."

"That is a lofty goal."

"But not insurmountable."

Benedict bit out his words between nearly clenched teeth. "Do I detect the possibility that you have now taken my warning to be something of a challenge?"

"It does not sound like much of a challenge to me."

"Goodness," I said, bringing their verbal fisticuffs to a halt. I felt I'd been dragged from one side of the room to the other. "Must I be forced to separate you like errant schoolchildren?"

Benedict looked at me sharply, then shook his head, a lone curl falling onto his forehead. He ran a hand through his hair to put it back where it belonged. "Forgive me, Felicity. I have become carried away. I will remove myself to avoid any further disruptions to your evening."

"You are leaving the ball?"

"No. I have seen an old school chum, and I will greet him before Thea can light my cravat on fire with her evil stare."

Thea raised her chin.

I wanted to ask if the school friend was a lord for Thea's benefit, but bit my tongue. Benedict's chagrin was heavy enough without me adding to it. He walked away from us, and Thea watched him leave. My eyes were clearly deceiving me, for it appeared that something akin to regret pooled in her eyes.

I tried to form a way to ask her about it when a familiar couple approached us, and I tucked that conversation away to have at a later time.

"Good evening, Mama," I said, giving my mother a hug. "Papa."

They each greeted us warmly, and I stepped closer to my husband while we spoke to them. James took my hand, his fingers gently running over mine, and we listened to Mama tell us of the wonderful events they'd so far attended and what was planned for the remainder of the week. I slipped into the conversation like I was dragging an old, familiar blanket over my shoulders, but it was made better by James's steadying presence.

My parents' visit to Chelton had been shorter than I'd anticipated and ended with an excursion to the hunting box before they traveled back to London, and we'd yet to see them again until arriving in London a few days ago. I would always love my mama and papa, but I was glad that I now understood the state of expectations I could reasonably have for my relationship with them.

The ballroom grew more crowded as time wore on until the instruments began to tune for the dancing.

"Mrs. Ormiston greeted us earlier," I told my mother. "She would like for you to find her when you have a moment."

Mama's eyes lit up, and I swallowed my repulsion at the eagerness she showed to hear the latest gossip—for that was undoubtedly why her friend wished to speak to her. It was all they'd ever before spoken of in my presence.

Papa stepped closer to James. "To the card room, son?"

James looked from me to Thea. "I intend to remain with Felicity this evening."

Papa smiled. "Suit yourself." He and mother both left, and we were once again standing by the wall in a line.

"We really ought to begin the introductions," I said. I did not wish to socialize, but we had a task to accomplish, and I was determined to see it done.

James looked to Thea. "Are you ready?"

She drew in a sustaining breath, surprising me a little. From the first moment we met she had seemed courageous and strong, but the way her hand trembled now, fidgeting lightly with the fabric of her skirt, I would almost assume she was nervous. I took her fingers and gave them a soft squeeze.

Thea looked up and held my gaze, her large blue eyes rounding.

"You needn't do anything you are not comfortable with," I said quietly. "That includes dancing or speaking to gentlemen. I know Lady Edith wants to see you comfortably established, but it is not a requirement that you marry by the end of the Season. If you do not find a man in the next few months, there is always next year."

She did not respond right away, but I held her fingers and her gaze so she would feel my sincerity.

"That is kind of you, Felicity, but it is easier if I do find a husband, and quickly."

"I do not know why," I said lightly, leaning slightly into James who stood at my side. "I am the mistress of Chelton, and as far I am concerned, you are welcome there as long as you'd like."

She gave me the softest whisper of a smile. "You are too kind."

"I will even promise to keep you and Benedict on opposite ends of everything."

She raised one eyebrow slightly. "Everything?"

"The house. The dinner table. The drawing room. The carriage."

She laughed lightly.

"I am the mistress," I reiterated. "It can be done."

Thea squeezed my hand back and lowered her voice. "Thank you, Felicity."

"Of course. Now, let us find a gentleman to introduce to you."

Thea nodded. "I am ready."

James winked at me, took me by the hand, and we made our way into the crowd.

A NOTE FROM THE AUTHOR

The idea for this book came to me in a flash while I was touring Chatsworth House in Bakewell, England (also known as Pemberley from the 2005 *Pride and Prejudice* film). While I chose to keep the town name the same as an homage to my ancestors, I moved it to Cumberland and changed the name of the Bradwells' house to Chelton. My ancestors were married in the Bakewell church, and I patterned the town in this book after the real town, but that is where the accuracy ends. If you looked for Bakewell in Cumberland, you would not find it there!

Likewise, Chelton is patterned after Chatsworth House, but I took liberties with the surrounding grounds. I kept the lovely bridge and river in, though, because they were too beautiful to skip. I also kept in the sheep that ran across the bridge when I tried to cross it the first time.

While Felicity struggles with an anxiety disorder, it would not have been diagnosed in that way at the time. Anxiety can manifest in many different ways and Felicity's experience is only one of them. I hope this book was able to give you a little insight into how one person might live and cope with social anxiety, especially if her experience is different than what you are familiar with.

This book is meaningful to me on a number of levels, and I hope you find some meaning in it as well. All successful relationships—whether they are romantic or platonic—require work and effort to maintain, and this story was meant to dive into the power of choice and how it relates to relationships. James and Felicity's relationship blossomed from their efforts to choose one another consistently. I think their love story is beautiful. Thank you, reader, for going on their journey with me. And guess what? It isn't over yet.

PLEASANTLY PURSUED

Thea Northcott cannot stand Benedict Bradwell, and the feeling is mutual. Or, is it?

Acknowledgments

If you are reading this, then thank you for getting this far in the book and reading my story! It is a special one to me, since it deals with matters that are close to my heart. When I set out to write a heroine with anxiety, I was careful to make her fears and worries extremely different from my own, but even though I'm not exactly like Felicity, I can relate to her concerns and her struggles, and I hope, if you've dealt with anxiety, that you can, too.

This book flowed easily for me (which isn't always the case) so I must thank, first, my Heavenly Father for blessing me with the inspiration for this story and the motivation to write it.

Thanks to my critique group and the SRR ladies for being a major support and many shoulders to lean on. The author community is fantastic, and I'm uplifted by so many wonderful writers each day.

Thank you Jacque Stevens and Molly Rice, my editors, for perfecting this story. You are both so talented, and I'm so grateful for your expertise and polish.

To my beta readers: thank you for helping me sort out the little inconsistencies and giving me the confidence that this book would be well-received. Heidi Stott, Brooke Losee, Emily Barton, Nancy Madsen, Sharleen Reeder, Maren Sommer, Ashlee Hunter, Rachel Stones, and Melanie Atkinson, you are all the best and I value your feedback! Even Ashlee, who only made it half way.

And finally, this book would not have made it to publication without the support of my husband, who not only inspires my chivalrous heroes, but keeps me laughing and loves me wholly. I would not want to be a stay at home parent with anyone else but you, and I think it's a good sign that we've been home together since March 2020 and are still happy. Here's to many more years—and many more romance novels—to come.

ABOUT THE AUTHOR

Kasey Stockton is a staunch lover of all things romantic. She doesn't discriminate between genres and enjoys a wide variety of happily ever afters. Drawn to the Regency period at a young age when gifted a copy of *Sense and Sensibility* by her grandmother, Kasey initially began writing Regency romances. She has since written in a variety of genres, but all of her titles fall under clean romance. A native of northern California, she now resides in Texas with her own prince charming and their three children. When not reading, writing, or binge-watching chick flicks, she enjoys running, cutting hair, and anything chocolate.

Made in the USA
Las Vegas, NV
04 May 2023

71586059R00199